Dedications

Especially for my brother, Rodney Hensley – who left Martin's Fork in Harlan, Kentucky in the early 1960s to find work in the city of Frankfort, Indiana – who has read my books an unreal number of times, which vicariously carried him back home to his beloved mountains.

For Robert Campbell, who left the mountains in the late 1950s to establish a business office after completing higher education, and his lovely wife, Frances.

In memoriam of my lovely daughter, Kimberly Lynn Harber, a high school business teacher, who faced an untimely death in 2003, and whose human spirit has been recaptured in the main character, Anna Laura.

A special thanks to: Crystal June Smiddy Adams for her unending support and encouragement.

Mountain Destiny

A novel

Pauline Hensley Harber

Mountain Destiny

This book is a work of fiction. Comments or statements within these pages are solely the responsibility of the author; Ascended Ideas accepts no legal responsibility for their authenticity.

An Ascended Ideas original

Ascended Ideas ePublishing
http://www.ascendedideas.com

ISBN 13: 978-0-9823969-3-3
Cover by Judy A Mason
Cover photo by Wilhelmina Ginter

Revised
Printed in the United States of America

Chapter 1

She came riding through the settlement sitting tall in her western saddle as her big Arabian horse made its way up the rough mountain and finally reached the top.

The mountain people stared from their small log cabins through small windows and from their porches. Never had they seen such a beauty. As she rode swiftly through the small settlement on the lovely mountain, her long dark hair blew slightly away from her face. Her full dark eyelashes intensified the beauty of her hazel-brown eyes. Her ruby lips, flushed high cheek bones and olive skin were the most beautiful sight the mountain people had ever seen. Her long slim legs and body were perfect. She was the picture of grace and poise.

The mountain people stood on their porches speaking quietly to one another, "Who can this be? Where did she come from?"

The whispers flowed from cabin to cabin.

After riding through the settlement without speaking to anyone, she came to a halt among the multicolored Redbuds, Dogwoods and wildflowers that grew in the rich mountain soil releasing their fragrance to the gentle wind.

A stream flowed adjacent to the clearing like a wild thing, hitting upon huge rocks as the water broke into thousands of shining bubbles as it splashed over the rocks, dancing into the air like white caps on the ocean.

The people now stood speechless staring at this awesome woman and her stunning horse so unlike any they had ever seen.

Speechless, Anna Laura sat staring back from a distance at the settlement of mountain people.

She wondered, "How do they survive? How do they educate their children? Do they have access to any medical facilities? Where do they get enough food? Are they able to grow enough to last throughout the year?"

She observed their actions and reactions, watching the many lovely children that ran through the meadows chasing butterflies, filling the air with laughter that echoed to the next mountain.

She turned and rode her Arabian out of sight in silence. She felt that trying to make any connection at this time would be in vain.

As she rode further through the semi-level mountains feeling the peace that the highlands brought to her soul; she felt so free.

She thought back to the days that seemed so long ago now, when she lived in the valley below on the north side of Brushy Mountain. Visions of her childhood, as well as her teen years, flashed through her mind. She considered how she had left at age eighteen. It had been ten years since she had left. It had taken a lot of motivation to complete her education. She thought of how only a few days ago she had come back to the Valley of Sampson to find all her loved ones were gone. She felt as though everyone she saw was a stranger.

The people at the sawmill boarding house had welcomed her for a few days of rest as a soft, but deep snow had fallen. It was spring time; she knew it would not last long. She loved riding her Arabian in the snow and was able to do so while staying at the boarding house.

Anna Laura remembered from her youth how the March snows, especially toward the end of the month, did not do any harm to the crops since the ground had already warmed and the snow was light and fluffy. It would not freeze anything.

The keeper of the boarding house allowed her to leave her red pick-up truck and horse trailer in a safe place. She left her keys with the keeper, John Asher, and his kind wife, Mary. She remembered telling them, "If I do not return within two years, the truck and trailer will be yours."

She had not made contact with anyone at home while she had been in Germany. There were too many sad memories in the valley at the foot of the tall mountain. Her memories were much too painful; at the time she had only wanted to leave them behind. She had seen far too much suffering in her own community. She had experienced hunger and lack of warm clothing to ward off the bitter cold. She had flashbacks of going to bed hungry and dreaming of proper food, then awakening to realize there was very little to eat.

While at the boarding house, she experienced a good feeling in her heart knowing that, through all the poverty, she managed to survive and endeavored to gain a high school education even though she was among the forgotten.

She remembered how she had cleaned and worked for the more fortunate people of the community and hid her money in a metal box for many years. Her willpower was extremely strong when temptations came telling her to buy the things she needed at the time instead of holding onto her future dreams; dreams that would break her out of the vicious cycle that engulfed her as well as many others.

"I will be different," she had vowed as a very young girl.

She knew one day she would break away from the poverty, illiteracy and loneliness. This kept her motivated. She knew if she could make it to some place in the big, wide world, somewhere there had to be some educational institution that would accept her as she was – extremely brilliant. Teachers in high school had encouraged her; they saw her potential. She knew if she could find her way she would be willing to work hard and strive to fulfill her dreams.

The outside world had filtered in to her community by way of battery operated radios as well and she had learned about the rest of the world through her high school education.

She was able to use her savings after graduation to catch a bus from Harlan to a city where she could take a flight to Germany. Her grandfather was of German descent which motivated her to research educational possibilities in Germany at the high school library. She had learned if one was willing to work hard, they could get an education for little or no money.

Anna Laura eventually came back to the present and rode on through a flat bench of the mountains feeling the cool breeze on her face. As hard as she tried, her mind could not let the latter part of her past die at the present. She focused on how she had worked to become a general surgeon and medical doctor.

She thought of the handsome, blond doctor that she had fallen in love with before graduating medical school. Knowing where she came from made her afraid she would not fit into Clint Knopp's world. His had not been a life of poverty, but one of privilege.

After working a year together in a great hospital, this wonderful man had asked her to marry him. She truly loved him. When he gently held and kissed her, she wanted the moment to last forever. Flashbacks of her past were always present. She feared that time would make a change and she would not be able to conform since his family was from royalty.

She had learned the ways of their world, but her heart sang a different song. Anna Laura knew she must return to her heritage; the mountains, the place she called home.

Far away, Clint's heart and spirit broke. He vowed to himself, "I will find her even if it should be at the end of the world."

He grieved for his tall, dark-haired lady who was not only beautiful on the outside, but on the inside as well.

Suddenly, Anna Laura realized she was a good distance from the settlement and should collect her gear and supplies from her horse and set up camp. Being in the wild, she felt she could get her thoughts together and put the past behind her - at least for the present.

The fire she built from the small branches she gathered glowed in the darkness and her horse stood hitched to a nearby tree. She lay on a quilt that she neatly spread on the bed of dry leaves. She was too tired to think and drifted into a peaceful sleep.

As she slept, she had dreams of what she had left behind. Awakening suddenly from her deep sleep, she was sad thinking of the man she loved with all her heart, soul and mind.

She looked toward the sky and prayed, "Please, God, help me to find my way. I must be here for a reason. Surely you have guided me here and there must be work for me to do."

A barely audible voice spoke, "Be patient and you will know what to do – my timing is not yours."

She remembered as a little girl how her mother told her not many days before she died, "My sweet child, time belongs to God, not to us. In your life everything will be done in God's timing if you put Him first in your life."

Those were memories that comforted her heart as the fresh spring breeze brought a soothing calm into her entire being.

Anna Laura sat on her quilt of many colors, the only tangible possession she had kept through the years that her momma wanted her to have. Her mother had hand sewn every stitch with her precious fingers. It was the only thing that had been given to her other than her mother's bible.

Anna Laura made sure the quilt went wherever she went. It seemed the presence of her mother stayed with this quilt. Anna Laura neatly folded the quilt and put it in a dry place. She then took soap and other necessities from the saddle bags and walked through the woods following the sound of a waterfall that ran over a huge cliff. Her eyes fell upon a waterfall that was hidden by trees, fully clothed in green leaves and accented by purple Redbuds and bright white Dogwood trees. This place was very private.

The rocks beneath the falls were flat and a very light array of color came from the continuous shallow flow of the splashing water. It was not slick, neither was it too rough. She could wash without worry of falling. As she stood under the falls bathing, she was a little chilled as the clear water and soap that lathered from the softness of the pure mountain water soothed both her body and mind. She felt totally rejuvenated as she walked back to her campsite.

As she walked back she took time to stop and pick a bouquet of wildflowers and sat on a rock holding them as she watched the yellow, red and blue birds flitting from tree to tree. It was as though they sang a mountain melody especially for her.

Her mind was at complete peace; she thought of nothing except the beauty that surrounded her.

Walking a little farther she laid the flowers on the ground when she spotted a blueberry bush that held a few ripened berries, most were green since it was early in the season.

She sat on a flat rock and had her fill of what nature had provided.

Upon reaching her campsite she was so filled with wild blueberries that coffee was all she needed. As she sat on a blanket sipping her coffee, she was so joyful inside that she spoke out loud, "God, I know you have ordered my steps. There must be work for me in these mountains."

Chapter 2

Anna Laura Gibson had brought as little as possible to survive, yet was surprised at how much she possessed when storing her goods beneath a cliff that was dry and safe. The air flow and temperature was perfect to prevent mildew and mold. Most important of all, her medical supplies would be safe. The area was spacious enough for several people to sleep if necessary when the rains came.

She now realized that living in the valley far below on the Kentucky side of the mountain had really inspired her when hearing that many people lived high in the Brushy Mountains. She then knew where her destiny lay.

She had to find her way to them and impart the knowledge that God had instilled in her by her willingness to learn.

Only God knew what lay ahead of her and only He knew that her heritage had made her a strong woman. Even she did not realize her capabilities; however, she knew with God on her side all things were possible.

Her mother had taught her that God would lead her through the valley of the shadow of death, as well as by the still waters. Anna Laura's strong personality had been formed before her momma died. Her momma's name, Ruth, was so fitting for her.

After drinking her coffee, she led her horse to a green meadow where he could get his fill of tender, green grass.

Anna Laura walked the short distance back to her camp. She combed her long, silky hair. As her eyelashes were long and dark, her olive skin and high cheek bones with a blush about them, she needed no make-up. Lipstick was all she needed. Her ruby lips matched the red plaid shirt she wore along with her blue jeans.

After tucking her shirt in, she put her leather belt through the loops and buckled it. The soft leather belt was one that had been given to her by Clint. The belt was very special as the belt buckle was gold with her initials engraved on it.

After the Arabian was full, he made his way back to Anna Laura. She mounted by putting her left foot in the stirrup, then lifting her long leg across to the other side, finally sitting with poise in the western saddle.

She ventured through the mountains finding even more cabins. Men, women and children were working their gardens where new ground had been cleared. Women were milking cows and the older children feeding hogs and chickens. They worked hard for their survival.

As she scanned the area, she noticed there was neither a school nor a church – and, of course, no type of medical facility. She knew that very moment these people were probably uneducated and lacking in healthcare.

Her heart wept for the mountain people and for herself because she felt she had met her calling, but knew a long road lay ahead of her. She knew mountain people would not be eager to accept a stranger, especially a woman, who had come to them alone. She knew their nature; they would be filled with suspicion.

Studying the area, she knew she would need money in order to help these people. She was sure very few of them had ever been off the mountain, most likely only a few of the men.

Anna Laura was well educated in various ways. She knew her geography. She knew beyond the other side of the mountain was a town called Cherry Valley, Tennessee. She also knew government grants were available for medical supplies, as well as educational needs and other necessities of life.

She set out early the next morning after she had bathed beneath the waterfalls once again and made herself presentable to enter Cherry Valley.

She rode into the small town. There, she inquired as to where the government office related to grants for the underprivileged was located. When she found the place, she walked in with as much dignity and confidence she could muster. Perhaps this would motivate the office people to listen to her reason for being there.

She was diverted to another more elegant office. The furniture and decor were very high quality. A tall, dark-haired, extremely handsome young man stood and introduced himself as Hank Gregory. She extended her hand, "I'm Anna Laura Gibson."

Hank was captivated by her impassioned story of the needs of the Brushy Mountain people.

She informed Hank, "Actually, I would say they are among the forgotten."

Hank was stunned to learn her educational background. He was silent for a couple of minutes wondering, "Why would this beautiful, intellectual woman come to the Brushy Mountains and want to help the poor, uneducated people that lived on the mountain and had for many years?" His thoughts were, "How can she sacrifice a medical career, she could choose to work anywhere in the wide world?"

After coming back to reality from his deep thoughts, Hank explained to Anna Laura, "This could take some time."

"I'm willing to wait. My momma taught me as a very young child that anything worthwhile is worth waiting for."

"Anna Laura, will you be able to come back to my office in one week? By then I should be able to give you more substantial information."

As Anna Laura stood to her feet to leave, the tall, dark-haired man stood and extended his arm to shake her hand.

Anna Laura couldn't help noticing he had the bluest eyes she had ever looked into. He was extremely handsome. She certainly was impressed as she noticed he was not wearing a wedding band.

"Ma'am, I will see you next week."

Hank's eyes were fixed on Anna Laura as she walked to the trail that led to Brushy Mountain. He had never encountered such beauty and grace in one person.

As Anna Laura rode up the trail in the quietness of the mountains, she had flashbacks of the day she told her fiancé that she must return to the mountains that she called home. Her heart felt as thought it was being gripped in a vise as she remembered the hurt she saw in Clint Knopp's eyes. He had tried convincing her not to leave, his blue eyes were the saddest she had ever looked upon. It was as though she was looking through the windows into his soul.

Anna Laura's heart ached with grief as the Redbud blossoms along the trail brushed her face softly, wiping the tears away. She remembered the sadness as she had walked away, knowing if she looked back she would find herself in his arms. She searched her heart and soul for her strong mountain resistance. By the grace of God, it still remained.

She could not accept that she belonged in Clint's world. She was sure she could be herself with Clint, but not his family.

She halted her horse beneath a huge oak tree then she asked herself, "Did I leave behind the person God intended me to spend my entire life with?"

At that moment her inner pain was so intense that she knew she must put her thoughts behind her and concentrate on her mission.

She arrived back at her campsite just before dark. She built a fire then spread her blanket on the ground. There she lay looking at the stars, the Milky Way, finding the most common constellations in the night sky. She drifted into a pleasant, much needed sleep; she planned to visit the settlement the next day. She felt so needed. She knew her destiny lay in these mountains. She truly believed this was her assignment from God; however, she deeply feared rejection from these people who had been secluded for so long and were not likely to take to strangers.

In the morning, she bathed, dressed and groomed herself then sat wondering what the upcoming days would be like. She pondered whether the handsome man at the grant office would really try to help her. She appreciated the kindness he had shown. The name Hank Gregory flowed through her mind in a comforting way. She remembered the sincerity in his eyes as he related to her the possibilities of getting help for the settlers.

As she sat sipping her coffee, again she wondered what could be happening to the one she left behind.

"Will I ever stop loving him or will he stop loving me? Perhaps he will continue on with his life and fall in love with someone new."

The very thought pierced her heart.

Clint had been adopted by a wealthy German couple who came to an orphanage in Boston when he was three years old. His parents had died in a car crash. He had been blessed that two wonderful people who could not have their own children took him to Germany and loved him as their own flesh and blood.

Anna Laura came back to reality as she dashed the last of her coffee in to the smoldering embers.

Chapter 3

Anna Laura saddled her horse and gracefully mounted wearing her green plaid shirt and Levi's. She lightly touched the flanks of her Arabian with the heels of her leather boots. She was comfortable in her simple attire. She began to feel a deep, consoling calm as she rode through the wilderness.

Suddenly, a flock of geese flew over, startling both Anna Laura and her Arabian. Coming to a halt, she watched them move over the mountaintop looking as though they were almost touching the blue sky. The fresh mountain air soothed her soul as it gently breathed over her skin and made her more alert.

Before she knew it, she was approaching the small settlement of log cabins, dabbed with clay mud to fill the cracks between. When riding into the settlement a huge, rough looking young man stepped into her path.

His voice was brusque. "Who are you? What are you doing here and what do you want?"

"I'm here to help educate and assist in the healthcare of the mountain people. I am not here to harm or take anything away from anyone."

"We don't want outsiders on this mountain," he replied.

"Sir, I once lived at the foot of this mountain in a little valley called Sampson before going to Germany and becoming a doctor. I came back and worked in Boston as a doctor for a few months. While there I had a deep heartfelt calling to come to the mountains beyond Sampson to help the mountain people I had only heard of while growing up. Are you familiar with the valley at the foot of Brushy Mountain?"

"Well, woman, I think you came to the wrong place. We don't need nobody." He frowned and spit his tobacco on the ground.

Anna Laura felt a little disturbed but knew if she had grown up in a forgotten land and made her way to Germany way across the sea, she could handle what lay ahead in these mountains.

As she entered the settlement, both men and women began to flock outside staring at Anna Laura and her Arabian horse. She introduced herself, then continued, "I'm here to help you. I am a doctor and I can also be a teacher for your children. I can be of help to you in many ways." The people continued to stare in silence.

Anna Laura began to feel uncomfortable as there was not a smile to be seen. Slowly, they began to disperse into their cabins. Anna Laura sat on her horse, somewhat mesmerized by the total unfriendliness of the people. She pondered for a moment and knew the only thing to do at the present was to turn her horse around, head back to camp and pray for a better tomorrow.

Her thoughts were, "There is always a tomorrow. I will be persistent. I do not give up easily."

As she rode out of sight a young, dark-haired, pale-faced girl, probably around seventeen stepped from behind a huge oak tree that hid her from her people.

"Miss," she replied, "I would like to learn your ways. You are so pretty and you talk so pretty. I would like to be schooled. I have heard talk of books and how they tell you about other places in the world. Today when I can, I would like to slip off and come see you."

"If you are sure you will not get into trouble with your family, please come for a visit."

"Well, it could cause an uproar, but I want to learn your ways more than anything in this world. I'll chance it."

Later in the day Anna Laura sat in her little mountain paradise that she had personally staked a claim on. She loved being encircled by the wild stream, the waterfalls, the Dogwood, Redbud and Sarvis bushes full of white blooms and the many colored wildflowers and the meadow of tall, green grass. The serenity of nature's splendor soothed her soul. The calm, heavenly sounds of nature were so different from the big cities where she had studied and lived; however, when living in the Valley of Sampson at the foot of the mountains she had experienced a hurtful, but quiet life. The God given beauty kept her human spirit alive. She was a dreamer. Her dreams of a better life had motivated her to leave the valley and endeavor to become educated as well as learning different cultures. Studying abroad was more rewarding. She drank in every experience. Although her endeavors were fulfilling she still had a yearning to return to her heritage and impart in some way the knowledge she had gained to the less fortunate.

Chapter 4

Suddenly, Anna Laura's thoughts were interrupted by the sound of soft footsteps snapping a small, dead tree branch nearby. She nervously turned to see the young girl, Mary Jane. In many ways, this girl reminded her of herself when she lived in the valley below as a young teenager. She looked frail and undernourished. Anna Laura remembered looking the same way.

As Anna Laura looked at Mary Jane, she imagined how pretty she could be with a bit of grooming. She extended her hand.

"I am Anna Laura Gibson"

"My name is Mary Jane Smith."

"Mary Jane is a really pretty name." Mary Jane smiled as she held her hands together nervously popping her fingers at the joints.

"Anna Laura," she nervously spoke, "I don't want to stay here all my life and be dumb, I rode off the mountain one time with my aunt and uncle over into Tennessee. The people acted different. I even seen cars. I've never been in one. Uncle Matt and Aunt Martha wouldn't take me back again. They said they could see the craving in my eyes for a different life, a life that I best forget about because I belong in the mountains."

"Mary Jane, what happened to your momma and daddy?"

"They come down with the fever when I was two years old and died. I can't remember them. People told me they were real good folks. Uncle Matt and Aunt Martha already had nine children. When I got big enough, Aunt Martha made me work real hard and whipped me a lot if I didn't do to suit her. Uncle Matt was my daddy's brother. He was kinder, but tried to please Aunt Martha. He never wanted to whip me. If they find out I am here, I'll get a hard whipping. I'd better go before they think I've been gone too long. I am supposed to be huntin' hickory chickens. Do you know what they are?"

"Yes, Mary Jane, I used to hunt them. They are edible mushrooms. I loved finding them when I was a girl. Mary Jane, my momma died when I was six. My daddy remarried. My step-mother didn't think highly of me.

She didn't make me work a lot, so I hired out to work for other women. I worked in their homes doing all kinds of chores. These women were married to men who were coal miners and made fair wages. My dad knew I had dreams of a better life and allowed me to save my money from the time I was nine-years-old until I graduated high school. I had studied about other countries so I went to Germany. My dad hired someone to take me to Harlan to catch a bus. From there I rode to an airport in Knoxville, Tennessee. I was given every opportunity in Germany for higher education. That's how I became a doctor."

"I want to help sick people, too, Anna Laura, or I might like to teach children. I don't know for sure."

"You may want to be a teacher, Mary Jane. Think of all the uneducated children on this mountain that you could help."

"Will you teach me, Anna Laura? I learn easy," questioned Mary Jane.

Anna Laura responded, "If given the opportunity, I will."

"I got to go now, Anna Laura."

"Mary Jane, I will be riding back into the settlement tomorrow."

"I'm glad, Anna. Is it okay if I call you Anna and you call me Mary?"

"Sure, Mary."

Mary went on her way. About halfway between the settlement and Anna Laura's camp, Mary Jane heard brush moving. She was frightened. As she moved faster the sound of steps were overtaking her. She began to run, but suddenly she was grabbed by someone big and strong. A gruff voice said loudly, "Little girl, you will pay." In the meantime, he covered her eyes with a rag, tying it at the back of her head, and threw her to the ground.

"We don't want a stranger on this mountain. They'll mess with how we raise our families. Others will come telling us how to live, what we can do and can't do. Do you get it, Mary Jane?"

The man, unknown to Mary Jane, threw her to the ground and kicked her head and body. She lay unconscious and bleeding.

Night hovered over the mountain, but the moon was full. Anna Laura lay on her blanket beneath the moon and stars. She felt a restlessness that she could not shake off. Suddenly she experienced a still voice within.

"Anna Laura, Mary is in trouble."

She tossed and turned for what seemed an eternity. The small, still voice nagged at her heart and soul and mind. She could not lie there any longer. She began walking in the direction Mary had gone. After a short distance she heard groaning. She recognized Mary Jane's voice. She ran through the woods filled with fear, but thanked God for the full moon, finally she saw a figure lying on the ground.

Anna Laura hovered over Mary Jane and removed the cloth that covered her eyes.

"Thank God you're alive, Mary. Do you know who did this to you?"

"No, Anna, I don't. They were big and tall and had a mean, gruff voice."

Anna Laura raised Mary Jane to her feet and by the effort of the two of them they were able to make it back to Anna Laura's place. Anna Laura laid Mary Jane on a soft, clean blanket spread over dry leaves. She went for her medical bag and supplies beneath the cliff.

Anna Laura carefully explained the procedures step-by-step as she cleaned and stitched the moderately deep cut. Luckily, the cut was near the hairline and the scar would not show.

Anna Laura administered a mild sedative that allowed Mary Jane to sleep.

Anna Laura fell asleep, but awakened in the middle of the night wondering how the mountain people would react when she rode into the settlement the next day with bandages showing on Mary Jane's wound. Her main concern was not to let Mary's Uncle Matt and Aunt Martha abuse her when they arrived at their place.

Anna Laura had brought a gun for protection in the mountain. She would never harm anyone unless it meant life or death; however, for the fractious people it could make them have second thoughts about their actions. She would keep it visible at all times; she had a special holder for it strapped to the side of her saddle.

It was only a couple of hours until the brightness of the warm sun filtered through the trees. Anna Laura was a little tired from the unexpected events of the night so she slept a little later than usual.

After showering and dressing, Anna Laura prepared blueberry flapjacks in the flat iron skillet. The aroma awakened Mary Jane. Never had she smelled anything like the fresh coffee and flapjacks. Her pain and soreness did not spoil her appetite.

Reluctantly, Anna Laura informed Mary Jane, "Mary, we must return you back to the settlement."

"I wish with my whole heart I could stay here forever," Mary replied with such sadness in her blue eyes.

Anna Laura helped Mary Jane onto the Arabian, then mounted herself and headed through the woods toward the settlement.

They dismounted at Jack and Ruth's place. Uncle Matt looked on from a distance from his cabin window. He made his way outside very hastily screaming at Anna Laura, "What have you done to Mary Jane?"

"Please, Uncle Matt, stop it! Anna Laura saved my life. Someone blindfolded me, threw me to the ground and kicked me till I passed out. Please believe me. If it wasn't for her I wouldn't be here."

Matt began to calm down, but looked at Mary Jane as though he almost wished she wasn't there. What she heard from Matt wouldn't compare to what Martha would dish out. Matt did care about his seventeen year old niece but he was so hen-pecked by Martha he felt he had to show bitterness. Martha ruled the roost, which left Mary Jane feeling desolate and Matt feeling a resentment that had become almost real.

After Martha walked back inside the cabin, Matt hurriedly and quietly thanked Anna Laura for saving Mary Jane's life. Anna Laura was confident that at last the ice had been broken just a little. Perhaps the people could see through this incident that Anna Laura could also be of help to others.

Most of the settlers were aware that Matt and Martha were mean to Mary Jane, but they never interfered.

Chapter 5

Anna Laura knew the time was right for her to ride through the settlement. There must have been at least twenty families. She was impressed at how most of the families accommodated each other in planting their crops. She then realized they helped each other at hog killing time, as well as harvesting crops.

The women came together to render lard from the fat of the hogs and divided it equally. The families had several children each so the population in the settlement alone was at least one-hundred and fifty or more. The settlers were really blessed to have found so much level land on the mountain.

Anna Laura rode through, observing, trying to find a bit of acceptance. As she passed family members that were outside doing chores she sensed the extension of more courtesy than the first day she rode through the settlement.

In spite of her more hopeful feelings, she was still a little uneasy. What had happened to Mary Jane left her concerned. Suddenly she could feel she was being watched. She rode steadily toward her camp. Once there, she realized someone had been there. The bizarre difference was that someone had made a miniature grave, the dirt heaped like a new grave in the mountains to allow the dirt to settle and not look sunken. Instead of a flower, a dead stick lay on the replica of a grave. Anna Laura was afraid. She knew this was a warning that she could end up six feet under.

She was determined to stay calm. As darkness dispersed the daylight bringing bleakness, the thought of a long dark night made her feel a little tightness in her chest. Fear could affect the body as she well knew. Night kept creeping in and she could not help the fear that crept up as well. She hurriedly gathered extra wood to keep the fire glowing; she wanted to light up as much of the area around her as possible. The full moon had just phased through to the new moon, which brought even greater darkness to the mountain. Anna Laura lay on her blanket thinking ahead. She knew that during the summer and fall season she would have to have a cabin constructed. The winter was harsh and no one could survive under the stars. Shelter was a necessity she would have to deal with.

She grew so tired that sleep finally came. Come morning she awakened to a spectacular sunrise in the eastern skies. The sound of the rippling waters, the fresh, clean air and the beauty of the mountains erased the fear that had occupied her mind earlier in the night.

She thought, "If someone had intended to harm me, they could have done it while I slept." The fear began to dissipate, but still the thoughts of what happened to Mary Jane made her realize there was an unstable, evil person lurking in the mountains. The thought occurred to her, "Perhaps there was someone who had no proper upbringing or was abused and unprotected."

Anna Laura dismissed the negative and prayed for protection. She now felt safe.

She headed for the waterfalls to shower and slip into her jeans and a pink silk blouse, tucking it in and wearing her special belt. She never wore it without thinking of Clint as she fastened the gold buckle. As she looked at the belt buckle, she tried convincing herself, "He is my past, far in my past. I must go on with my life. I must let go."

She then thought of the tall, dark, handsome man at the government grant office. She figured he was near her age, perhaps a year or so older.

Anna Laura came back to the present, finished grooming, saddled the Arabian, mounted and headed toward the settlement. As she had gained a little rapport with Mary Jane's Uncle Matt, even though it was mostly negative, she did not feel as apprehensive. She hoped for a positive day. Much of the apprehension left her and her positive spirit was returning. She rode through the mountains feeling beyond a doubt she would have a better day.

As she rode into the settlement, people were taking a day of rest. It must be Sunday. People sat on their porches enjoying the sun that beamed its warmth onto their porches.

As Anna Laura rode through, she saw many smiles. The tale of her saving Mary Jane had spread through the community and brought a feeling of trust to the people. They began to see Anna Laura as an angel of mercy rather than an intruder. At last she could feel peace in her heart and mind.

One couple, Steve and Lilly, who were standing in their fenced-in yard called out, "Anna Laura, would you like to sit at our table and share our meal?" Anna Laura was absolutely stunned.

Lilly and Steve smiled. They were a good-looking couple.

Steve displayed his unusual sense of humor right away and Lilly had a smile that never seemed to leave her face. Their inward goodness was reflected in their kind eyes.

Anna Laura dismounted and hitched her Arabian to the fence. As she walked up the steps, her natural gracefulness displayed itself. Anna Laura formally introduced herself to Steve and Lilly. The couple extended their hands, "We sure are happy to have you on our mountain."

Walking into their home, Anna Laura was surprised to look upon the lovely furniture and the cleanliness of the cabin. She learned Steve had built their furniture. Their table was made from pure cherry wood; the trees cut from the mountain timber.

Anna Laura admired the ladder back chairs and the rocking chair by the fireplace as well. The table setting was beautiful; Steve had bought glass dishes from time to time when making his trips to Cherry Valley. The dishes were a semi-transparent, pinkish color.

The meal was delicious. There were shucky beans seasoned with pork, fried potatoes, cornbread fritters and apple pie made from dried apples sat in the middle of the table. Everything had been cooked over the fireplace in cast iron cookware. This was so different. Even in the Valley of Sampson, Anna Laura's family had a cook stove.

As the three sat at the table, the young couple talked about their only means of transporting goods and how they bartered their mountain productions for things they could never have on the mountain without such exchanges.

Anna Laura asked, "Do you ever plan to leave Brushy Mountain?"

"No, probably not" Steve replied, "We've been here all our lives."

"Do you have any form of education for the children on the mountain?"

"No, ma'am, we don't," Steve sadly replied.

"If the children should leave the mountain in years to come, how will they survive?"

Lilly spoke up, "We don't believe they will ever leave."

Anna Laura finished swallowing the tasty apple pie. "Believe me, I don't want to hurt you, but they are probably already wondering what lies beyond these mountains and are yearning to find out one day."

Steve and Lilly looked a little sad, perhaps a little irritated.

Anna Laura immediately changed the subject. The last thing she wanted to do was to provoke the wonderful couple that had invited her into their home. It seemed to Anna Laura this couple was probably the most looked up to couple and rocks of the settlement. Changing the subject, Anna Laura inquired, "Do you have a church?"

"No, we have never given it much thought as most of us serve God in our own way."

"The Bible tells us not to forsake the assembling of ourselves together. Don't you think it would be wonderful to have a church in the settlement where everyone could have Christian fellowship together?"

Steve replied, "Well, we never thought much about it, did we, Lilly?"

"No, Steve, but I bet it would bring us all closer in our hearts and spirits."

"What about a school house?" asked Anna Laura.

"We don't have one. We all feel that all the children need to know is to work with their hands."

"I'm afraid I totally disagree. Your children need to know how to read, write and do arithmetic."

Steve stared out the door, deep in thought. "Well, we have never been blessed with children, but many others have."

Anna Laura suddenly changed the subject again and began to praise them for their good works, their talents of building, producing food and their survival in general.

"Steve, Lilly, I appreciate your hospitality. The food was great! Thank you so very much. I really must be getting back to my campsite."

Steve and Lilly thanked Anna Laura for her visit. "Will you please come see us again?"

After Anna Laura had ridden out of sight, many neighbors gathered at Steve and Lilly's place inquiring about the stranger. The couple related to their neighbors Anna Laura's concern about a school and church. The crowd whispered among each other. This was definitely a shock, something they had never thought of.

As Anna Laura rode back to camp, she began to think, "I must talk to the most influential person in the settlement." She had an idea that this person was likely to be Steve. She rode into her camp feeling excited; she had surely made a breakthrough.

She turned her Arabian loose to graze in the green meadows. The Arabian made a beautiful picture standing in the tall, green grass as she passed by, heading to the falls to allow the powerful waters from the mountain to wash over her and soothe her soul.

The sun still beamed through the trees, warming her body. Coming back to the camp and building a fire, she stood in the flickering light. As she thought about the day, she felt hope, hope for a better life for the mountain people, especially the young people. She knew the children would not always live in the rugged mountains. Time would bring change for them as it had for her. She knew education was the key. She recalled passing the graveyard as she rode into the mountain settlement. There were mostly small graves. She so wanted to use her medical expertise to save children, as well as others.

She lay under the stars staring into the beautiful lit up sky contemplating on how wonderful it would be to have a school, a church and a medical clinic. She recalled a vacant area bordering the settlement that would be the perfect site for what could forever change lives.

Anna Laura slept peacefully, dreaming of a better life for the mountain people. She awakened very early. She washed and groomed herself before heading off the mountain to Cherry Valley to the government office.

Chapter 6

Anna Laura experienced the greatest feeling when leaving her horse at the stables. The joy she was experiencing seemed like it would burst right out of her chest; her heart was so warmed. She remembered feeling that way as a child when something very simple, but good, happened in her life.

Suddenly, Hank Gregory called from the other side of the narrow street, "Anna Laura, it is so good to see you."

Hank could hardly hide his excitement as he talked with her. He had dreamed of seeing her again, but did not want her to be aware. Hank had spent many sleepless nights feeling that when he met Anna Laura the very first time that it was definitely love at first sight. He admired not only her beauty, but her courage and ability to come to an unfamiliar land; the mountains that were so desolate compared to her new world, to help those who had no connection to her in any way.

Hank was hesitant, but finally asked the question, "Anna Laura will you have lunch with me at the Hemlock Inn?"

Anna Laura's answer came quick, "Indeed, I will."

The restaurant was called the Hemlock Inn because it was built of square hemlock logs. The Inn sat near the foothills of the small town and tall hemlock pines covered most of the area above the Inn.

As they walked across the small town of Cherry Valley, Anna Laura asked out of curiosity, "Hank, are you from Cherry Valley?"

"No, I moved here from Nashville, Tennessee."

Anna Laura and Hank walked into the huge restaurant. The atmosphere was delightful. Cherry trees were in bloom, the blossoms a lovely pink that made one feel happy just to feast their eyes on such beauty. Cherry trees grew near the clear stream and on the green, grassy site that lay beyond the Inn. It was quite a sight to look upon. The huge restaurant window allowed a clear view of the beauty of the cherry trees and the mountain of hemlocks.

Anna Laura looked lovely in her pink silk blouse, gray riding skirt and gray boots. Her lips were perfectly shaped, shining with pink lipstick. Her long, dark hair shone and her olive skin was flawless. Today she wore small pearl earrings that added a hint of innocence.

Hank could not take his eyes off his companion. He experienced a little guilt since he had a girlfriend back in Nashville. He had not made a commitment; however, he was sure that Ingrid's feelings for him were deeper than his for her.

As Anna Laura sat at their table staring out the window, she asked, "Hank, do you think the government is planning to accommodate the mountain people?"

"Yes, Anna Laura, you will be getting a substantial grant, providing it's used for education and medical facilities, as well as clothing and other basic needs."

"Oh, Hank! That is wonderful! I am totally elated. I'm at a loss for words!"

"You don't have to say anything," Hank touched Anna Laura's hand. "It is real, you can believe it."

Anna Laura blushed as Hank lifted his hand to touch hers. After finishing their divine lunch, they walked to Hank's office. Anna Laura signed several papers accepting the grant.

"Anna Laura, it will likely be a couple of weeks before the grant money will be accessible. I will open an account, which will enable you to write checks to cover your purchases."

Suddenly, Anna Laura said she had better get on her way to reach the mountain before dark. She extended her hand, "I will see you in two weeks, Hank."

Hank loved the sound of Anna Laura's voice. It was somewhat different as she had been in Germany for ten years.

Anna Laura headed to the stables for her Arabian. He was rested and fit for the trail that would take them from Cherry Valley to Brushy Mountain.

Before beginning the steep climb she stopped by a clear stream for her horse to drink. As she began her climb, she took her handgun from the saddle bag. She didn't really anticipate trouble, but wanted security and wasn't so naive that she believed one was always safe in the mountains.

Anna Laura safely made it to her campsite, the only home she now occupied. Someone had paid her another strange visit. The blanket she had slept on had random burns on it. Another strange warning, she thought, but deep in her heart, she was at ease.

God gave her peace in her heart and soul, only a peace that God could give. She always recognized this peaceful feeling in times of trouble. She had been taught by her momma as a small child to put her trust in God. Each night she prayed for his protection. She knew she was covered by his blood spiritually. She also knew he expected her to use wisdom throughout her life.

Anna Laura put her saddle away as well as other items and headed for the waterfalls to bathe. Feeling chilled from the fresh mountain air, she put on her soft, warm flannel gown. After a snack she brushed her teeth at the clear stream near her camp. She laid a fresh blanket on the leaves. For a while she lay staring toward the sky filled with twinkling stars as she thanked God for the blessed day she had encountered.

She drifted into a peaceful sleep as she thought of all the wonderful things the grant money could provide for the mountain people who were so afraid of change or leaving the mountain. Anna Laura slept like a newborn babe. In the morning, she adorned herself, brushed her Arabian, then had a delightful breakfast of blueberry pancakes and coffee. She saddled her horse, mounted and rode toward the settlement.

As she slowly rode through the woods following the familiar trail, she rehearsed how she would explain that she would be receiving a grant and how it would be used if everyone was in agreement, maybe not everyone, but the ones who influenced the lives of the settlers. Perhaps Steve and Lilly would be the couple to approach as she had established a relatively peaceful connection with them.

Anna Laura hitched her horse to a rail and made her way across the yard, up the steps and tapped on the door, feeling very anxious. She composed herself, trying to appear very confident.

Lilly opened the door. Surprisingly, she called out with a smile on her face, "Steve, we have a visitor, Anna Laura is here."

Lilly asked her in and they sat at the cherry wood table Anna Laura adored. Lilly served coffee for the three of them; it was strong, but very flavorful.

"Steve, Lilly, I have the best news ever! I'll explain to you as best I can. The government has given a grant for your mountain people who are lacking in education, medical treatment as well as clothing and shoes for many. I have already learned during my short-time here that mountain ways are difficult for most. How do you think mountain people will respond to this act of kindness?"

"Well, Anna Laura, change is a hard thing for mountain people. They may not be educated, some not as clean as they should be, some lacking in food if they don't preserve enough to last, but they're still prideful. I guess the better way to put it is they are easily insulted."

"Steve, the grant won't cover a church building. Do you think you could get several of the men together to build a church?"

"I don't rightly know, but I am game for seeing what I can do."

"Steve, do you think we could call a meeting and tell the people all that I've told Lilly and you?"

"I can try, but I can tell you now some that are so set in their ways will act plumb crazy. Well, Anna Laura, we will try. Tomorrow I will go from house to house. When do you want the meeting?"

"There is a big level place around the back side of the settlement. There will be room for everyone there," Lilly replied.

"Steve, do you think we could set the meeting for Sunday? Today is Wednesday, that will give you a few days to spread the word."

After returning to her campsite, Anna Laura began preparing her presentation. By Friday she was well-prepared. Meantime, Steve thought of ways he could approach the people. He went from door to door asking the people to come to the meeting. Anna Laura had a couple of days to be free. She was well-prepared and wanted to get the meeting off her mind. She decided to do some riding into an area she had explored. By candlelight she even wrote to Clint hoping she would one day mail the letter from Cherry Valley. There was still an emptiness in her heart for the one she left behind.

Dearest Clint,

When I finish my mission, if you have not met someone else and made a new life for yourself, I will return to Germany. The royalty and wealth of your people do not matter to me. I would belong to you, not your family. Please write back and let me know how you feel. I do love you, Clint.

Anna Laura

Anna Laura slipped the letter into her saddle bag. As the moon was new, candlelight was not bright enough. Anna Laura did not want to be in total darkness so she lit a fire more for light than heat. As she gathered wood for the fire, someone grabbed her from behind.

The man was huge; no doubt he had heard of the upcoming meeting. What he didn't know was that Anna Laura was trained in karate. By the time the man was thrown into the darkness of the mountains, he was terrified and ran away.

By Saturday Anna Laura realized that the man was not her real enemy. She then realized he had left the strange warnings at her campsite before. Anna Laura talked with Steve and Lilly about this huge young man.

"Steve, just how many people do you think are against my wanting to help the settlement?"

"You know, Anna Laura, I don't want you to go getting hurt and I also don't want you to leave. We need help on this mountain. Our children are suffering. We want them to have a better life than we have and have had in years gone by. Maybe our children and grandchildren can get an education and learn new stuff about the rest of the world. Maybe they can get good jobs somewhere beyond the Brushy Mountains. What really troubles me is the ones up here on the mountain don't want nothing to be different. Me and my Lilly have always dreamed of a time like this; that maybe God would send a change. We certainly never dreamed He would send a young doctor like you."

"Anna Laura, me and Lilly staked a claim on a big piece of ground beyond them woods over there. I'd be safe in saying there's near five acres. It has always amazed me how flat it is on this big ole Brushy Mountain. It's odd that it would be so flat when the trails leading off to Kentucky and Tennessee are so rough and steep. Nobody can get up the nerve to leave these mountains because they are afraid of the unknown. My daddy and mommy were among the first settlers here on the mountain. Well, I guess their mommy and daddy were. We'd be the third generation. People have been here for a long time. This generation might have life a little easier because we've learned from our parents. Seems like every generation gets a little wiser. Look at that cherry table. I got tools over in Tennessee and learned to build my own house furnishings."

"Steve, that cherry table is one of the most original pieces of furniture I have ever seen."

Chapter 7

Steve's mind suddenly made a transition from his own blessings.

"Anna Laura, I know the weather will be good for a few more months. What will you do when winter comes on? What do you do now when it rains?"

"I lay my blankets and quilt under a huge rock that has safe, clean space under it; however, I prefer sleeping under the stars while the weather is nice."

"Now, Anna Laura, you'll freeze to death under a rock this winter. I mean to tell you the snows are big, the winds from the north whistle and blow, it's so cold we just about have to hole up inside but for caring for our livestock and bringing in wood from the shed. We have our food under our floors; we have a square door and wood steps to go down. We put it in the middle so that water don't get to it. We bury cabbage upside down in our gardens so it won't rot and put our taters in a hole and cover them. Keeps them from freezing. Over the years we got glass jars to can jellies, apple butter and other stuff that we keep on shelves inside our cabins. We dry beans and apples. Berries and nuts grow wild up here and plentiful."

"Yes, Steve, I know. I really enjoy the fresh berries."

"Anna Laura, I just got to tell you, there's bears, wolves and panther in these mountains, they don't come near our homes, but beware they could come where you camp."

"Steve, I pretty well keep a small fire going, which I feel will warn them off my campsite. I heard as a child that a fire at night keeps the wild animals away. I am really not afraid. I keep a gun nearby, I shoot well. I refuse to live in fear."

"I'll tell you what, Anna Laura, I'll see if some of the accommodating gentlemen will help build a log cabin for you before winter comes on. We can build make do furniture for you. Our wives can help make you a feather bed to lay on. They all save feathers after plucking the chickens that we eat. When us men go to Tennessee we bring back muslin cloth for our wives to work with. We take the extra food we raise in our gardens and pick fruit from our trees and barter for stuff we can't make or raise up here in the mountains. Our forefathers already had cattle, horses, chickens and pigs. Even a few goats roamed the hills. We keep them multiplying. We love this kind of life, but it ain't easy. There has been many a one died 'cause they couldn't survive this kind of life. Flu and fever take a lot of people. We sure need a doctor."

"Steve, that's the main reason I'm here. I also want to see children escape poverty and being uneducated just as I have."

"Anna Laura, what really caused you to come back and come to the mountains?"

"Steve, I feel that God has ordered my steps. I am from the valley below as you know, but went to another country to be educated. I feel at the present I am a missionary in my own country. Seems a little strange, but God's ways are not always our ways. Our flesh desires to take the easy way. The plans God has for us are not always easy, but if we endure he rewards us in the end when the calling he puts in our lives is fulfilled."

"Anna Laura, you sure have a lot of faith."

Lilly broke into the conversation, "You are a mighty brave girl."

"Lilly, it is the Holy Spirit that dwells in my heart that gives me courage and relieves fear."

Steve broke into the conversation, "Anna Laura, the people have agreed to meet with us on Sunday."

"Thanks, Steve, for passing the word around. I've always heard that word of mouth travels fast in the mountains. Lilly, Steve, I'd better head back to my camp."

"We'll see you tomorrow, Anna Laura. You be careful now."

"Don't worry, I'll be fine."

Anna Laura mounted her Arabian and headed through the settlement. Some watched with anger and some with pleasant anticipation as Anna Laura rode through.

Chapter 8

Anna Laura entered her own little paradise. To her it was all she needed at the present. After finishing her evening rituals of bathing at the waterfalls and enjoying the fragrance and wildflowers in the clean mountain air, she lay on her momma's quilt that always gave her a certain amount of security.

As she lay staring into the beautiful sky, memories of a happier time warmed her heart. The good times she and Clint had spent together were hidden away in her heart; however, she felt a bit of confusion as thoughts of having lunch with Hank a week prior seemed to break into her thoughts of Clint.

Suddenly, she realized Hank was falling for her as she remembered the way he touched her hand and the way his eyes made contact with hers. She was attracted to Hank, but what she felt could not compare to what her heart held for Clint. He was her first love; young love filled with emotion, but innocence as well.

Anna Laura fell asleep as she stared into the star-filled sky. Her sleep was sweet.

She was awakened by the sun rays beaming through the trees. She felt so peaceful as she made breakfast, but also couldn't stop wondering how the settlers would react to the meeting that was to take place.

Anna Laura wanted to look really presentable so she dressed in a pale yellow shirt and jeans, her special belt and leather boots.

As she spread light orange lipstick on her lips to match the light yellow shirt, she felt pretty. She was completely relaxed. Suddenly her horse stood on his hind legs neighing in fear. Looking to the ground, a huge rattlesnake was in the process of striking her horse. She drew her gun and took the snake's head off with a single shot. She calmed her horse and rode toward the settlement feeling a little anxious.

She made her way to Steve and Lilly's. As she rode into their yard, they stood calmly on their weathered, gray porch waiting for their new friend.

"Anna Laura, hitch your horse to the rail and we'll walk to the meeting grounds," Lilly spoke softly.

As they walked, Steve suggested that Anna Laura use the huge, flat rock that lay at the back edge of the meeting grounds for a platform. Anna Laura was surprised to see that so many people had already gathered for the meeting. After everyone arrived, Anna Laura took the platform.

She began, "Folks, I'm here to help you, to enrich your lives, as well as the future of your children. First, let me explain. Within a week, I will be receiving a government grant which is money. I want to build a medical clinic to treat the sick and prevent untimely deaths. Medical supplies will be purchased with part of the grant money. I am a trained doctor."

The crowd whispered to each other.

"The next important thing is to build a school house, a place to educate your children. Grant monies will be used to bring books and necessary materials to the mountains. I am prepared to teach, as well as to care for the sick. Your children will be taught to read, write, spell and recognize numbers and how to use them."

Many were excited while others looked as though they had bit into a persimmon that wasn't ripe. Some had the expression of a horse eating saw briars. For the most part, the settlers looked hopeful.

Anna Laura knew there would be opposition, but was sure the good would outweigh the bad. She knew her heart discerned to her, by the help of a few positive, hard-working men and women, she could fulfill this dream and change generations to come.

After the meeting was finished a nice couple, George and Mary Fowler approached Anna Laura, "Will you have dinner with us?"

Lilly and Steve were also invited.

When Anna Laura took her place at the table she thought, "I haven't seen anything that looks this good since I was in Germany." The wild turkey that George had killed was a baked golden brown. The shucky beans, baked potatoes, blueberries boiled into a sauce and biscuits were a real treat for Anna Laura.

As they sat around the table after finishing their meal, the two couples related to Anna Laura that many others would support her endeavors. The mountain people were really good at reading facial expressions. As the two couples observed the crowd when Anna Laura spoke to them, they were elated to see a pleasantness that they had not encountered in years. The looks of hope on the people's faces were heartwarming. Even the children listened with anticipation and hoped for a better life.

Anna Laura could hardly sustain the joy that flowed through her heart and soul. She wanted to let out a loud scream of joy, but only smiled a beautiful smile of grace and thanksgiving. She offered to help in cleaning up the kitchen but Mary and Lilly would not allow her to.

This had been a wonderful day.

Chapter 9

Anna Laura headed back to her temporary home. She had learned home could be any place where one was peaceful. It could be under the stars or under a cliff. Then she approached a wild stream that ran toward the Kentucky side as she had wandered upward. She watched as the wildness of the stream splashed and rolled like waters of wrath, feeling her body chill from the mist of cool water.

She thought about tomorrow, the day that she would be riding off the mountain to Tennessee. She entertained the thought of having lunch in the lovely restaurant with Hank. She closed her eyes and envisioned his dark hair, his blue eyes, his tall form and his slightly dark skin, but, most of all, his smile. Suddenly, she opened her eyes and felt guilty; she had thought of Clint. He was so far away. She wondered if she would ever see him again. The same thoughts had occupied her mind so many times before. She believed she had a love for Clint that would never die, yet she was still a bit drawn by Hank's charm.

Her heart was torn in different directions. She whispered to herself, "No one can replace Clint."

Monday morning arrived and Anna Laura awakened early. She would soon be heading for Cherry Valley. She blundered around half asleep gathering her supplies for bathing and washing her hair. As the early sun beamed in, she laid her brown riding skirt, underwear and cream colored silk blouse across the bushes near the waterfalls. The sun had already filtered in and, being June, the air was warm and the clear water was soothing. Her silky hair dried quickly as she brushed it in the warm air and brightness of the sun.

She mounted her Arabian and joyfully headed down the mountain. She had eaten blueberries when she first awakened and knew they would sustain her until she had lunch with Hank.

Within a few hours, she reached the edge of Cherry Valley and stabled her horse; she still felt as fresh as a rose in the early morning dew.

Anna Laura tapped on Hank's office door and Hank immediately opened it. He knew it was Anna Laura. As he stood before her, again she could not resist noticing how handsome this dark haired, blue-eyed man was. It was very obvious to Anna Laura that Hank was elated to see her again.

It was late in the night in Germany. Clint stood on his balcony looking over the city wondering where the love of his life could be.

"Will I ever see her again?" he asked himself aloud. He pondered how his family and friends had introduced him to prominent young ladies. He enjoyed the time he spent with them, but no one could compare to Anna Laura. He had been captivated by her free spirit. She was graceful and beautiful, yet did not pretend to be someone she was not. There was nothing fake about her. He loved deep sea fishing and camping with her. He had never known anyone like her and knew he never would. He was always amazed that lipstick was the only thing she needed to enhance her beauty.

As he stood there in the cool of the night gazing toward the city lights, he thought of her loveliness. He remembered how she treated everyone equally as a doctor and a person. She loved and cared for the poor, as well as the wealthy; their status did not matter to her.

He wept inside for his Anna Laura.

As Hank stood still holding onto Anna Laura's hand with a touch of courtesy, he gently asked," Anna Laura, are you ready to have lunch at the Hemlock Inn?"

Anna Laura had enjoyed the atmosphere before and had anticipated lunch with Hank so she gave him a quick, "yes."

As they sat again in front of the big window, Anna Laura was relaxed. As they ate lunch, Hank relayed to Anna Laura how much grant money would be available. She knew at that moment she would be able to do everything needed for the people of Brushy Mountain.

As they walked toward the office, Hank gently slipped his hand over Anna Laura's. She wanted to pull away. Clint was the last to hold her hand. She experienced guilt as she still held him so dear to her heart.

After reaching the office, Hank became professional and discussed how he could have medical supplies, educational supplies, clothes and other necessities delivered to the mountains.

"I had better head home. I definitely do not want to be overtaken by darkness before I reach my campsite."

The two of them stood to their feet.

"Anna Laura, I am very fond of you," he then lightly kissed her beautiful lips. Anna Laura flushed. "Would you like to come down one weekend and ride up to Nashville with me? We could tour the city, the suburbs and look at some of the Grand Ole Opry stars' homes. I will make a reservation for you at the Andrew Jackson Hotel. It is really nice. Not far from the hotel is Church Street. Lots of nice places for a lady to shop."

"Hank, I will definitely give thought to your invitation.

Later, as Anna Laura's Arabian climbed the mountain, she feared that out of longing for Clint she could possibly be developing feelings for Hank. She still wanted to see her handsome Clint. Her feelings were mixed, but the fact still remained she still loved Clint.

Regardless of who she would one day marry, she wasn't sure she could ever let her love for Clint go, which would not be fair to the person she took for her husband. At that moment, she questioned herself, "Why did I let our different backgrounds separate us? I could have fulfilled my mission and he would have waited." Tears flowed down her pretty face like rain over a windowpane.

After arriving at the place that she now called home in Brushy Mountain, she lay staring at the stars as the fire glowed and in her heart knew she was where God wanted her to be. She remembered the Biblical scripture, "There is a time and a place for all things."

She knew this mission was not forever, but did not know how long it would last. Anna Laura drifted into sweet sleep, but shortly after was jolted by an intense clap of thunder. Lightning quickly followed, sending long streaks across the skies. She sprang to her feet, grabbed her blanket and made a dash to the cliff where her belongings were stored. She did some quick rearranging and laid her blanket in a safe, dry place. As her momma's quilt was a little damp, she hung it from the sides where small rocks extended from the walls. As the rain poured, making a relaxing sound splashing on the huge rock that sheltered her, she snuggled under a blanket and peacefully slept once again. Her Arabian was sheltered beneath the huge trees that were fully clothed with branches covered thickly with leaves.

By morning the rain had stopped, the freshness of the air, as well as the sun, made its way through the opening into the space where she slept.

Anna Laura endeavored to drag herself from her comfortable nest. She knew she had to prepare for the settlement meeting that would take place the next day. Anna Laura found a makeshift altar, a square rock in the clearing and knelt to her knees to ask God for wisdom. He had given her knowledge to acquire the needed monies that would change lives. She now needed the wisdom to know exactly how to use it when it came. She prayed, "Please, God, give me the wisdom to gain the trust of these people who are so afraid to trust."

She spent the day walking through the woods enjoying the God-given nature, picking berries and greens. In the distance she could hear the call of wild ducks as they soared over the mountains to the river far below. She felt like a free spirit as she breathed the pure air and the fragrance of the wildflowers.

The day swiftly passed; it seemed to be gone before Anna Laura realized. She would still have just enough daylight to prepare supper and shower.

As she strolled toward her place, her mind carried her back to walks in Germany and how exciting it was when she first arrived. The years of study raced through her mind.

Her mind was filled with the memory of standing before a huge fountain, pondering how it was unlike anything she had ever seen. As she stood mesmerized by the beauty of the water the fountain displayed, she felt eyes upon her. Suddenly a handsome, young man startled her as he stepped softly beside her and introduced himself as Clint Knopp.

She stopped in her tracks, speaking aloud to herself, "I must let these memories go and concentrate on the present."

Anna Laura performed her evening chores, showered at the falls and made her bed beneath the cliff as she feared it might rain again. Once more she snuggled between the warm blankets in her flannel nightgown as she was a little chilled from the fresh water that the heavy rainfall brought. Never had she rested so peacefully; the day of walking in the fresh air had completely relaxed her.

She wanted to get to the settlement early to spend time with Steve and Lilly before the meeting. As she mounted to leave, she was confident. As she rode, her confidence dissipated and uneasiness seemed to creep into her mind. For a moment she questioned herself.

"Can I be a testament to the human spirit, and the Holy Spirit that I am driven by, to change lives for the better?" She knew in that moment of time she must be strong and steadfast and unmovable from her convictions.

She rode into Steve and Lilly's yard. She had a few minutes before the meeting. As she dismounted, Steve brought corn to keep the Arabian occupied. After talking with Steve about the feelings of the people that he had talked to, she walked with the couple toward the meeting ground. She knew she could not waver in her conviction.

She recalled the words of the scriptures, "He who wavereth is like a wave of the sea driven with the wind and tossed." She vowed silently to herself, "I will stand strong and impart the knowledge I hold that will make these lives better, at least the future generation. As she thought of the small children and teenagers, the scripture, "Withhold not good from them when it is due; when it is in the power of thine hand to do it" came to her mind.

She now was reassured that God allowed her to do what she was engaged in and no one could stop her. "Barriers will come, but I will overcome them." She had learned as a child to endeavor for what she believed in.

The closer she came to the meeting area, the higher her spirit seemed to rise. Before stepping onto the huge rock to explain to the people of whom only a few had ever been off the mountain, she remembered the scripture, "The Lord thy God is in the midst of the mighty." Anna Laura had studied her Bible that her momma left her.

Her grandmother, Anna Marie, had learned to read as a child and read the Word avidly. Her desire was for Anna Laura to do likewise, regardless of where her destiny led her. Her momma held her on her lap and read to her at night by the light that flickered from the coal oil lamp before electricity finally made its way into the valley. Her momma taught her one very special thing about the Bible; Anna Laura knew the Bible was a promise book, as well as a guide for ones path through life.

She stood tall and beautiful on the huge rock adorned in a long Victorian lace dress with pearl buttons down the front and on the sleeves. She looked like a princess. The young girls and women stood in admiration of her poise and beauty. The men admired her looks as well, but not her charisma. Men in the mountains found it hard to see a woman in control of anything. Anna Laura knew that God used women throughout biblical history, so she was comfortable with what she was doing.

She asked, "Is there anyone who would like to open this meeting with prayer?"

"No!" Someone responded.

Anna Laura began a prayer of humility. "Whosoever therefore shall humble himself as a little child, the same is greatest in the kingdom of Heaven. Lord, thou has heard the desire of the humble, thou wilt prepare their heart, thou wilt cause thine ear to hear. And whosoever shalt exalt himself shall be abased and he that shall humble himself shall be exalted. Better it is to be of a humble spirit with the lowly, than to divide the spoil with the proud. God resisteth the proud, but giveth grace to the humble. Amen."

The people, not being educated, perhaps some words from Anna Laura's prayer they could not understand, but in context they understood that she was not a proud person and regardless of how poor and uneducated they were they could still have the undesirable characteristics such as being too proud to accept change and help.

Anna Laura began, "Ladies and gentlemen, young women and men and children, I have gone off the mountain seeking money from the government which has finally come through. The monies that have been made available can provide you with tools to build a medical building, a schoolhouse, books and supplies for all ages, even you that are older, also a church and Bibles for everyone as well as Bible storybooks for the children. This can open up a whole new world for your children and for you. Some of you will never leave Brushy Mountain except by death; you will want to be buried over there in the Brushy Mountain graveyard; so you will never leave the mountain except when Christ splits the Eastern skies. Your children and grandchildren may want to prepare to leave these mountains, especially when you have passed on."

Those opposed to change began to be rude and yelled negative words toward Anna Laura. She held her peace and was silent until the frustrated people saw her humbleness and calmed down. She definitely did as the Bible said, she heaped coals of fire on their heads. Everyone became so quiet, the only sound was the fluttering of the leaves as the wind stirred through the trees.

Anna Laura continued to share the news of what the grant monies could do. "We will have medical supplies to save babies and older children from dying of influenza and pneumonia, and other childhood diseases. Look at the small graves over in the graveyard; most of the deaths of the young can be prevented as well as many adults."

She saw rivers of tears sliding down the faces of both young and older women. The men dropped their heads feeling sorrowful.

"Your children can learn more about God, about faith and love. We will have Sunday school to educate you about preparing for a new life. I know you love this mountain, but there is more. I love it as well, but do not want to spend the rest of my life here. How many of you men will help build a medical building, a doctor's office, a schoolhouse and a church?"

At least twelve hands went into the air. Steve spoke up loudly, "I will donate the land. The buildings can be built on the same acreage."

The people whispered among themselves. Some were opposed but a greater number were elated which spoke volumes; clearly more were for the program than against it.

"Thank all of you," Anna Laura spoke over the voices from the crowd, "All of you that are interested in helping with this great step toward a better life meet here next Sunday at noon."

Steve and Lilly invited Anna Laura for dinner. Dinner was in the middle of the day, supper was in the evening; this was a part of mountain culture. Anna Laura felt great relief as she walked toward Steve and Lilly's home.

As she walked, many of the people from a distance admired her. They whispered to each other, "I wish I could look and act like her."

Most of the mountain women and girls possessed natural beauty. They only needed the clothes, the shampoo and other aids to enhance their beauty.

After the meeting, Anna Laura sat at the table with Steve and Lilly enjoying the splendid meal that sweet Lilly prepared. She was filled with joy as the responses from the people were far more than she had expected. She certainly believed that God's word was real when it said, "God's word is full of promises for His people." She knew this very moment that assurance of His guidance had come her way.

Anna Laura helped Lilly clean the table, extended her gratitude as Lilly walked outside with her expressing her thankfulness as well.

As Anna Laura mounted her horse to ride side-saddle in her lovely dress, she softly spoke, "Lilly, I could not have done this without Steve and you."

Upon reaching camp, she took off her beautiful dress, stored it safely in a long linen dress carrier, then folded it and stored it in the case she had brought her clothes in. As she bathed at the falls, she relaxed as the water splashed over the rock she stood on while her thoughts carried her thousands of miles away. Her heart was in the mountains, but yearned to be in Germany with Clint. She began to concentrate on how many months or years would pass before her mission would be fulfilled.

"Will he still be there? Will the sacrifice be worth what I have given up?"

The scripture, "For the needy shall not always be forgotten," came to Anna Laura's mind, reassuring her. As she stood beneath the clean waters that washed over her, she asked herself, "How could I go away and forget these people to fulfill my own life?"

Anna Laura purposed in her heart that very moment, there is a time for all things. Again, she lay under the big, open sky taking in the beauty of the stars and moon. Just as she began to relax she heard voices and became a little startled.

"Who's there?" She called out as the voices came closer.

"Please, Anna Laura, we need help. Our mommy is so sick. She can't even sit up."

Anna Laura rubbed her sleepy eyes, trying to see who was calling on her. Before her stood two small children: a boy around seven and a little girl about six.

Anna Laura collected her thoughts and went to the cliff for her medical bag. She called for her horse. She sat the children on the horse, one in the front of her and one behind.

"Show me the way, children."

As they did not live in the settlement, Anna Laura had never seen them before. They had no problem directing Anna Laura around the mountain in the opposite direction from the settlement.

"What are your names?"

In unison they answered, "Joel and Susie."

Anna Laura chatted with them, trying to make them feel comfortable. The distance was at least a mile east of her campsite in the rougher part of the mountain.

"Thank you, God, for a full moon," Anna Laura spoke out.

The children told Anna Laura that in the past they had played near her camp and were hiding in the woods during the special meeting. There they learned that she was a doctor. They also told her that they wanted to go to school. As they rode the path through the moonlit mountain, crossing rough areas of rocks and old rotten trees, Anna Laura guided her horse very careful and enjoyed listening to Joel and Susie. She tried diligently to take their minds away from the trauma they were going through.

Suddenly, Anna Laura saw a light glowing through a small window, she was sure this was their house. With sadness in her voice, Susie whispered, "Anna Laura, we are home."

Anna Laura got off her Arabian, stretched her arms upward to assist the children as they lightly slid into her arms and to the ground.

"Follow us, Anna Laura."

"Let me get my medical bag."

The three walked into the cabin. The floors were of split logs, rough, and a bit dirty. Dirty clothes lay in the corner. A slab of side bacon hung beside the fireplace where the family cooked. One had to be careful when moving around to prevent greasing their head by rubbing against the slab of salty cured meat.

"Where is your momma?"

"She is in that little room." Joel pointed.

The bed was dirty. There was an unpleasant odor in the room.

"Anna Laura, this is our momma." Joel whispered, "Her name is Martha Wilder."

"Where is your father?"

"We don't know. He was real mean to our momma one day, hurt her real bad. He hit her in the back and chest. He made her nose bleed, then knocked her on the floor. She didn't wake up for a long time. He left that day and never came back."

"We've tried to help momma," Susie chimed in. "She's been gettin' real bad off. She held on to stuff trying to cook for us, but she can't do that no more."

"Let me look at Martha while you keep an eye out for my horse."

"We can do that," they replied as they walked through the shabby room and out the door.

Anna Laura took out her stethoscope and put it to Martha's chest. Never had she heard lungs so filled with infection. After breathing in, Martha could not turn over; her temperature was dangerously high. Anna Laura knew she was near death. She spread Martha's chest with Vick's salve then covered the ointment with a warm flannel cloth. She took the penicillin from her bag, praying that Martha would not be allergic. Next, she pressed through the crowded kitchen and found a pan, filling it with pennyroyal. When the tea was done, she had Martha sip it lightly.

Martha began to sweat within thirty minutes; her fever had broken.

"Who are you? Where did you come from? Where are Joel and Susie?"

"Martha, I am Dr. Anna Laura Gibson. I came to the mountains a couple of months ago. Your children found me and asked that I help you. Martha, they truly love you."

"They're all I got to live for. Times sure have been hard for them. Their daddy is mean. I hope to my God he don't come around no more. He likes to make people suffer. Don't let him come back here. Whippin's make love turn to hate. Where's my youngins?"

"They're outside with my horse."

Anna Laura went out to check on the children. She caught a glimpse of a man at the edge of the woods. She discreetly took her rifle from the leather case and fired a couple of shots over the timbers. The man ran like a scalded dog. She had no fear of him returning.

"Susie, Joel, come inside with me." They were elated to see their mother breathing better and the signs of fever gone. Her face was no longer red. They embraced their momma, letting her know how thankful they were to still have her. She meant the world to them.

Anna asked the children to step outside. She took a small pistol and shells from her bag. She placed it under the mattress made of corn shucks. "If you should need to, Martha, use the pistol to protect Joel, Susie and yourself. God will understand that you can't let your husband separate you from your little ones. He wants you to protect them, as well as yourself."

As it was near morning, Anna Laura took a knife and cut a piece of the hanging bacon. An iron skillet sat nearby and she placed it over the fire and fried the bacon along with eggs that lay in a small tin pan. The children ate as though they were starved. Thankfully, Martha was able to eat a fried egg.

After applying the Vick's once again, Anna Laura laid a warm cloth on the sick woman's chest. "Now, children, I must be going home. Be sure to give your momma sips of tea and rub Vick's salve on her chest." The children nodded at her directions.

Anna Laura so hated to leave, but she knew she must return and rest before she took the long, hard trip the following day. She was exhausted, but experienced no problems on her way home.

The fog began to lift and the sunrise was absolutely breathtaking. Each time that she approached the beauty in the mountains it was as though it was for the first time. This sunrise was unlike any she had ever seen. She was engulfed in a heavenly place as she saw the glistening of the dew on the wildflowers, the mountain laurels and the many shades of green leaves that covered so many different types of trees.

She rode slowly taking in all of the beauty her heart, soul and mind could hold. Knowing she had helped Martha to live and Joel and Susie would still have a momma inspired her to continue fulfilling her mountain destiny. In spite of her joy, she still feared Martha's husband would return and bring harm to Joel, Susie and Martha.

She pondered for a moment, "Perhaps if I visit often enough he will stay away."

Upon reaching camp, Anna Laura knew she really needed to head to her special falls to cleanse her body as the house she had spent the night in was unsanitary. With Martha being sick for weeks in the mountain shack, she wasn't able to take care of the chores; however, Anna Laura could tell that normally Martha was a clean housekeeper.

The soap and shampoo lathered in the soft mountain water as Anna Laura cleansed her body. Alone with the abiding freshness in the air and the proud waters that rinsed her body, she felt totally relaxed on the outside and the inside as well because she was not too proud to do all that she could for the little forgotten family that dwelled higher in the mountains in the little shack.

Anna Laura felt fresh and rejuvenated though she had been through quite an ordeal and lost a night's sleep. She constantly thanked God for the perfect health that he had blessed her with. He did a special work for her immune system and she knew that; he had equipped her well for her destiny and she would be forever thankful. She believed as a Christian that God never gave anyone an assignment that he would not see them through if they were faithful and willing to sacrifice. For the present, she knew she had saved Martha's life, but knew not what the future held.

Even though she had only a few hours of sleep, Anna Laura would not miss her appointment in Cherry Valley. She climbed on her Arabian dressed in a black riding skirt, black leather boots and a red silk blouse. Subconsciously she hoped Hank would find her attractive, and at the same time, wished she was headed out to see Clint. She held him so dear to her heart; the memories of his loving kindness were stored in her heart and soul.

She asked herself, "How can I care for two fine gentlemen? Is there something wrong with me?"

Time had swiftly passed and before she realized it she had already entered Cherry Valley. She dismounted gracefully and led her horse to the stables. As it was Saturday, the town was more busy than usual.

Hank had made preparations for her to meet him in his office, even though it was Saturday. Walking toward his office made her feel awkward as it seemed every eye was upon her. She knew some of the supplies had already arrived so she was very excited.

Hank met her at the door. He greeted her with a huge smile, wanting so much to embrace her, but yet not comfortable to follow his feelings. He took her hand, "Come, Anna Laura, see what you think of all the supplies."

Tears swelled up in Anna Laura's eyes as she thought of how the books and medical supplies would change the destiny of the children of Brushy Mountain.

As the tears began to slide down Anna Laura's pretty face, Hank so wanted to hold her in his arms, but he knew how reserved Anna Laura was.

After looking at the books and medical supplies for awhile, Hank realized that she must be hungry after the long ride.

"Anna Laura, are you ready for a good lunch?"

"Yes, Hank! I'm starved!"

As they sat in the huge restaurant, she again admired the mountain views; the Hemlocks and the grove of delicate pink cherry blossoms beyond the window. The color lit up the entire area with nature's beauty. She knew the pink cherry blossoms would probably be out of season when she returned again so she feasted her eyes on their inexpressible beauty.

As Hank talked of the future of the Brushy Mountain people, she knew these were precious moments that would never be forgotten. In the meantime, she had to take control of her mind as it wondered back to the dinners she and Clint shared on high balconies of nice restaurants overlooking the waves and the vast ocean of blue as far as they could see. A heart that held feelings for two wonderful people was more than confusing.

Hank and Anna Laura continued their conversation over dessert and fresh brewed coffee. Hank related to Anna Laura, "I will find someone to deliver the supplies for you. You'll still be able to make purchases with the checks as needed. I know the roads are narrow, but the owners of the stables have just what we need. There is a young college student who works the stables during the summer. His name is Jess, a very nice young man. I believe he will be available."

Hank stood and pulled Anna Laura's chair back as she stood, then lightly guided her through the restaurant as his hand supported her elbow. They headed for the stables where the owner had everything ready as Hank had already given him a quick call from his office.

Jess took the wagon to Hank's office and the three of them loaded the readers, arithmetic and spelling books. This would be the foundation for the beginning of education for children on Brushy Mountain. The medical supplies were loaded and secured as safely as possible.

Anna Laura's heart was filled with joy. Hank was amazed just to look at Anna Laura's face. She looked even more beautiful. Anna Laura mounted her Arabian and Jess followed behind with the narrow wagon. They would travel slowly and with special care.

Hank waved to Anna Laura as she gave a big smile that showed what she was feeling inside.

The two headed up the mountain. Anna Laura noticed the clouds were moving swiftly and beginning to turn a little dark. Uneasiness seemed to set in. Jess and Anna Laura climbed higher as the clouds darkened and moved faster. The fear that overwhelmed Anna Laura was all about the supplies in the narrow wagon. Even though they were covered with a canvas, she knew they could still get wet. The wind was rising and whipping the branches of the trees as the rain began to fall. She silently prayed for God's protection. She began to think about where they could take cover if the weather became really severe. Suddenly she remembered a huge hanging rock not too far up the mountain from where they were. She knew the area was large enough to accommodate the horses and wagon loaded with supplies as well as the two of them.

"Jess, the rain is coming down harder and the cover won't protect our supplies for too long with winds like this."

As the trees swayed toward the earth, Anna Laura felt out of control. She prayed, "Please, God, you gave us these supplies. I believe you will see they reach those who need them so desperately. I know you love the mountain people so I am trusting in you."

Suddenly, Jess almost screamed, "Anna Laura, up there is a huge hanging rock!"

They moved faster as the rain became harder. They made their way beneath the towering rock. Jess was amazed, "I have never seen anything like this."

Checking the supplies, they found everything was dry. The rain continued and it was suddenly as if a huge curtain dropped, blocking what light was left. Jess had brought along an old kerosene lantern; Anna Laura was stunned as the lantern lit up the open space. She brought snacks that she had picked up in Cherry Valley from the saddlebags.

Each had blankets that were not wet. As they were sure they would be there all night, they spread them on the soft, silky dirt. They sat on the blankets as the warmth beneath the rock took the chill from their bodies and their clothes; the small fire they had built really helped and soon they were feeling almost dry.

"Jess, do you have plans other than working the stables?"

"Yes, ma'am. I only work on weekends and summers and attend college during the week in the fall and spring. I only lack one year before graduating."

"That is wonderful, Jess!"

"I plan to be a teacher."

"Will you be teaching elementary?"

"Yes, ma'am."

Finally, they became tired and fell asleep on their soft blankets.

The morning brought sparkles of sunshine through the trees and under the hanging rock. Anna Laura and Jess got their gear together and headed up the mountain without hesitation.

When reaching the campsite, Jess built a fire from the dry wood stored under the cliff. Anna Laura wasted no time getting the coffee boiling and the flapjacks frying; they were both famished. Jess had his first taste of blueberry flapjacks and was very impressed.

Chapter 10

A new day was about to begin. After washing and dressing, Anna Laura and Jess were ready to move on to the settlement of log cabins. Just before Jess and Anna Laura were about to leave, Mary Jane came down the trail. She looked really pretty as she had tried very hard ever since she met Anna Laura to keep herself well groomed.

"Jess, this is Mary Jane."

"Nice to meet you, Mary Jane."

Shyly, Mary Jane replied, "You, too."

Mary Jane had never been to school, but that didn't mean she was dumb. She knew the ways of the mountains and had a great innate ability. All she needed was a chance to develop her dormant potential. One of her greatest talents was identifying medicinal plants on Brushy Mountain.

She was now seventeen and no one had ever discovered her secret garden. As a lonely child, she stumbled upon the area where wildflowers, Rhododendrons and daisies among others, grew. Even delicate bushes of sparrow grass grew in her garden. Just beyond the garden, a meadow of green grass grew abundantly. In the middle of the meadow, a huge rock stood. Actually, it was taller than anything growing around it. Mary Jane saw it as being one of a kind as it was a conglomerate rock. The gravels of many colors embedded in the huge rock amazed her. To the right a clear, small stream flowed, smooth and gentle. So many times as she lay listening to the clear water slowly rippling over the rocks, she stared into the blue sky and wondered if she would ever leave the mountains.

Mary Jane knew that only the men ever left the mountains. Obviously a child and wife might have an opportunity, but not likely more than once in a lifetime. The first settlers came from the valleys beyond both sides of the mountain and went back for a young bride who would probably never leave the top of Brushy Mountain.

Mary Jane dreamed the opposite. Her dreams were of a charming, smart, good-looking man coming to the mountains and taking her away from the difficult life she lived. She had heard talk among the settlers of schools in small towns and communities off the mountain.

"Mary Jane, Jess and I are about to take supplies out to the settlement. Would you like to come along?"

Mary Jane shook her head; she did not feel comfortable in the presence of Jess. She figured he was smart in the ways of the world beyond her mountains. She had an urge to be alone in her secret garden, her place of serenity where she could feel comfortable.

Jess and Anna Laura headed for the settlement. Once they got there, the children ran behind the narrow wagon shouting with glee. Their hearts told them a different future lay ahead of them; knowing that books were in the wagon was the most exciting thing they had ever experienced.

Steve and Lilly had one of their buildings prepared for storage until the school and other buildings were completed. It had been thoroughly cleansed and shelves had been built by Steve and a couple of other men. It smelled of fresh Hemlock. With the help of Steve and Lilly, everything was placed in order.

Jess felt a bond of trust when introduced to Steve and Lilly. Jess looked toward the sky and discerned that he should leave for Cherry Valley. He definitely wanted to return home before dark.

"Anna Laura, I'll head back out."

"Jess, you be careful. I'll see you at the stables next weekend."

Jess was a good-looking young man, of medium height and muscular build. His blonde curly hair, blue eyes and tan skin were definitely an asset for a young man who was self-sufficient and paying for his own education. He was from a middle-class family of good character.

Mary Jane had no idea how taken Jess was by her good looks, her quiet nature, even her poise and grace that she had dwelled on possessing after she met Anna Laura. Jess was sure she had tried in no way to impress him as she had gone her own way.

He could feel in his heart that she possessed great potential for life's calling. Jess thought of Mary Jane all the way down the mountain, wondering under what conditions she lived. He could not help but wonder if she was mentally abused. He saw the frailness that had carried over from her childhood as well as the presence of innocence. He knew in his spirit he would not soon forget her.

The girls he knew and courted were different, not in a bad way, just different. He saw a sense of security in them that did not exist in Mary Jane. He could tell that she was a loner and lived in her own world of dreams, wondering if life would ever be different.

Jess arrived at the stables before he realized as his mind had not been off Mary Jane for one minute.

Chapter 11

Back on Brushy Mountain, Anna Laura asked that Steve and Lilly schedule another meeting. As she rode back to her campsite, she began to feel a need for rest, but was filled with anticipation.

When night came, as Anna Laura lay on her quilt observing the beauty of the skies, feeling the warmth of the summer moving in, she thought of all the gardens of fresh vegetables and fields of corn she had passed and of looking out over the grounds near the settlement of log cabins. She thought of how hard the women worked preserving and canning the fruits and vegetables that had already ripened and knew this would continue until fall was almost gone as they replanted crop after crop.

She began to ponder on what she would do when fall came and went and winter came on. She could not endure the winter in a campsite under the night filled with stars, nor could she survive for long under the huge rock. She fell asleep staring at the Eastern star with a prayer in her heart.

Morning seemed to come quickly; she had not awakened a single time. She experienced a renewed strength as she did her morning chores. When all was done, she headed for the settlement.

Lilly met Anna Laura on her porch wearing a big smile. Lilly was older than Anna Laura, but had a natural beauty and a warm heart. Nature had treated her well. God had given her a heart of love and compassion which enriched her health mentally and physically, each affecting the other in a positive way which brought good health.

Lilly called to Steve, "Anna Laura is here."

Steve instantly appeared from the building that held the supplies. He found it hard to stay away from the books. The pictures hinted at stories that intrigued him.

"Come on in, Anna Laura. Me and Steve have some good news for you."

Anna Laura was filled with anticipation.

"Well, Anna Laura," Steve began to speak, "the men have gotten together and are figuring on building you a cabin over on our land where the meetings was. We know there's no way you can stay in that campsite, nor under that cliff. We know you wouldn't want to live with other people."

Lilly smiled as she spoke wonderful words that were sweet music to Anna Laura's ears. Lilly began, "Anna Laura, the women will share our canned and preserved food with you. We will oblige you with chicken, eggs and hog meat. Most of the folks on this mountain feel like you are an angel of mercy sent by God to change things for generations coming on. Most of the people want their children to look for a better life than they had."

"Lilly, I may not have lived my life on Brushy Mountain, but I know poverty and lack of education among my people over in Sampson. I was blessed that even though I lost my momma at an early age and my daddy remarried a woman that resented me, that did not stop my self-motivation and a desire for a better life. My daddy stood by me regardless in a discreet way. He shared my dreams as we sat under the big oak tree and talked away from my step-mother's presence. I worked hard. Also, I was pretty much a loner like Mary Jane is right now. I am so thankful that I left the Valley of Sampson. I finished high school and left the valley beneath the mountains that held no opportunity for a young woman. My dreams, hopes, endeavors and faith led me down the path of becoming a doctor. If I could succeed, so can these children. They will learn that it takes endurance, struggle and lots of faith. I hope to impart these characteristics to them. We must always remember God helps those who endeavor to help themselves."

Lilly listened intently and her heart was stirred. She realized that life had not always been easy for Anna Laura. Steve spoke out, "Anna Laura, the schoolhouse and doctor building will be built in the same place where your cabin will stand. The schoolhouse will be a few hundred feet away, but the doctor building will be closer to your cabin so you can get to it faster and keep a watch out for your supplies."

Anna Laura sat in amazement. This was the second greatest news that she had heard since coming to the mountains, the first being the grant that Hank worked so diligently to get for the settlers.

"That's not all, Anna Laura, we'll build a church, because we know you really believe and trust God. Many eyes were spiritually opened because you came to these mountains."

"Steve, I want to flourish spiritually to change lives just as the huge trees in these mountains have provided homes and are in the process of providing a school, a church and a doctor's office. The God given provisions will be appreciated and looked on for their contributions to a life changing experience for generations."

Anna Laura was so happy that everything seemed to be falling in to place. She had supper with Steve and Lilly. Lilly's chicken and dumplings, cornbread and apple pies were the best ever. Anna Laura's stomach felt as though it would not need food for a couple of days.

After the table was cleared, Anna Laura went on her way feeling all bubbly inside.

Suddenly, she could feel eyes upon her. She brought her Arabian to a complete stop. She got off the horse to listen more intently. 'Perhaps it is in my imagination,' she thought.

Anna Laura was suddenly hit on the head from behind and she found herself dazed from the pain. Placing his hands under her arms, a huge man dragged her. She could not see his face as her vision was extremely blurred. Next, he blindfolded her, then brought her to her feet and put a rope around her waist, pulled her to higher ground.

"You haint got no cause coming in our world up here in these mountains."

Anna Laura was nearly in shock; she could not speak a single word. She was dragged to a cliff that hung high with space beneath it. There she was tied up, her hands behind her and her ankles together.

The following day, Anna Laura's horse showed up in the settlement. Those that were busy working toward the progress of the settlement were alarmed. Steve fed Anna Laura's horse as more and more people gathered out of concern. Steve and Lilly's yard was quickly filled with neighbors. Everyone was upset and wanted to help.

Mary Jane came near their home when hearing the commotion. "Steve, Lilly, what's going on?"

"Mary Jane, Anna Laura's horse showed up without her. John and Roy Taylor hurried to her campsite, but she wasn't there. It's believed she didn't make it home yesterday."

Mary Jane wept inside. She vowed to herself, "We will find her." She knew she had better get home before Aunt and Uncle missed her. Later she would slip away as she often did to spend time in her little garden.

Everyone set out to look for Anna Laura. Darkness hovered over the mountains before they could find her. Mary Jane traveled by foot choosing her own path, but could find no clue as to what had happened to Anna Laura. The searchers headed back home knowing they would set out at the break of dawn to search again.

Somewhere in the predawn hours, Anna Laura heard voices coming near. This time it was two men. Their voices were gruff and illiterate. Anna Laura began to panic. This was a feeling she had never experienced before. Her heart raced as fast as her thoughts as two men entered the cave.

"We'd better git her outta here." They literally carried her; one took her legs and the other her arms. She could tell they were climbing upward. Beyond the level land of the settlers there were higher ridges.

Anna Laura silently prayed, "The Lord is my light and my salvation; whom shall I fear? The Lord is the strength of my life; of whom shall I be afraid?" A calmness flowed through her entire being after meditating with God.

The men whispered as if she could not hear them.

"We'll leave her up here so the wild animals will take care of her."

Anna Laura prayed silently again, "I shall no more be a prey to the heathen, neither shall the beasts of the land devour me; but I shall be safe, and none shall make me afraid."

She did not know how far they traveled, but it seemed as though they had left her somewhere high in the mountains. The men had called each other by the names 'Rock Head' and 'Cold Tater' as they talked. She lay wondering after they left, "Why were they called Rock Head and Cold Tater?" She learned later that Rock Head got his name because his dad was abusive when he was a boy. He had hit Bobby in the head with a rock at about age five. No medical attention was available. People just assumed he was never right in the head so people called him Rock Head. Cold Tater was called by that name because his momma and daddy were lazy and did not provide for him. So, little Billy went from house to house begging for cold potatoes that people had left from supper. He put them in his pocket and ate them to keep from starving.

The boys' parents had died when they were around thirteen. They feared if life on the mountain changed and people left, they would never survive so they wanted to scare Anna Laura off the mountain. They literally tried to scare her to death, but she believed they did not intend to kill her.

Anna Laura managed to turn her face to the ground. She heard water gushing beside her so she rolled until she could lie on her back, exposing the ropes that imprisoned her to the water that would hopefully loosen them. She finally succeeded. The ropes stretched gradually as she moved her legs and arms against them. At last her limbs were free. As she uncovered her eyes, she realized it was dark and she was in a strange place. She made her way to a nearby cave; she was a little afraid as she crawled in since snakes were abundant in the mountains. Thankfully, the cave was unoccupied.

With it being summer she was able to dry out somewhat and eventually get warm.

Anna Laura suddenly remembered the Proverb, "When thou liest down, thou shall not be afraid; yea thou shalt lie down, and thy sleep shall be sweet."

Anna believed the scriptures as she prayed. She drank the rainwater that fell from the rocks above the cave so she would not dehydrate. Finally, sated and at peace, she fell asleep.

Daylight began to filter through to the cave where she slept, the sunbeams eventually making their way to Anna Laura's place of refuge.

She crawled from the cave, feeling stiff, hungry and a little weak. She first made her way to the stream and drank the clear, cool water. She immediately spotted a mulberry bush nearby. The long purple berries were the prettiest fruit she had ever looked upon.

After sitting in a pool of water that had a huge sandrock beneath she splashed water over her entire body and head to wash away the dirt and debris, she was rejuvenated and made her way back to the mulberry bush.

The berries were so plump and juicy. She had her fill and immediately felt her strength returning. She knew to follow the stream downward. It would lead her near her campsite or the settlement.

She walked downstream carefully; she was already bruised and definitely did not want a broken bone.

All fear left her as she repeated the 23rd Psalm. She did not fear evil and it was as though she had been through the valley of the shadow of death and now she walked beside the still waters that flowed gently down the mountain.

The settlers were headed up the mountain again. They spotted the tracks of the men. The earth was soft and the rain had not been severe enough to wash them out.

Finding the ropes that Anna Laura had left beside the stream, they were very puzzled. They saw no tracks since she had waded the stream quite a distance until it was feasible for her to walk beside it.

Steve informed the men, "We will go farther around the ridge. Some to the left and some to the right."

Anna Laura had been following the stream for a couple of hours, resting occasionally as her body was not at full strength yet.

Suddenly, the area seemed familiar. Below she heard water splashing on a hard surface as though it had a ways to fall. Upon coming closer she realized she was above the falls where she usually bathed. She pondered on the easiest route down. She slipped and slid on soft ground where the foliage was not very high, mostly fiddlehead ferns. Reaching the bottom, she knew she was home safe.

After getting fresh clothes and bathing, she found her Arabian in the meadow grazing.

"Thank you, God!" she repeated over and over. Her Arabian meant the world to her. As his saddle was still on him and now dried by the sun, she mounted and headed for Lilly's house. She knew her friend would be worried.

As she rode through the settlement, young children jumped, laughed and shouted joyfully.

"Anna Laura! Anna Laura! You're alive!"

Anna Laura's eyes filled with tears and they slid down her pale face. She saw at that moment how much she was loved by the settlement people.

Anna Laura possessed the strength of a mountain woman. As she stood on Lilly's porch after the women and children had disappeared to their houses, her mind became troubled for those who were still looking for her.

The last vestiges of daylight were about to be swallowed by the darkness. She knew the mountain was rough and the men traveling by horseback could be in danger of their horses tripping over rocks or even walking over a cliff.

Meanwhile, the group of men was sadly returning home without Anna Laura. Steve became fearful. He confided in his friend, Jerrod McCoy, "She's been lost for two days and one night. I fear we'll never see her again."

Jerrod replied, "Now, Steve, don't give up. I sure believe God sent her here to help change the lives of our children and their children and right on down the line. I know we learnt a lot over the years from our forefathers, but we want our children to be learned and to leave these here mountains and find good jobs and an easier life than we've had."

Steve looked so desolate and sorrowful.

"Now, Steve, I believe her calling will come to pass. What God says goes."

Nodding in agreement, Steve felt a little better.

Just as the last of daylight was leaving, the men arrived at the edge of the settlement. Riding around the bend, Steve saw Anna Laura's Arabian tied to the hitching post in front of his porch. The weary men were no longer tired when they saw Anna Laura walk out on the porch. It was not so dark that they could not make out who she was. They began whooping and hollering and even looked to the star filled sky to offer gratitude to their God. They knew her return was a miracle.

They still had no idea why she had disappeared. Steve got off his horse, slightly limping and walked over to Anna Laura, "You sure look a lot better than I expected. How on Earth did you stay alive? The rain poured like a cloud had busted."

"Steve, it's a long story. When the timing is right, I'll tell you everything."

Anna Laura felt compassion for the two men who had done this to her. She knew they were a product of their environment and did not want harm to come to them. She intended to find out all about their lives. She realized they were afraid of change and afraid they would not survive when change came.

"Anna Laura," Steve commented, "now that this time of trouble is over, we will commence working on the schoolhouse, the doctor's office, a church and a cabin for you before winter sets in. Winters are awful cold up here."

"Thank you, Steve, and everyone else as well. Please know you have proven everything I needed to know, God works in mysterious ways. God in all his sovereignty rules the universe. There are times he allows bad to happen in our lives to bring good." Again, Anna Laura loudly spoke, "Thank all of you."

"Welcome!" Many voices responded through the near darkness.

Anna Laura knew at this moment, "These are such genuine people. I truly trust them and they trust me as well."

Anna Laura mounted her horse and headed to her campsite. With the stars in the sky she could see well enough. She felt wonderful and experienced a peace inside that only God could give.

Once she was lying down, conversations between her mother and her friend, Tildy Ann Nicely, rang in her ears, discussions about the hardships of their lives. She remembered her momma's words, "Always, no matter how hard things are on the outside, God can let peace flow through your heart and soul like a winding river."

Anna Laura was filled with tranquility. As it stirred inside her being, she fell asleep knowing her guardian angels were encamped all around her.

Tomorrow would be the dawn of a new day. She slept peacefully on her momma's quilt in her warm, flannel gown.

Chapter 12

Progress was in the making. The sun rays beamed through the many trees as Anna Laura awakened. She believed it was going to be a good day. Her body was in a state of recovery from all the traveling as well as the despair she had experienced. She felt as happy as she did the day she set out to follow her destiny.

She walked through the splendor of the huge trees and wildflowers. As she walked, she thought about her future plans as well as the construction that Steve and Paul had talked of the day before. She knew it was not just a dream. She could see all the buildings in her imagination. They would soon be ready. She would not allow herself to doubt it.

She had been so deep in thought, she had not realized just how far she had walked. Looking up, she saw a cabin sitting in a clearing. She was reluctant to call on the people. It was evident that this family was probably outsiders. She had not realized that anyone lived this far out.

Anna Laura immediately headed home, but could not dismiss from her mind the blond, humble-looking woman that she had seen out by the small shed near a cow that she was likely going to milk. Also, she had noticed a man of small stature higher on a hill pitching horse weeds into a hog pen. Anna Laura's mind traveled a million miles as she walked home. It took some time to get the scene out of her mind.

Since it was Saturday, she made her way toward the settlement. From a distance, she could hear hammering and cross-cut sawing.

Riding into the settlement, she could see the wonderful plot of land that Steve and Lilly had donated. Her spirit soared to the height of the blue and amber floating skies beyond the next mountain.

The children ran up to Anna Laura and began interacting with her. Rock Head and Cold Tater were lurking in the woods nearby listening. They were really ashamed of the unkind act they had committed against Anna Laura. They were thanking God no harm had come to her from the wild animals of the mountains.

As they listened to Anna Laura discussing her future plans relative to school with the children, they experienced shame as their eyes met. These two young teens who had known nothing but hurt and in turn wanted to hurt others, now felt it dissipate as they listened to Anna Laura.

Each of their minds was occupied by the same thoughts, "We're eighteen and nineteen, maybe we can still learn." Neither of them had any idea of the natural ability they possessed. Being treated as misfits all their lives, and given what their lack of education had disposed them to, had made them feel stupid. Their real names were Bobby and Billy, but those did not seem genuine to them as they had only heard the degrading names they had carried from childhood. They suffered such guilt they were afraid to make their presence known.

Anna Laura introduced the first level reader to the children. She chose one related to the mountains; familiarity would be a good beginning. The children were intrigued by the colorful pictures above the printed words illustrating what was written below.

After introducing the books to the children, Anna Laura strolled through the scope of the future buildings that would be a part of changing generations. She began to concentrate on where the archives would be kept; it would be of great importance to keep medical and school records. An extra room built onto her cabin for this purpose would be viable. The medical records could help in the future as some diseases could possibly be hereditary. Perhaps lives could be saved in generations to come if the records were safely kept and made known to them.

As Anna Laura stood amid this new beginning for the mountain people, she knew there would be conflict as some had always lived in their own worlds; they had known no other world so did not miss what they had never had.

She would do anything within her power to establish a personal and trusting relationship with those she had not been able to communicate with. There were times she experienced an overwhelming joy in knowing she had not been in Brushy Mountain for many months, but yet her accomplishments were far greater than she had expected. Still, she realized it was only the beginning of her hope for the mountain people.

Hopefully the buildings would be completed after the crops were harvested and before cold weather set in. Anna Laura stood beyond the new development scanning the woods and ridges from a distance wondering if people lived in those areas. She remembered when she had gone with Susie and Joel to help their loving mother when she was deathly ill and how crude the father was. Anna Laura's heart told her there were possibly other isolated families in those hills and ridges.

Chapter 13

Anna Laura pondered as she looked toward the mountains, "I must see who lives west of the settlement."

She rode back to camp, packed a lunch and set out on her journey, guiding her Arabian through the rough terrain. After riding about an hour west of her campsite, she got a glimpse of smoke rising above the treetops. She would not turn back; she had to know what lay beyond. Her first impulse was to ride a distance above the smoke; perhaps she would not be seen.

Peering through the large trees high on the hill, she stared down into the hollow where the terrain spread outward. She saw a moonshine still. She had seen them when growing up in the Valley of Sampson while exploring the wooded areas. She remembered how detrimental the 'shine was to women and children where the husbands and fathers were always intoxicated. The Federal agents called revenuers had come, confiscating the liquor and taking or destroying the stills.

The whiskey seemed to put a pure demon in many men. It seemed they were either mellowed out or were prone to become violent. Either way, they acted stupidly. Anna Laura was sure this was why Joel and Susie's momma had suffered so many beatings. She was sure the two precious children were also beaten by their father.

Anna Laura eased away from the scene before being seen. During her ride back to her campsite, she contemplated what to do and how, or who she would approach about the moonshiners. Distilling moonshine was definitely against the laws of the land.

The night was filled with stars and the air was warm but not uncomfortable. Her experience on this particular day was bewildering. As she lay looking toward the star-filled sky she knew she would return to the same scene the following day. Her main concern was for the many children the scattered families had. She lay awake half the night praying for spiritual guidance.

She awakened to a bright morning, had breakfast, groomed herself, mounted her Arabian and took the same path as she had the day before.

Today, she would focus on locating the dwellings of the illegal whiskey makers. Income tax evasion was punishable by law. Anna Laura was sure the moonshiners carried the 'shine to the valley below and sold it to those who indulged, but were not in what they thought was a safe place to produce their own. Anna Laura perched high on the ridge above the stills. She could hardly believe her eyes when she saw at least a dozen children in the area.

She knew these children deserved a better life; however, her question was, "Dear Lord, what can I do?"

She knew in her heart it was not the right time for her presence to be made known so she headed home.

On her way, she rode through the settlement. The progress was great. The buildings were going up faster than she expected. She had a nice visit with Lilly, but did not speak of the moonshiners.

"Anna Laura, let's me and you go see your cabin."

"I'd be delighted, Lilly."

As they got closer, Lilly asked, "What do you think?"

"I'm absolutely amazed. It feels so good to know I'll have real shelter before winter."

"Anna Laura, before you leave, let's have a piece of apple pie and coffee."

After the wonderful treat, Anna Laura headed home. Her mind was totally engulfed with the thoughts of the children she had discovered that day.

After showering and getting settled in for the evening, Anna Laura began thinking of steps to take toward stopping the moonshiners. She knew in her spirit these women and children must be suffering just as Joel, Susie and Martha had for so many years.

As Anna Laura's spirit wrestled with how to handle the moonshine situation she thought of Hank.

"Tomorrow I will ride off the mountain to Cherry Valley and ask Hank's advice," she thought to herself before falling asleep.

She slept well and awakened early feeling that she would be advised well.

She dressed herself nicely, still feeling the desire to appear attractive to Hank. Somehow she wanted Hank's approval even though she was still in love with Clint. There were times her heart ached with grief as she wondered if Clint had met someone new or might even be married by now. Regardless of how much she loved Clint, she could not leave the mountain people who so desperately needed her.

She could not know her thoughts of what Clint's life was like were completely off course.

Clint's heart was filled with hurt each day as he secretly grieved for Anna Laura. At present, he did not have a life outside his medical career. He literally worked almost night and day living in hope that Anna Laura would return.

As much as he loved Anna Laura, his hope of her returning began to dwindle away. Beautiful, elegant, wealthy women were constantly being introduced to Clint by his co-workers. When on a date all he could think of was his beautiful Anna Laura, of her high spirit; she was a genuine human being who never pretended to be someone that she was not. Clint only saw the lovely, kind and caring person that she was.

He asked himself many times, "Why can't I let the memories go? Why can't I stop loving her?"

All that he could think of was that she was unlike anyone he had ever known. He had so hoped that Anna Laura could have accepted belonging in his world. This was all that mattered to Clint. Status meant nothing to him.

A huge portrait of Anna Laura still remained over his fireplace. The picture of her wearing the full length creme colored Victorian lace dress, her long dark hair hanging loose and shining and her skin color and full lips a perfect color. Her smile was beautiful, her teeth were perfect and as white as the mountain snow.

Clint could not bring himself to take the picture down. Every day he spent time looking at her picture and remembering the lovely times they spent together.

Suddenly, Anna Laura came back to reality to find herself nearing the bottom of the mountain. Time had passed quickly as she rode down the mountain lost in thoughts of Clint.

Chapter 14

Anna Laura arrived in Cherry Valley and took her Arabian to the stables to Jess.

"How are things going, Jess?"

"Very well, Anna Laura."

She could tell that Jess had something on his mind. Just as she turned to go to the street, Jess spoke his mind.

"Anna Laura, how is that pretty, young Mary Jane doing?"

"She is doing well. She's an extremely intelligent girl. I've given her access to books that we took to the settlement. My intuition tells me she has a very high IQ. I believe she has a desire to pursue nursing, but is torn between nursing and teaching. Perhaps she will become both to accommodate the mountain people. Maybe in the future the state will pay for medical care and teaching positions on the mountain. I feel sure Mary Jane has the ability to do both."

Jess's eyes lit up with interest and excitement.

"Jess, one day I will bring her off the mountain to Cherry Valley."

Jess grinned shyly in response.

Anna Laura made her way to Hank's office and lightly tapped on the office door. Hank recognized the delicate sound; there was no other like it. He walked to the door filled with expectation.

Opening the door, Anna Laura's eyes met Hank's. He could see her excitement, but yet also anticipation.

" Anna Laura, this is a pleasant surprise. What brings you to Cherry Valley?"

"Could we go to the Hemlock Inn Restaurant and talk over a light lunch?

"Sure, Anna Laura."

Anna Laura radiated with beauty as she walked beside Hank. He felt so warmhearted and filled with joy just hoping Anna Laura would demonstrate in some way that she had feelings for him beyond friendship and business relations. As Hank slipped Anna Laura's chair back from the table, she sat down gracefully.

While having lunch, Anna Laura began inquiring as to what she could do about the moonshiners.

"Are there lawmen that can come to the mountains and stop the men that are running the whiskey? Hank, women and children are suffering as a result. You would not believe the shacks I discovered farther west into the mountains. I thought the settlement had problems, but there are by far more problems spread throughout the mountains. Not as many people, but a much sadder situation."

"Anna Laura, I know of one really accomplished officer that works with the Federal authorities in apprehending moonshiners. As you already know, income tax evasion is involved as the whiskey is carried off the mountains and sold. I have heard a great deal about young Lieutenant Samuel Adams who works very diligently supporting the revenuers that are called out to go to the mountains in many areas. Adams sometimes accompanies the revenuers if the situation could be one in which the moonshiners might be aggressive. Here in Cherry Valley, Bill Mullins, Emanuel Long, Clyde Smith and Mark Gibbons usually do the job where there is little danger."

They decided Hank needed to see the trail himself so he followed Anna Laura to the stables, then to the trail that would lead him up the Brushy Mountains.

The directions were easy enough as there was only one trail that was widened by travel over the years. The mountain men had gradually broken up rock and removed enough trees to have a narrow road that a wagon could travel as long as it was not too wide. Anna explained the route well.

" Anna Laura, the revenuers may have a truck that will maneuver up the wagon trail and in some parts of the mountains if the noise wouldn't alert the moonshiners. They may prefer to travel by foot or horseback for that reason."

"I know there's one still not too far from my campsite that will be accessible by truck. I have kept watch on one particular house while they carry 'shine in jars inside the house. In the valley where I grew up, men dug holes under their floorboards, and made a square door that could be lifted up to bring their 'shine in and out. It was well hidden. I heard the husband and wife call each other names, Hattie and Jow-Bo. They had a gang of children. Hank, the one thing that really worries me is that eventually the moonshine will be brought into the settlement and to the decent people living outside the settlement in the ridges. I've heard talk that it can get pretty bad around July 4th. Sometimes I feel a little afraid for myself if this should happen," she admitted. "Hank, there are many people in the mountains whom I have not met. I recall hearing someone scream as I rode about a mile from my camp. I followed the sound, but had to be careful not to be seen. I saw a beautiful young blond girl, probably around eighteen years old. Actually, she looked clean to be living in a rundown shack. Just as I was about to ride down to where she stood and talk to her, an older man, whom I assume was her father came out from behind the shack, screaming, 'Crissy, where are you? Get in this house. Your mommy needs you. Do you think you're special?' Then he struck her across the face with his open hand. The momma ran out of the shack pleading, 'Please, let her be, Patch.' Patch screamed, 'Millie, mind your business,' and struck her across the face, too.

"I could see these lovely women were trapped. Perhaps when school is in session, I can make a way for Crissy to attend. Hank, this is just a small example of what the 'shine does or causes the men to do. It was very obvious that Patch was drunk on moonshine. I saw him go behind the shack and bring out a jar from beneath some boards and guzzle it down. When he passed out, I knew it was a blessing for Crissy and Millie."

"Anna Laura, as this situation seems to be worse than I thought, I'll inform Lieutenant Adams in Nashville. I'm sure he will get the revenuers on the job. Don't you worry; Adams will not stop until the mission is successful."

"Hank, I hadn't realized how fast time has passed. I'd better head toward Brushy Mountain; I don't want to be overtaken by darkness before reaching home."

Hank stood in silence wondering, "Does she realize how I feel about her?" He watched until she rode out of sight. He stood for a while remembering how he had asked her to go to Nashville with him for a weekend. He decided that moment to ask her to agree on a date the next time they met.

He would stay with his Aunt Daisy and Uncle Joe and make reservations at the Andrew Jackson Hotel near 5th Avenue in Nashville. With Church Street being only a couple of blocks away, she would have access to the many shops. Perhaps they could visit the Grand Ole Opry at the Ryman Auditorium.

"Perhaps I'm only dreaming," Hank thought. "This woman is so different. She came from some poverty and a valley which was a breeding ground of illiteracy." It was hard for Hank to comprehend a young woman having enough self-motivation to go where she wanted to go and to become all that she wanted to be and still have such compassion for the less fortunate. "Most would have never looked back."

Chapter 15

Anna Laura made it safely back to her proclaimed place of serenity feeling sure Hank would do exactly what he had told her.

The following day, Hank contacted Lieutenant Adams in Nashville, Tennessee asking him to authorize the local revenuers to go to Brushy Mountains and seek out the moonshiners. Adams agreed something needed to be done, but said he would bring his own men.

Anna Laura lay under the heavens the night she arrived home from Cherry Valley thinking of Crissy and Millie whom she had seen hit across the face only a few days earlier. She was determined to help Crissy. She so much wanted to talk with her again.

Morning finally came and Anna Laura did her usual routine. She then saddled her Arabian and headed in the direction where she had seen Crissy.

As Anna Laura rode through the woods, she became a little sidetracked by a special area that she could not resist. The sun beamed through the trees striking a waterfall, which reflected light rays of many colors. Everything was so still except for the sound of a mourning dove. Suddenly, in the quietness Anna Laura heard soft steps. She turned to catch a glimpse of Crissy. She called softly, "Crissy, please come and talk with me."

Like a frightened fawn the girl stood looking and listening intently. Then she delicately walked toward Anna Laura as she climbed down from her Arabian.

"Crissy, I suppose you're wondering how I know your name."

"Yes, I am."

"Crissy, I'm Anna Laura. I came to Brushy Mountain a few weeks ago. I was scouting the ridges and ended up above your home. I saw your dad mistreating your momma and you. I had to return in hopes of seeing you again. Crissy, by late fall we'll have a school house completed down in the settlement and school will be in session. Would you be interested in learning?"

"Oh, yes ma'am I would be obliged to let someone teach me. I want to be somebody. Will you help me?"

"Crissy, I'll do everything I can."

"Can I just call you Anna?"

"Of course you may."

"Anna, I can slip off while dad is with the other men making moonshine. They are mean men like my dad."

Anna Laura gave Crissy directions to her campsite.

"Perhaps I can go ahead and begin teaching you to read, Crissy."

"Oh, will you, Anna?"

"If you should come by and I'm not at my place, I'll be at the settlement. Do you know where the settlement is?"

"Yeah, I do. I hide sometimes and look that way."

"You can come to the settlement and look for me or wait for me at my campsite. I'm never gone very long."

"I will, I will! I promise." Crissy suddenly became a little nervous. "I'd better get back before my dad does."

"I'll see you soon, Crissy."

"Goodbye, Anna."

Crissy broke out into a run like a little wild thing. Fear of being caught overtook her emotions. She thought, "If he catches me near Anna, I'll never ever see her no more."

Luckily, she made it home before Patch. He wore a patch over his eye because he was drunk one day on shine, fell forward and a sharp stick stuck into his eye and destroyed it. So now he wore the patch because it looked so horrible. His real name was Burton Walters.

When Crissy arrived back at the shack, Patch was not there. When she relaxed, her momma saw a look on Crissy's face that she had never encountered before. The look was of hope, not despair.

Millie didn't have much, but she was clean and had taught Crissy likewise. Even though Patch was crude, when he carried moonshine to some valley below that had a store he brought sewing goods and Millie was able to sew dresses for Crissy. Nothing fancy, but this enabled Crissy and Millie to look nice. When Crissy was a little girl, Millie made little flowered dresses. As Crissy grew into a young woman, Millie sewed styles that complimented Crissy's age and shape. Some of the mountain people were ignorant in many ways, but also gifted in many different ways that helped them survive.

Meanwhile, Anna Laura rode to the settlement. She was filled with joy as progress was being made. She was elated to know that she would soon be sleeping under a roof again, even though it would be small and with winter coming on in a couple of months she would be heating water and bathing in a metal tub. She definitely would miss her waterfall, which had been a gift from God all these months.

Every day she observed progress being made. Crissy was able to sneak by Anna's place for reading lessons in the early mornings three or four times a week. Anna Laura was sure Crissy was a child prodigy - well not a child anymore, but a young woman. Within three weeks she was reading at sixth grade level.

Anna Laura was sure by the time school began in the new school house in the settlement, Crissy was likely to be reading at college level. What a great challenge this was for Anna Laura and Crissy. To do this for one person in a lifetime would be worth every hardship Anna Laura had endured or ever would endure.

The Psalm "Blessed is he that considereth the poor; the Lord will deliver him in the time of trouble" seem to flow through Anna Laura's mind as she lay on her quilt listening to the stream slowly rippling down the mountain. As it was summer, the water seemed to flow more calmly.

Anna Laura lay thinking of how God had delivered her safely many times as she fulfilled her God-given destiny.

Chapter 16

Anna Laura heard the whimpering of children just as daylight filtered into Brushy Mountain. As the children came closer, she saw Joel and Susie.

"Children, what's wrong, what brings you here so early in the morning?"

"It's momma. We don't think she's breathing. Daddy got real crazy from drinking that clear stuff from a glass jar. We hid out in the trees and heard momma crying. In a little while we seed daddy running as hard as he could run. He acted like he was wild, like wild hogs we seed in the mountains before. He was running down the mountain.

"We run to see to momma. She had blood on her head and her purty face. Please come and help her, please Anna Laura. Will you come with us?"

"Yes, children. Let me get my medical supplies."

The three of them ran to Anna Laura's Arabian, and managed to get on the horse. They arrived at the shack. The children slid off the horse as Anna Laura got her feet out of the stirrups. Anna Laura hurriedly grabbed her medical bag.

The children were hovering over their momma when Anna Laura rushed in to the shack.

"Children, please step outside."

The shack was only two small rooms, which held a table, two beds and a fireplace. Anna Laura tried to protect the children as much as possible.

Anna Laura took Martha's hand in to hers as she felt for a pulse. She tried again and again. She listened for a heartbeat as tears slid down her face when she looked down on beautiful Martha. She stood in silence praying, "Dear God, give me strength to tell these precious children their momma is dead."

She walked outside to find Joel and Susie sitting on the ground, their arms around each other as the tears flowed down their innocent little faces.

They looked up to see tears in Anna Laura's compassionate eyes. She did not have to say a word. Together they said, "Momma is dead. He killed her." Then, they began to cry.

Anna Laura sat on the ground holding Susie and Joel as their small bodies shivered from near shock and wept along with them.

"Anna Laura, are you going to leave us by ourselves?"

"No children. We must go to the settlement and have Steve and the other men come for your momma. Children, you will miss your momma, but remember Heaven is going to be sweeter with your loving momma there."

Again, the three of them mounted the Arabian and headed toward the settlement. As they rode down the mountain, the sobs of the children eased.

"What will happen to us? We're afraid of our daddy. We don't want to see him."

"Don't worry, little ones. I'll see that you are taken care of."

They were still broken but Anna Laura could tell by the sound of their voices that some of their fears had faded.

Upon reaching the settlement they made their way to Steve and Lilly's. Steve and Lilly were Anna Laura's rocks; a couple she could lean on.

Steve and Lilly ran out into the yard as Anna Laura hitched her Arabian and helped the children to the ground.

"What's wrong?" cried Lilly.

"Let's go inside," Steve said as he took the children by their trembling hands.

"Momma is dead," The children spoke at the same time, trying not to cry.

Lilly took the children into the kitchen and prepared breakfast as Anna Laura told Steve all that the children had related to her.

"The last they saw of their dad, he was running and stumbling down the mountain."

Steve knew where they lived and knew there were massive cliffs in the area as he and his friends had picked huckleberries there.

"Anna, I'll get three or four men together and we'll head out to the rough side of the mountain beyond the shack. Chances are, Jake has not survived."

Steve rounded up men that were young and strong and headed out of the settlement, then upward toward Jake and Martha's home. From there, they would try tracking old Jake.

Within the hour they reached the shack. They hitched their horses to a rail and proceeded on foot. They walked and stumbled a long distance downward.

Suddenly, Rob yelled, "Steve! The small saplings are near laying down in a straight path towards the Hanging Rock. It sure is a long ways to the ground from the top of the cliff. A man wouldn't stand a chance."

Rob could plainly see that Jake's body had rolled over the moss and small huckleberry bushes. The rest of the men came down with care as they made their way down the mountain beside the Hanging Rock.

They reached the bottom where the ground was a bit level in front of the huge cliff's base.

Steve and Rob laid eyes on Jake at the same time. Their eyes met knowing Jake was dead.

They knew Jake wasn't a bad man except when the demon moonshine got in his blood and stimulated his brain, making him a different person.

After Jake realized he had most likely killed Martha, he must have run wildly down the mountain and over the huge hanging rock. The cliff was called the hanging rock because when they were young boys they stole a hog, cleaned it and cut it into hams, bacon, shoulders and pork chops and hung it under the hanging rock. There it stayed cold and safe in the winter and kept them from starving. Steve knew Jake had been an orphan along with a couple of his friends who were left to fend for themselves.

The men carried Jake up the hill on a stretcher they made from small poles. When reaching the shack they laid him across one of the horses then went inside the shack where Martha still remained.

Anna Laura was there when they arrived.

Kind hearted Lilly had kept Joel and Susie. Steve and Lilly were a bit older than Anna Laura, but had not been blessed with children.

Anna Laura had already bathed and dressed Martha. She looked so peaceful as her body lay on her bed, almost as though she was asleep.

Martha had married Jake for survival. Her parents died during a flu epidemic in Brushy Mountain when she was only fourteen. She had grown up in this same small shack. She was afraid of being alone and orphan Jake, who was somewhat older, had no home so they were married.

In later years, she gave birth to Joel and Susie. Martha was humble and loving just as her parents were. Being taught the Christian way of life by her parents, she passed it down to her children. As personality is formed at an early age, Joel and Susie were very blessed that they had their momma until they were five and six.

Jake tried to listen to Martha, but could not overcome the drinking which he had been exposed to at an early age.

With all the bad that Jake had done, Anna Laura still felt sad because he had no one to teach him as a small child after his parents disappeared, leaving him to keep company with anyone who would help him to survive.

The men brought Jake into the shack. Anna Laura pronounced him dead. Then she headed to Lilly to help comfort the children.

Steve and his friends bathed and dressed Jake in clean clothes. They closed the doors and went to retrieve a sled. They would return in a couple of hours for the bodies. The sled had good size runners that would enable their horses to pull the bodies over the rough ground.

Steve, John, Jack and Jim ate and rested for a short while then headed after the bodies. Meantime Rob rounded up a few men to build the pine boxes and dig the graves. Everyone was willing to help. In a time of trouble, the mountain people came together.

As Lilly and Anna Laura explained the plans to bury their parents, and where Jake was found, the children's blue eyes were the saddest the ladies had ever seen. As Anna Laura and Lilly looked into the children's eyes, the windows of Joel and Susie's souls, they wept inside. The only thing they could do was reach out to them and hold them close.

Susie managed to say, "What's going to happen to me and Joel? Where will we stay? We'll be afraid in the shack way back yonder by ourselves. There's wild animals in them mountains and people that make that bad stuff that daddy drunk."

"Don't worry children," Lilly replied, "You'll stay with me and Steve for now."

Anna Laura's eyes filled with tears. The thought raced through her mind that perhaps Steve and Lilly would keep them permanently. She thought of how beautiful the two of them were inside and out. Lilly had the fairest skin and eyes as blue as the sky. She was of a healthy build, well proportioned and her hair was long and blonde, but she wore it up in an old fashioned hair style. Steve was ruggedly handsome with a tall, muscular frame and dark skin, brown eyes and hair.

Anna Laura hurt inside just thinking of the graveside service.

The Reverend Paul Reed would conduct the services. He was soft spoken and had great insight into human relations. He would be considerate and choose his words wisely not to make the situation worse for Joel and Susie. The reverend came to the mountain from time to time and held meetings under a huge tree. It was fortunate he happened to be on the mountain at this crucial time. Anna Laura pondered on how this had worked out and how everything is in God's timing.

The graves were finished and the pine boxes completed when the men arrived with Jake and Martha. It had taken longer than they anticipated as they had to move the sled slowly.

Lilly's older friend, Sally Short, brought hand sewn quilts to line the boxes that Jake and Martha would be laid in.

There would not be an all night vigil as was the usual custom in the mountains. The evening sun was sinking low; they would be buried that same day for the sake of the children.

Anna Laura and Lilly had already seen to the bathing and grooming of the children. Cindy Lou Britton brought nice clothes and shoes for Susie and Joel as she had children the same size.

The children were stunningly beautiful. Never had they experienced the luxury of this type of clothing on their bodies.

Martha had done the best that she could with what she had to do with. Her love and kind ways and moral teachings would by far surpass any material things that would come the children's way.

Joel and Susie were kept in the house until time for the burial.

Steve's niece, Scarlet sang "Amazing Grace." Her voice would humble any human being. Her talent was so natural that the words flowed effortlessly.

After Scarlet sang, the reverend spoke kind words as Joel and Susie stood by the graveside holding on to Anna Laura and Lilly. They were secure in their presence even though they knew their parents would be forever gone as Anna Laura and Lilly had very carefully explained to them earlier.

Lilly and Anna Laura took Joel and Susie to Steve and Lilly's before the graves were filled and covered by beautiful white daisies gathered from the fields by the settlement children. The children were filled with compassion for Joel and Susie even though they did not know them. They were anxious to be their friends.

Joel and Susie were now safe with Lilly and Steve.

The evening was near spent so Anna Laura headed home. She hugged Susie and Joel. "I will see you soon. Lilly and Steve will be really good to you. No one will harm you."

Anna Laura did some serious thinking that night as she lay beneath God's given beauty. She felt warm and calm, did not feel hostility toward

Jake as she had before. She was at peace. In some ways, she experienced sadness for Jake after becoming aware of his lifelong circumstances; however, that did not make what he had done right.

Anna Laura knew when Friday came she would head off the mountain to pursue her endeavor of contacting resources to bring help to the mountains to deal with the moonshiners. She began to think of how many other families were spread throughout the mountain that are suffering as an end result of moonshine. She knew there must be other mothers and children trapped in abusive situations.

Tomorrow she would spend time with Joel and Susie.

She thought of things she could do with them to take away some of the pain that gripped their tender hearts. She knew they loved their momma and just as it had been with her as a child, no one could truly replace their mother.

The only good memories of their dad were when he was not under the influence of the filthy moonshine he was so obsessed with. Unfortunately, the pleasant memories were few and far between.

Anna Laura prepared herself as the sunrise began to lighten the eastern sky then headed out to see Susie and Joel.

As she rode into the yard, they ran out on the porch. Lilly was right behind them.

"Anna, Anna," they yelled in anticipation. They had already grown to love her. Had it not been for her, they may have been left alone in the mountains without anyone knowing, at least anyone from the settlement.

As they sat on the porch, Anna Laura held them close, all was silent. No tears, no words, just love and compassion.

"Lilly, will it be well with you if I spend the day with the children?"

"Sure, Anna Laura, I have special things to do, I will be sewing on my treadle sewing machine. I have measured the children's sizes. When you return they will have lots of play clothes."

The children smiled as did Anna Laura. They rode to Anna Laura's place. As they sat on the quilt, Anna Laura began talking to them.

"Children, we are going to do fun things today. Our first adventure will be to find a mulberry bush. Have you ever tasted those long, purple berries? They are so good!"

"No, ma'am, we never have," Joel replied.

While walking through the woods they held tightly to Anna Laura's hands. She could feel their insecurities.

"Children, there is a mulberry bush." Grass grew under the tree, so when the berries fell they were clean and not smashed. The three of them sat under the tree and had their fill.

Susie softly spoke, "Anna Laura, these are the best berries we ever ate."

Suddenly Joel began to laugh. "Anna Laura, your teeth are purple."

"Joel, your teeth are purple, too!" They laughed at each other.

"Children, let me take you to my private waterfall. Have you ever played in the water that runs over a huge rock from high in the air and falls far below on a flat sand rock?"

"No, Anna Laura, we never did. Momma was afraid for us to leave sight of the shack."

"Well, children, you're going to have more fun then you ever dreamed of having."

The children followed the path with Anna Laura leading the way. Suddenly their eyes lit upon the most beautiful sight they had ever seen. Flowers surrounded the falls as the water splashed down on the flat rock. They were totally mesmerized by such beauty.

"Anna Laura," they both yelled, "can we get in that water?"

"Yes, yes, run for it! It's okay if your clothes get wet."

Joel and Susie jumped, splashed each other and sat in water that had pooled farther back in huge eroded bowl-shaped areas of the rock.

Anna Laura stood under the rippling water as it ran smoothly over her face as she tilted her head slightly back, letting her hair fall away from her face.

She was elated just to be able to get the children's mind off the trauma of the past few days.

They played in the water until they were tired. They were a bit chilled so Anna Laura took them to a huge, flat rock that took in full sun.

As they lay on the rock warming, Anna Laura stated, "Joel, Susie, I know how you feel to some extent. I lost my mother when I was near your age. It wasn't easy. Every night I prayed, 'Jesus, help me. I need you, my momma is gone, and she always told me you would take care of me.' Children, you must be strong and believe and ask Jesus to be with you when you feel hurt in your heart. He has already given you a new momma and daddy that will love you"

"Anna Laura, do you think he has give me and Joel to Lilly and Steve? They are good to us."

Joel spoke up, "I wish we could stay with them forever and ever. They said they would keep us for now. I heered them telling you that."

Back at the settlement, Lilly had taken a break from sewing to make the noon meal for Steve.

They sat quietly at the table. Suddenly, Steve said, "Lilly, I know you've always wanted a boy and a girl. For some reason, you were never with child. Do you want to keep Joel and Susie for good?"

"Do you mean it, Steve?"

"Yeah, I mean every word of it, Lilly."

Lilly grabbed Steve around the neck in an elated hug, almost choking him.

"Well, Lilly, before you choke me to death, it's settled. The children are ours."

Steve went back to his work and Lilly back to her sewing, both thanking God for the children.

She could hardly wait to tell Anna Laura and the children.

Anna Laura, Joel and Susie's clothes had dried by the sun as they talked of many things. Anna Laura told them of how they could be schooled and how wonderful it would be to learn of far away places. She had loved the same things so much when growing up. She knew from the time she was really young she would one day leave the valley at the foot of the tall mountain.

Now, she could teach Joel and Susie and many others that another world existed beyond their mountains.

"We should be getting back to Lilly and Steve's. We don't want them to worry about us."

Anna Laura could see the change in Joel and Susie's countenance. The trauma was fading a little from their hearts. She could now see a spark of hope and security.

The three headed for Anna Laura's place, then mounted the Arabian and headed for Steve and Lilly's.

Lilly had already stopped her sewing and prepared a wonderful supper for the five of them.

The sun had already set in the west; the evening was wearing on as Lilly stood waiting for her three favorite people. Steve was excitedly getting cleaned up from his day of working. For him, this too was a special occasion. He knew announcing the good news would be one of the greatest moments of his life. He and Lilly were in their mid-thirties, they had made a decision that day they never dreamed they would ever make. There had been no reason to think they would ever be this blessed.

Finally, Anna Laura, Susie and Joel rode into the edge of the yard.

Lilly stood grinning like a possum, as Anna Laura's grandma would have proclaimed.

"Children, Lilly sure looks happy to see you."

Lilly embraced the children as soon as they stepped foot on the porch and gave Anna Laura a special hug. She excitedly said, "Come on in."

They walked in to see a special table covered with a table linen and special dishes that Steve had bought Lilly for her thirty-second birthday. There was even a white candle burning in the middle of the table. Susie and Joel had never seen a candle before. The small dancing flame gave them the calmest feeling.

The roasted wild turkey was brown and plump. Everything looked so appetizing. Joel and Susie could hardly keep from licking their lips. They did not know the best was yet to come. To them, the pies they saw in the homemade pie cabinet were the greatest thing they could experience that evening. The brown, fluffy meringue tantalized their taste buds.

Steve walked in looking clean and handsome with a huge smile on his face that showed his white teeth, his dark skin making them look even brighter. All the time Joel was thinking, "I wish he could be my dad."

Each took their place at the table, Joel sat next to Steve, Susie next to Lilly and Anna Laura at the head of the table.

They blessed the food together as they joined hands in unity.

As they ate, the children talked of their day's adventure with a special glow on their faces.

Joel and Susie became very quiet after finishing talking about their glorious day. They began to worry what the future held for them and wondered how soon this wonderful experience would end. They both were quiet, thinking of how they had an Uncle Jeb and Aunt Nervie. "Could we possibly end up on the rough side of the mountain with them in another shack?" They had seen both of them drunk on moonshine and they acted terribly. It was normal that the two of them were having the same thoughts.

Suddenly, Steve spoke out, "Me and Lilly have something special to say. Lilly, you tell them."

"Joel, Susie, we have decided to keep you children as our own. We want you to be our little boy and girl."

Joel bounced from his chair, locked his arms around Steve's neck and Susie did the same with Lilly.

Anna Laura just sat with tears sliding down her face. Silently, she prayed, "I knew You would, I knew You would make a way for these children. Thank You! Thank You, God!"

The children could hardly contain themselves. They were suddenly silent, so was everyone else.

Susie and Joel joined hands and looked upward.

"Momma always told us You would take care of us if she ever had to leave us."

Their speech was already becoming better from being around Anna Laura. They seemed to thank God so eloquently. They now felt secure, loved and wanted. They knew in that moment that life would be good.

"Thank you, Steve, thank you, Lilly."

Steve chimed in, "Children, would you like to go with me to feed the animals?"

"Yes! Yes!"

Anna Laura and Lilly joined hands and prayed for a wonderful future for Steve and Lilly's home. This was more than Anna Laura could have hoped for.

"Lilly, I'd better head back to my place." Anna Laura spoke as her emotions surfaced. "Thank you for everything."

She shed tears of joy all the way home.

<h1 align="center">Chapter 17</h1>

Anna Laura went to the falls, bathed and washed her hair as she would be leaving for Cherry Valley early the next morning. Her hair must dry before she could lie down.

She lay under the heavens sleeping like a baby that night. Never had she experienced a more peaceful feeling.

Morning came with brightness and the sound of a dove echoed through the hills. There was a heavenly feeling in the air that flowed in the area of Anna Laura's special place that God had allowed her to occupy.

Anna Laura had her coffee and fresh fruit that she had picked from Steve and Lilly's orchard the previous day. She then brushed her teeth at the stream so her breath was as fresh as the pure unpolluted air of the mountain.

She adorned herself in a silk blouse and a riding skirt of sage green. Her chosen lipstick was a muted orange and she wore her hair long, loose and straight, parted on the left.

After the Arabian finished eating, she saddled him and mounted.

As she rode down the mountain, she could not bear to think that moonshine was causing the same cruelty to other women and children through the mountains as it had to Joel, Susie and Martha.

All she could think was, "It has to end. I know it will not be easy, but it must be stopped."

She prayed fervently there would be no bloodshed for the cause.

Halfway down the mountain, she stopped to hobble her horse and to allow him to pick tender green grass from a small bench of the mountain.

She lay in the soft green grass staring at the still, blue skies. She thought of the Psalm: "The Lord lifteth up the meek. He casteth the wicked down to the ground."

In her spirit she knew the children and women she was going to battle for were meek; therefore, God would lead her in the right direction.

[95]

Anna Laura arrived in Cherry Valley around noon. She and Hank had lunch at the Hemlock Inn. The atmosphere was soothing after the long ride off Brushy Mountain.

Hank proceeded to inform Anna Laura of his progress on the problem.

"Anna Laura, I've contacted Lieutenant Adams. He'll be in Cherry Valley next week. He'll have a crew of revenue agents ready to come up the mountains. They'll rent horses here in town. The moonshiners that are caught will be brought off the mountain and jailed in the facility in Cherry Valley until their trials and sentencing take place. Then they'll be escorted to the prison near Nashville, Tennessee. I would like to ride up with them if you feel comfortable with my being on the mountain. I am anxious to see the settlement and the progress that the grant has helped bring to the mountains."

"That will be great, Hank."

"Of course, Lieutenant Adams will be riding up with the revenuers. When I expressed your concern, he was extremely interested in coming to Brushy Mountain. Tennessee has never been very concerned with Brushy Mountain before. Everyone thinks of it being more of a part of Kentucky. When looking on the map, I found that particular area was on the Tennessee corner. That doesn't mean that some families don't occupy the Kentucky side."

It was obvious that Hank would go beyond the call of duty to help Anna Laura.

"As I rode up the Kentucky side, I didn't see any homes," Anna Laura replied.

"Anna Laura, have you thought about going up to Nashville for a weekend?"

"Yes, Hank, I have. When this ordeal is over, we'll talk more about it. I feel sure at that point I would enjoy a weekend: that would be a nice change."

Hank smiled, "Any time will be fine, maybe in the fall of this year."

"Sounds good to me, Hank. Could we walk to the stables? I don't like getting back on Brushy Mountain too late."

Hank was hoping she would ask. As he assisted Anna Laura in mounting onto the saddle that Jess had secured on the Arabian, their eyes met. Hank gently lifted Anna Laura's chin and lightly kissed her pretty, full lips. She did not resist.

As Anna Laura headed up the mountain, her feelings were mixed. She asked herself, "Am I falling for Hank? He is among my class of people and I do feel comfortable with him."

As her horse plodded along, she had flashbacks of her time with Clint. She knew no one could ever fill the void in her life other than her blond-haired, blue-eyed, handsome Doctor Clint Knopp.

She began to think, "Most likely I will never go back to Germany when my mission in Brushy Mountain is fulfilled. How can I ever forget Clint? I have feelings for Hank, but they do not compare to what I feel for Clint and that isn't fair to Hank. I feel so guilty. I believe Hank is falling in love with me, but I don't know how to handle the situation. The last thing I want to do is to hurt Hank."

Before realizing, Anna Laura was near her campsite. Her thoughts had separated her from time.

As she stood under the falls bathing again, her thoughts carried her away. She was first in Brushy Mountain, next in Cherry Valley, then higher in the mountains.

There was so much to do.

When she made it back to camp after bathing, Crissy was waiting for her. She had returned the books Anna Laura loaned her and was ready for more. She had also mastered her penmanship. Her reading ability was unbelievable.

As it was a couple of hours before dark, Anna Laura quizzed Crissy about what she would like to study for a career. Crissy did not hesitate, "I want to deliver babies and help women who are suffering. I want to be a doctor. I know that one day I'll have to leave these mountains to go to medical school. I also know you can prepare me for that."

"Yes, Crissy, I can if you're willing to work hard."

"Oh, Anna Laura, I'll do everything you say. I have nothing but time."

"Crissy, I know you will succeed. There will be a way, Crissy. My momma always said God helps those who help themselves. She always said, you take one step and He will take two."

"You know what, Anna Laura, I really believe that is true. Your momma must have been a good momma."

"She surely was, Crissy. I wish I could have had her longer."

Crissy spent day after day in her secret utopia studying and going to Anna Laura when she needed special instructions.

Chapter 18

Sunday morning came after Anna Laura had spent a Saturday alone enjoying the mountain breeze while she planned wonderful things for the Brushy Mountain people.

As she rode toward the settlement she was anxious to tell Steve and Lilly about her visit to Cherry Valley. She had faith Steve would tell only the men he trusted that the revenuers would soon be coming. It would be detrimental for those who opposed the law to find out about their plans. Chaos was definitely not needed.

Anna Laura, Lilly and Steve walked through the new construction area which would come to be called 'The Place of Hope.' Anna Laura was surprised at all the progress that had taken place the past couple of days. She was filled with joy.

Anna Laura related to Steve and Lilly, "The search for moonshiners will take place in late fall. Steve, when this is over, we may have to build housing for the women and children who are left behind. They couldn't survive in the rough mountains alone."

"Don't you fret, Anna Laura, we'll provide shelter and the good book asks that we give a tenth. I am sure a tenth of our crops will feed the women and children. Everyone will pitch in and provide a place for them to live until each can have their own."

"Steve, I know the women are strong and are accustomed to bringing in wood to keep warm, among other necessities for survival. I know they'll work together. After all they've been through, they will be happy with whatever we're able to give to start their new lives. Steve, the children will be schooled and will be in church on Sunday to learn about the Bible through the Children's Bible books."

"I know it will work," Steve responded with a pleasant grin.

Anna Laura glanced toward where the children were playing. She was overjoyed to see how Susie and Joel were accepted by the settlement children. This certainly put a smile on her face.

Anna Laura took Steve and Lilly by the hand, "I am so grateful and blessed to know the two of you. Without you, my accomplishments would be much less."

"Anna Laura, we surely are thankful you came our way. Four months ago we never dreamed things on Brushy Mountain could be like they are now. We wake up every morning with a new hope rising inside our minds. We've got hope for our young people that we never had before."

"I must be getting home as I need to prepare lessons for a young girl from the higher mountains."

"Wait, Anna Laura! Let's take a look at how your cabin is coming along."

As they came into view of the building site, Anna Laura stood in awe. The logs were round Hemlock pine. Every log was near the same size. The fireplace was already being constructed, the rock came from the huge streams that rushed off the mountain over time and had worn them perfectly. Lilly anxiously spoke out, "Anna Laura, your kitchen and front room will be here together. Over here will be your bedroom and that room, you talked about storing your records of sick people and school records. Up in the loft there will be a lot of room to store stuff."

Anna Laura thought, "I most likely will be here near two years."

This was the allotted time she believed her plans could come to pass. She would be in the twenty-ninth year of her life, still young, considering her accomplishments.

As Anna Laura walked toward her Arabian to head home, Joel and Susie ran to hug her around the legs. They truly bonded with her as she was their earthly savior the day they first came to ask for help for their good momma.

As Anna Laura rode home, she thought of how she hadn't seen Mary Jane in a few days. She was a little apprehensive about her. Mary Jane always had to sneak away from her aunt and uncle to visit Anna Laura. Perhaps she had not had the opportunity.

Anna Laura was so hopeful that Mary Jane and Crissy could become friends. It would be wonderful if they could study together. Mary Jane had already learned to read and do basic arithmetic. In the beginning Mary Jane was so sure she would like to become a nurse; at the present, she was not as sure. After seeing Jess when he came up with Anna Laura to bring supplies and learning his college studies were preparing him to be a teacher, she began having second thoughts. Now she wondered if she might rather be a teacher.

Anna Laura knew that Mary Jane was taken, heart, soul and mind by Jess' looks and kind personality. He spoke so gently and looked so pleasant when he briefly talked to her. This kind behavior was not what she had seen in the men in her so-called family. Mary Jane now had a new hope other than her schooling. Like Crissy, she had a secret utopia in the lonely mountains where she sat to dream and Jess now featured in her future dreams. Her biggest fear was whether she would see him again.

When they had first met, Mary Jane had been taken by Anna Laura's feminine ways and lovely manners. She was catching on very fast. At times Anna Laura had seen her as she practiced her speech and the way she carried herself. She wanted so much to be graceful.

That very night when Anna Laura slept, she had a dream. She had not dreamed during her sleep since she had been on Brushy Mountain. She dreamed a small plane landed on a large clearing on the mountain as she stood looking over God's given beauty. When the plane came to a complete stop, Clint stepped out dressed in street clothes and was as handsome as ever. She walked toward him with open arms, but he only handed her a letter and climbed inside the plane and was in the air again in a matter of minutes. She stood with tears streaming down her face as the plane left the mountains soaring behind the clouds that hung over the next mountain.

She nervously opened the letter.

Dearest Anna Laura,

I love you with all my heart and always will, but I must make a life for myself. I am now engaged to be married to a young lady from a royal family. Anna Laura, as you know, royalty means nothing to me, but I must go on with my life.

Remember me always,
Clint.

Anna Laura suddenly awakened, the dream seemed so real. She lay looking toward the star strewn sky in deep thought, "Is this a sign that Clint has found someone else?" Her heart ached with grief until the sun beamed in onto the rippling stream reflecting rainbow colors from the water hitting lightly upon the rocks that stood vertically, creating a mist as the water splashed against them.

She began to think positively. *Maybe when my mission is over, Clint will show up and we will go some place like Prince Edward Island and be married. Perhaps I will only think of the two of us and not about his royal family.*

Bringing her thoughts back to reality, she remembered her plans to scout the mountains and find Mary Jane. She made herself ready for the day, mounted her Arabian and headed in the direction of Mary Jane's secret place.

She was not there. Anna Laura guided her Arabian over the rough terrain and began an upward climb. After thirty minutes or so she heard a faint voice. She followed the sound and saw a cave. The thing that bewildered Anna Laura was the fact that small poles were attached to trees on each side of the cave completely securing the inside. Huge nails held the small poles to the trees. There was no escaping for the person held captive there.

Anna Laura hurriedly got off her Arabian, almost running to the cave, but being careful to walk around the sides and down. It could be dangerous to go straight toward the opening. As she peeped in from the very end of the cave, she saw sweet Mary Jane lying in a fetal position groaning softly.

"Mary, Mary!" Anna Laura cried out.

Mary Jane began to move her body slightly.

"What happened, Mary Jane? Who brought you here?"

"My uncle and some strange man called Buddy Little. Uncle wanted to marry me off to him and I ran away trying to get to you, but they caught me and brought me here saying I would never learn the way of this world, and I was going to stay in these mountains forever."

Anna Laura found a rock that was big enough to hold with both hands and began beating against the back of the poles pushing the nails from the trees. It took so long that twilight was coming on by the time Anna Laura freed Mary Jane. She was extremely weak, hungry and dehydrated.

Anna Laura gave her water, then managed to get her on the Arabian. She slowly took her charge down the mountain trail. The bit of daylight that was left was a God-given blessing.

"Mary Jane, you are going to stay with me. I will not allow your uncle to take you."

When they reached Anna Laura's campsite, she realized this is was the first place the men would come looking when they discovered Mary Jane was gone.

"Mary Jane, we must head for the settlement and find a safe place for you."

As they approached Steve and Lilly's, Lilly peered through the window into the dimness of the late evening as the sun was sinking low. She found it hard to identify the girls. She stepped out on the porch.

"Lilly, this is Anna Laura and I need your help. I found Mary Jane very near death in a cave high in the mountains. Her uncle and his friend, Buddy Little, planned to let her die there if they could not scare her into marrying Buddy. I'm sure they'll hit my place first. Lilly, what shall I do?"

"Anna Laura, I know if we talk to Rob and Jane they will hide her out. They have an extra room in their loft that's open to the rest of the cabin."

Steve headed to their friends' home to inform them of the situation. Their reply was an instant, "Yes."

No one seemed to be stirring outside, which was good. As it was in the dusk of the evening their movements went unnoticed.

Jane prepared a bath for Mary Jane while Anna Laura made sure she ate and drank adequately. Mary Jane bathed and dressed in Jane's flannel gown. The bed was extremely soft and clean. Being in the cave for two days had been terrifying. Mary Jane seemed to feel as though she had died and gone to Heaven, but she knew this was earthly comfort as she closed her weak eyes to sleep.

Anna Laura took one last look at Mary Jane and eased out of the loft. She headed back to camp. She dressed in a soft nightgown and settled for the night beneath the rock that hung over the nice, clean earth. She felt safe there with her rifle by her side. Around midnight she heard voices of men above the cliff. She prepared herself for battle. She assumed Buddy and Mary Jane's uncle had learned that Mary Jane was gone and figured Anna Laura would be the one who rescued her.

She loaded her rifle and waited for the two outlaws. She watched closely as they blundered around her camp. The fire she had built still shed light enough for them to be seen.

Anna Laura listened closely as they talked.

"We'll find Mary Jane and you talk about sorry, she'll be one sorrowful girl and that doctor of a woman, the no good thang that came in these mountains nosing around, we'll git her too. She shoulda never came to Brushy Mountain. Wonder where she's at?" Buddy whispered.

"See that big ole rock up yonder, I bet you a dollar she's a hid there with Mary Jane."

As they neared the cliff, Anna Laura cocked her rifle and opened fire, only meaning to scare them. The bullets flew all around them, stirring up the dirt. Anna Laura had never seen two men running as fast, stumbling and at times hitting on their knees and hands. There was just enough moonlight to show them as they ran.

She could hardly contain her mirth. As they scrambled up the mountain, she began to giggle and laughed until she hurt. She was certain they would not return.

Anna Laura's thoughts were, "Mary Jane can stay with me and study with Crissy." Anna Laura knew in her heart the lives of these two young women were headed for change. She vowed to herself, "I will not relinquish Mary Jane to those crude men."

[105]

Chapter 19

Anna Laura was now ready to deal with Crissy's well being. No one would stop her from saving this young woman from a life of abuse and loneliness.

To Anna Laura's surprise early the next morning Crissy showed up at her campsite. "Crissy, what are you doing here at the break of dawn?"

"Anna Laura, early last night after going to bed I overheard Momma and Daddy talking of how they were planning to leave Brushy Mountain and head back to Virginia where their folks once lived. Daddy argued with Momma, he told her I wanted a different life. He knew where I've been sneaking off to. He followed me here. He knew I'd been learning from your books.

"He told Momma, 'Millie if you'll go with me I won't drink the bad stuff no more that makes me crazy.' And she told him, 'Well, Patch, I will go for the sake of my Crissy, I want her to have a different life to mine.'

"I fell asleep. When I woke up, they were gone. They must have left at daybreak. I was afraid of other mean men in the mountains and got here as fast as I could."

"Thank God you are here. You are welcome to live here with me."

Anna Laura knew before winter came her small cabin would be finished, but what about Crissy and Mary Jane?

She would use the room intended for storing records for a bedroom for the girls and keep the files in the attic. She could now dismiss this worry from her mind.

Crissy and Mary Jane enjoyed every moment they spent with Anna Laura at the campsite. They experienced more security than ever before. They could feel motherly love from Anna Laura even though she was not much older than them. Being a maternal figure came easy as she had not had that experience at the age the girls were. She did not want them to feel as she had, therefore, she put great effort into making them feel secure.

The girls were gaining an abundance of knowledge even before school was in session. They would likely be educated enough to help teach the small ones or even the older ones that were beginners. Anna Laura would teach the girls advanced classes in the evenings. She would advise or help when they needed it. With their intelligence, very little monitoring was needed.

Crissy and Mary Jane were now free from the horrible abuse they had known. With the help of Hank, Anna Laura had petitioned the courts in Cherry Valley for guardianship over Crissy and Mary Jane. As there had been no legalized custody by their relatives, there were no problems.

Cold Tater and Rock Head seemed to accept the fact that Crissy and Mary Jane were permanently in Anna Laura's care. The boys were not ignorant; they simply had no steady guidance as children. Anna Laura had pretty well put enough fear in them that they kept their distance. She sensed in her heart that there was hope for them if they were exposed to a better way of life. Perhaps before leaving Brushy Mountain she could reach them in some way, at least teach them not to be hostile and to become aware that they could get by without confrontation. Hopefully, they could learn that some people and properties were off limits to them.

The thought crossed her mind that perhaps she might even get them to scout out moonshiners for the revenuers. Even in an isolated place like Brushy Mountain they had been stereotyped as children, a state which followed them through adolescence into young adulthood. Anna Laura had hope for them even though they had committed serious acts that could have sent them to jail had they been in an area where the law was better enforced. Their upbringing had disposed them to physically hurt people to get what they wanted or to get attention, even though it was negative attention. They needed a reason to conform to a proper way of life and Anna Laura believed she had the answer.

<h1 style="text-align:center">Chapter 20</h1>

It was now time for Anna Laura to make her weekend trip to Nashville with Hank. She cautioned Crissy and Mary Jane to be careful while she was away.

"Girls, I want you to sleep under the cliff. It's safer there. I'll also teach you to shoot this gun; each of you give it a try, it isn't difficult."

They were a little apprehensive, but mastered the task. Anna Laura feared Mary Jane's family might come around trying to cause trouble and wanted them to be able to protect themselves.

Anna Laura made herself ready early the next morning as the fog lifted on the mountain and the sun eased its way in. She rode off the mountain, taking her prettiest clothes for the weekend. She arrived in Cherry Valley, stabled her Arabian and went to meet Hank at the Hemlock Inn for breakfast.

Anna Laura was a bit apprehensive about going to Nashville, but knew if Hank's aunt and uncle possessed the same characteristics as Hank she would be comfortable. Anna Laura gracefully slipped into Hank's nice car and he closed the door and made his way to the driver's seat. They then headed south toward Knoxville then west toward Nashville.

As they traveled, Hank wanted so much to tell Anna Laura his true feelings for her, but was afraid of moving too quickly.

They arrived around mid-afternoon.

First, they contacted Lieutenant Adams about accompanying the revenuers into Brushy Mountain. Anna Laura was sure a personal meeting would be more effective so they arranged to meet him around four that afternoon. Afterward, they headed to Hank's aunt and uncle's estate. The couple had insisted Anna Laura stay with them instead of paying for a room at the hotel. Anna Laura was extremely impressed with the huge property. The plantation style house was Anna Laura's favorite. The land was beautiful with big grassy fields and trees edged the huge home as well as a small river that gently flowed on the north side.

Hank and Anna Laura were greeted by the couple on the huge porch that spread across the entire front of the house with its huge columns accentuating the entire home.

"Aunt Daisy, Uncle Joe, this is Anna Laura." Already, they were extremely impressed by her grace and poise, as well as her looks and intelligence.

After the introduction, Anna Laura was taken to the guest room by a young maid.

Hank relayed to Aunt Daisy and Uncle Joe before going to his room, "Aunt Daisy, Anna Laura and I have an important business meeting in Nashville before dinner."

"That will be fine; dinner will be served around 6:30."

Anna Laura bathed and put on her favorite cream color Victorian style dress. She wore her hair long and loose.

Hank gave Lieutenant Adams a call and they headed to his office on Broadway.

"Lieutenant Adams, this is Anna Laura Gibson. Anna Laura, Lieutenant Samuel Adams. Lieutenant, Anna Laura is very concerned about the illegal moonshine that is being produced in Brushy Mountain. Believe it or not, deaths have actually resulted from men drinking and becoming irate and aggressive."

"Hank, I feel that I can assist you in weeding out the moonshiners. I have a task force that can be sent in to the mountains to eliminate the production. Give me a couple of weeks to get everything ready. I'll send my best men, perhaps I will accompany them. Actually, I've always wanted to visit Brushy Mountain. It's hard to believe families still live up there, after all, it is the 1930s."

Adams advised Hank, "It might be a good idea to get a couple of men to help, men that no one would suspect. Someone inside would probably know those involved and where they're dispersed throughout the mountains."

Immediately Anna Laura thought of Cold Tater and Rock Head. From the time they were children they had roamed the mountains and probably saw far more than they needed to see and maybe indulged in as they got older, which most likely influenced their behavior toward Mary Jane and others. Anna Laura's imagination was going every direction. She believed helping others would change their lives as they had never been considered anything more than dumb mountain boys.

Anna Laura eyed the clock on the wall and informed Hank that they should be going as it was already 5:30. She definitely wanted to make it back to the plantation at least thirty minutes before dinner. Anna Laura and Hank bid Lieutenant Adams goodbye. As they left, they gave him the address to the Hemlock Inn in Cherry Valley and told him he would find complete courtesy during his stay while accomplishing his mission on Brushy Mountain.

Hank and Anna Laura felt very confident as they drove to Aunt Daisy and Uncle Joe's.

"Tomorrow, we'll go to the Grand Ole Opry if you would like, Anna Laura."

"I'd be delighted. I'd also like to do a little shopping in downtown Nashville as well."

"We'll make time for shopping either before or after the Grand Ole Opry."

"That will be great, Hank. Thanks."

Anna Laura wanted to buy Mary Jane, Crissy, Joel and Susie a couple of outfits and shop a bit for herself as well.

They quickly entered the huge house and freshened up for dinner.

Anna Laura was absolutely intrigued when walking into the huge dining room. The big windows were open and the Victorian lace curtains moved slightly with the light breeze. The fresh, sweet scent of roses and other flowers carried into the dining room.

It was not yet dark, but candles glowed and flickered making the dining area cozier. Even though there was a maid present, Daisy did her own cooking and was the best in the area.

The dinner was country style. Roast meat, fresh red potatoes roasted with mild herbs sprinkled over them. Every fresh vegetable imaginable lay around the huge roast. Homemade rolls were huge and light. The garden salad and homemade dressing were almost exotic. The fresh iced tea had been brewed to perfection; the fresh lemon and cane sugar making the tea a captivating drink. Huge homemade chocolate pies with thick golden brown meringue sat in the pie cabinet.

Anna Laura had not looked upon a meal this lavish in years, if ever.

The four enjoyed their meal immensely, as well as the conversation, which was focused on Brushy Mountain and the people who lived there. They were very impressed by Anna Laura; she seemed to fit into their kind of world, very down to earth people, even though they possessed wealth.

Anna Laura had a personality that could adapt well. She could have fit into royalty in the past, but had feared rejection.

After the wonderful dinner, they sat on the balcony that overlooked the estate and talked of Anna Laura's past.

Daisy and Joe were really keen on Anna Laura. They were already hopeful of a relationship between Hank and Anna Laura that might one day lead to marriage.

Anna Laura departed to her room after a time and Hank to his. Daisy whispered to Joe, "Those two are a match from Heaven."

Joe had already sensed that Anna Laura may have had someone special in her past. He could read between the lines in parts of their conversation. He could see that Anna Laura's affection did not manifest itself in the same way Hank's did.

Morning came and they shared a delicious breakfast before heading off to downtown Nashville. Anna Laura shopped with great anticipation for Crissy and Mary Jane. She bought them hair brushes, shampoo, make-up and perfume. She was very capable of choosing the right colors to complement their hair and skin colors. She also shopped for Joel and Susie; They had never worn store-bought clothes and would be as elated as Mary Jane and Crissy.

After a nice dinner at the Burning Embers, they headed for the Grand Ole Opry. Anna Laura loved the music and enjoyed herself to the fullest.

As they drove back to the plantation, she thanked Hank.

"Hank, this has been a wonderful evening. It couldn't have been better. I haven't been this relaxed in such a long time."

"Anna Laura, what ever makes you happy makes me happy."

As Hank covered Anna Laura's soft hand with his, she felt all bubbly inside, but her inner spirit could not dismiss Clint long enough to know if she could possibly have feelings for Hank.

Upon returning to the plantation, they had wonderful conversation with Uncle Joe and Aunt Daisy about their visit to Nashville, but went to their rooms fairly early that night.

Anna Laura was filled with guilt as she lay awake for hours remembering her Clint who she had left behind. She kept telling herself, "I could possibly have fit in, but would they have ever truly accepted a Kentucky mountain girl?"

Chapter 21

Anna Laura looked across the vast, beautiful land to see the sunrise in the eastern skies. This had been a wonderful and blessed weekend, she pondered in her head. Anna Laura was pleased that she was asked to stay at the plantation instead of the hotel downtown. The plantation was like a paradise after living in the outdoors for several months.

Her only fear was that she knew Hank was falling in love with her and she also knew she still had deep feelings for Clint. "How can I ever stop loving him?" She knew the only way she could be sure was to see him again; to touch his handsome face, to look into his blue eyes and be held in his arms.

His absence sometimes put doubt in her mind. If only she could see him again there would be no doubt. She was consumed with guilt that very moment as she was sure of Hank's feelings for her. She also knew Hank was too much of a gentleman to pressure her in any way. She purposed in her heart to fervently pray from that day forward that Hank would meet and fall in love with someone else. Anna Laura really believed in prayer.

Soon, she was ready to head back to Brushy Mountain. She dressed casually and went down for breakfast.

Daisy and Joe greeted her with a smile telling Anna Laura, "We really are taken by your genuine charm, as well as your beauty and intelligence."

They even mentioned that Hank was their only heir and would one day inherit the plantation.

As Hank and Anna Laura walked outside, Daisy and Joe stood thinking the same thoughts, "What a perfect couple." Joe smiled at Daisy. "Daisy, they belong together."

"You know, Joe, we have met many young women that Hank has dated, but never an Anna Laura."

Daisy and Joe watched until they were out of sight.

The trip back to Cherry Valley was extremely pleasant. Hank came so very close to telling Anna Laura he loved her, but kept it to himself.

The two of them had accomplished their mission. They were sure the lieutenant would be true to his word.

Anna Laura knew her mind would never be at ease until the families of women and children were free from abuse that was brought about by moonshine and wicked men. Their upbringing and the moonshine had molded their lives.

Hank and Anna Laura arrived in Cherry Valley in mid-afternoon. Anna Laura was tired so she stayed the night at the Hemlock Inn. To be able to sleep three nights in a row on a real bed was wonderful. She had almost forgotten the luxury of a bed and a roof other than a hanging rock over her head.

She fell asleep thinking of how excited Crissy, Mary Jane, Joel and Susie would be with their new clothes. She knew the make-up would excite the girls even more. She could only imagine how a touch of make-up would enhance the natural beauty the girls possessed.

Sunday morning seemed to come quickly. Anna Laura was off to the Hemlock Inn Restaurant to have breakfast with Hank.

"Anna Laura, I would like to ride up on Brushy Mountain with you today."

"Why not, Hank? You can make it back to Cherry Valley before dark if you only spend a couple of hours on the mountain."

They headed to the stables. Hank rented an appaloosa, a saddle horse with black and white spots on its rump and loins. A western saddle would be more comfortable for Hank as he had not ridden in rough terrain often. He definitely made the perfect choice of horse, it was sure-footed and calm. Anna Laura was impressed. The ride up the mountain was intriguing for Hank.

When arriving at the campsite, Hank was totally entranced by the surrounding beauty, the waterfalls, the water nearby that ran down the mountain like a wild thing, the soothing, rippling stream beside the campsite, the huge, healthy trees, the fresh air and the sun rays that filtered between the trees into the area.

He was intrigued that this delicate, beautiful, but strong willed woman chose to live under the skies. Learning the hanging rock became her shelter when needed amazed him even more.

Suddenly, Mary Jane and Crissy came into the clearing as they returned from their morning walk. Anna Laura was shocked to see the girls had found a new friend. Their companion was stunningly beautiful.

Anna Laura detected immediately that she was at least part Cherokee Indian with her long, straight, black hair and ebony eyes, as well as her olive skin and perfect features. One could have described her as having the face of a goddess. She was of medium height and perfectly proportioned.

Anna Laura noticed from the corner of her eye that even Hank took a second look. The newcomer looked to be around nineteen or twenty years of age.

"Anna Laura, this is our new friend who we came upon while gathering berries. We found her sitting by a stream, her feet in the cool waters trying to relax and soothe her spirit. Her dad came to Brushy Mountain many years ago from North Carolina. He brought her here when she was only three; She just turned twenty. Someone in these mountains killed her dad; a crazy drunk white man did it because he was an Indian." Crissy's eyes were filled with tears as she related the girl's brief history to Anna Laura.

"Her dad was killed about three weeks ago."

Anna Laura introduced Hank, "This is the man responsible for the good things that are taking place in Brushy Mountain. He works for the government and was able to get grants for us."

Crissy was not quite finished with her story so she introduced her newly found friend. "Hank, Anna Laura, this is Selena. She buried her dad all by herself. Mary Jane and I were so sad for her. We knew you would be happy if we brought her home with us. We went to her cabin and got her things. She has pretty clothes that she sewed. Her dad managed to go to North Carolina and take herbs about twice a year and trade for necessities and special cloth, thread and needles and scissors. We brought her belongings."

"Anna Laura, can she stay with us? She already knows how to read. We'll teach her more. Her dad got books for her. He had learned to read before he came here."

"Crissy, I'd be happy to have Selena stay with us."

Hank was amazed at the way Anna Laura so calmly handled the situation.

"Hank, you have at least an hour left. Let's ride out to the settlement. Most of the people are very polite and hospitable."

As the two of them mounted onto their horses and rode away, Selena was totally taken by Hank's looks. She smiled at Crissy and Mary Jane.

"That Hank is the best looking man my eyes have ever looked upon."

Anna Laura first introduced Hank to Steve and Lilly.

"Anna Laura, let's show Hank our new buildings."

Hank was amazed at the progress that had taken place in such a short time.

"Let's go to our house for apple pie and coffee." Steve wanted to sit at ease and talk. They talked of their future plans. Steve spoke with sincerity.

"Hank, please believe what I am about to say. I thank you from the bottom of my heart for all that you have done. I know Anna Laura has worked hard in making things happen, but if you hadn't a helped it couldn't be happening. You have really helped us Brushy Mountain settlers. The biggest thing is what it's going to do for the children's future."

"Thank you, Steve."

Hank looked toward Anna Laura. "I think I'd better get back to Cherry Valley before dark."

As they rode away Lilly couldn't help expressing her opinion, "Steve, I think they are a fine match, both tall and good looking."

"They are both good workers. They sure can get things done."

When reaching the campsite, Hank bid the girls goodbye. He was still a little stunned by Selena's beauty and personality. He had no idea that such beauty existed in these tall mountains.

Anna Laura was very aware that Hank was finding it hard not to let his curiosity show concerning Selena. If she could have looked through his eyes into his soul she could have seen multiple questions floating around. She did not feel jealous as she was constantly filled with thoughts and questions about Clint.

Hank made a safe trip to Cherry Valley. As he traveled he had very mixed emotions. Meeting Selena had absolutely stirred his heart.

On the mountain, Anna Laura became more acquainted with Selena. She suddenly remembered she had not given the clothes and make-up she had bought in Nashville to the girls. She also knew she could not treat Mary Jane and Crissy and leave Selena out. She began to think of how close she and Selena were in size and how their skin colors were so much alike and their hair as well. She looked at the beautiful dress she had bought for herself, which was light purple and would complement Selena in every way. The extra hairbrush, shampoo, soap, toothbrush and other necessities would be perfect for Selena as well.

Anna Laura said to herself, "I really do not need anything." To give was something she loved to do.

When giving the beautiful clothes to Selena, Crissy and Mary Jane, they could not hold back tears or smiles. Selena was stunned that Anna Laura thought enough of her to give to her what she knew the woman had purchased for herself. Selena had always been filled with faith and believed that God had allowed this small miracle to show her Anna Laura's true heart.

After the girls received their gifts and thanked Anna Laura, it was time to settle in for the night.

"Selena, I have an extra blanket. Crissy, Mary Jane, give her a little help in piling dry leaves to lay the blanket on. You'll be surprised, Selena, how comfortable it will be, especially under the stars. Here's an extra blanket to cover yourself with. The air gets a little cool at night. Once we're settled, I'll show you the most common constellations in the sky."

Selena was amazed. She had never really noticed as she was rarely outside after dark.

Selena lay late in the night looking at the beauty of the starry sky. She had been taught that there was a Heaven and a real God beyond the sky. Selena was secure. This was more than she ever dreamed could happen. She had basically been in hiding for three weeks in fear of being taken like her dad had been.

Somehow, Anna Laura's strength and lack of fear made Selena feel safe. Selena already had a lot going for her. She was by far a stronger woman than she realized. Her dad had been a good father and husband to her momma. Both her parents had taught her the basics of reading, writing and numbers.

Their departure from North Carolina came about because life for the Indians was changing drastically. Her dad felt life would be better in the mountains. He had learned of a few people walking to North Carolina from Brushy Mountain and was impressed but was misinformed and given false hope. Their journey had been very hard, but they had been really happy and did really well until the moonshiners became more prevalent and began to invade their privacy, moving higher into the mountains out of fear of being caught.

Selena was blessed the day she ventured farther down the mountain; she had wondered so many times what existed beyond her home high near the top of the Brushy Mountain.

Just as she was making her way down, she had seen a couple of drunk men stumbling away, one carrying a shotgun. As Selena hid quickly behind a huge oak tree, almost afraid to breathe, she heard their voices in a low, broken tone brought by the drunkenness, "There will be no more Indians in these mountains excepting that girl of his and she'd better be a keeping hid or she'll get the same thang as her ole man got. The main thang is that we got Big Eagle."

Her father had been called Big Eagle because he was swift and strong. It seemed that regardless of the way he was treated or the emotional hurt he experienced, as the old saying went "like the old eagle he soared again."

Selena wept for her dad, as well as for her momma and baby twin sisters who were stillborn, daily by the shining waters that rippled down the mountain. Selena wished with all her heart there had been a doctor like Anna Laura in the mountains at that time.

Selena wondered what would have happened to her had she not wandered down to Mary Jane's secret place. She knew God had ordered her steps that special day.

It was as if God had a straight view into her secret place that nature set aside as special; a place that had brought three broken spirits together to help each other and come to know a special person like Anna Laura.

Chapter 22

A new life had begun for Selena, Mary Jane and Crissy. They were learning from the advanced books that Anna Laura cherished.

Mary Jane had made up her mind to be a teacher and Crissy wanted to be a midwife. Selena still was not sure what the calling of her life would be. One thing for sure, she could sing like a bird, the soft melodious sound floating toward the sky. Perhaps she would be a writer, or maybe a singer. She thought she could be an investigator. When talking with Anna Laura she uncovered a broad spectrum of talents. She had cunning, quiet ways that opened her heart, soul and mind to things that others overlooked. Anna Laura detected this rare characteristic in Selena very soon after becoming a part of her life. For a split second, Anna Laura entertained the idea that Selena might get involved in tracking the moonshiners as a start; however, considering how her dad's death had occurred, she knew this might not be a good idea.

As the day ended and everyone lay down to sleep, Anna Laura knew there was one thing for sure, when the day came that the girls would leave the mountain, Hank would direct them toward financial aid to achieve a higher education.

Anna Laura drifted into a peaceful sleep thinking of the future of the three girls that God had entrusted to her.

When morning came, Anna Laura came back from the waterfalls looking as fresh as a rose covered by the morning dew. While the girls took turns bathing under the falls, Anna Laura laid out new clothes. They were close enough in size that accommodating the three of them would not be a problem.

Excitement overwhelmed the girls as they took turns dressing in clothes right out of the department stores in downtown Nashville, Tennessee. Anna Laura had curtained off the area beneath the cliff with muslin for privacy.

The new undergarments of soft cotton made them feel feminine. They were intrigued by the soft cotton night gowns in pastel colors which they would be wearing when night came. The riding skirts, jeans, shirts and even dresses were more than they ever dreamed of owning.

Selena dressed in a lavender blouse. The color complemented her olive skin and long, dark, silky hair. Crissy chose a light pink that flattered her blond hair and blush complexion. Mary Jane possessed features similar to Anna Laura. She chose a baby blue that actually complimented her blue eyes as well as matching the blue sky that day. They all wore modest jeans.

The girls trailed behind Anna Laura as she rode toward the settlement feeling really good about themselves as well as a closeness to Anna Laura. They were like a real family.

Anna Laura had chosen to ride the Arabian in order to carry her rifle. She wanted to be cautious, especially as Selena was now in the group. Her plan was to find a horse for each girl. She was sure Hank would be able to take her to an auction one Saturday when she visited his office in Cherry Valley.

When passing through, they traveled by Mary Jane's former so-called caregivers. They had a look of anger on their faces, but did not say a word.

As they entered the edge of the settlement, Selena got a few stares that made her uncomfortable, but she would be fine.

Anna Laura took them straight to Steve and Lilly's.

"Steve, Lilly, Joel and Susie, meet Selena. Joel, Susie, say hello to Crissy and Mary Jane. You remember them, I'm sure."

Steve enthusiastically cut in, "Let's take the girls and Anna Laura to see the progress of the school, church and doctor's office. And we don't want to forget Anna Laura's cabin, do we, Lilly?"

To Anna Laura's surprise, the extra room that Mary Jane and Crissy were to share was far larger than she had realized. There would be plenty of room for Selena and even more if needed.

After living as they had, the room would be a luxury for the girls, with the possible exception maybe for Selena. She most likely had a more suitable place to live as she had caring parents.

Anna Laura was overjoyed by the progress on the buildings. As they toured the school, she began to think, regardless of the career the girls chose for their futures, they could help in the beginning to teach the Brushy Mountain children.

She could hardly wait to see the excitement that would come with learning for the children. She could visualize a new world opening in the minds of those who had never experienced opportunity.

She knew in her heart that one day Mary Jane would be a certified teacher. She could plainly see that teaching was an innate ability that lay dormant in the young woman from her early years. She recalled how Mary Jane's face lit up like a Christmas tree when she was able to aid Crissy in the learning process, although Crissy had likely been a prodigy from the very beginning. Anna Laura had no doubt that Mary Jane would be the number one person to open a new world to many children on Brushy Mountain. Anna Laura was blessed to have spent many evenings teaching Mary Jane.

As Anna Laura, Mary Jane, Crissy and Selena made their way back to camp, Anna Laura led her Arabian. She and the girls were filled with excitement at what they could accomplish when the buildings were finished and everything fell into place. Steve had assured her that all would be completed in a matter of weeks.

Anna Laura planned for Crissy to help with teaching as well as assisting in medical affairs when needed. Selena would be Mary Jane's right arm in teaching. Meanwhile, in their spare time, all three would be preparing for higher education that would likely enable them to follow their destinies beyond Brushy Mountain forever.

Chapter 23

Anna Laura had planted a vegetable garden in early spring. She and the girls worked it when the shade came over in the evenings. They were able to work at least an hour or so. Working in the garden together was a precious time, a time for special conversations about their futures. They talked of their dreams of better lives and of one day meeting their Prince Charmings.

Crissy chimed in, "I think Mary Jane has already met hers. I believe his name could be Jess."

Mary Jane blushed the color of the tomatoes that were beginning to ripen around them.

While working, Anna Laura talked to them about how to be graceful. At times she laid her spade down and demonstrated graceful walking, bending and squatting to pick something up. They enjoyed their work as they learned about important issues. Anna Laura wanted so much for them to have grace, poise and self-confidence, but yet the high spirit of a strong mountain woman. She had been fortunate enough to attend a finishing school in Germany that polished her natural grace. Her momma had a similar natural grace about her as well. Some were born that way.

After relaxing, showering and eating a healthy supper, they sat under the full moon, the stars, and the amazing Milky Way listening to the lonesome sound of the whippoorwill as well as the crickets and the hoot owls. The girls sat absorbed in this new world of communication as opposed to their former life of feeling so terribly alone, especially Crissy and Mary Jane. Brushy Mountain had been their only contact but Selena's folks had not always been there. She had been treated like a princess by her dad even though life was hard since they were rejected and isolated, although they had made it back to North Carolina a few times over the years.

Anna Laura knew she would work with Selena in releasing her fears related to her dad's death. Finding him shot to death and digging her own father's grave to bury him had been extremely traumatic. Anna Laura was sure the images surrounding his death and the aftermath would not easily depart from Selena's mind, but she had no doubt Selena could overcome the tragedy. She could see the strong human spirit that existed within the girl. She knew Selena had an accepting heart and allowed the Holy Spirit that her gentle soul possessed to comfort her. Her momma had taught her of God's spirit at a very young age. As a child's personality is pretty well formed by age four, Selena was blessed to have her momma during those precious years. Her momma knew what an asset it was to have the Holy Spirit within through life's endeavors and had passed that on to her daughter.

One of Anna Laura's greatest desires was to play a part in changing lives that were hurting. She bubbled with joy inside; a warm feeling swept through her soul just to look at how the three girls had changed from the first time they had met.

Over a short period of time she had seen the disappearance of fear and lack of confidence, especially in Crissy and Mary Jane, dwindling away. A new strength had emerged for these young women, making them strong and self-confident. Anna Laura vowed to serve as a strong role model for these girls as long as she was able.

As the new day dawned, Anna Laura knew she should take the girls to the settlement to help in any way needed so they could get their new home ready before winter came upon them, even if it was chinking clay into the cracks between the logs.

It would be fun for the young ladies to dig in the clay banks, even artistic as they smoothed the clay between the logs. They could imagine how pretty it would be when it dried, also knowing it would keep out the cold when the harsh winter came. They already knew how bitter the winters were in the mountains. They had spent many winters not protected from the raging winds, snow and ice storms. Crissy and Mary Jane had endured many days and nights shivering from the cold, blustery weather.

They could also help the settlers in the harvesting of their gardens as the people would be providing for Anna Laura's household. The young ladies realized there would be no harvest as Anna Laura's garden was only large enough to serve during the producing seasons.

They would be working with wonderful people like Steve, Lilly, Rob and his wonderful wife, Jane. They would be extremely busy until late summer and fall passed; however, they knew they would be rewarded with special time as well.

They knew Anna Laura's ways.

They dreamed as they worked what it would be like to teach in late fall and winter. They imagined how wonderful it would be to be in church on Sunday and to be able to help Anna Laura treat the sick folks in the mountains and the settlement. Dreaming came easy as dreams were the very thing that had sustained their emotional health over their young lives. A desire to live a fruitful life gently swirled in their minds like a whirlpool that gradually moved.

After discussing what their chores would be, Anna Laura and the three lovely girls were filled with motivation for a new way of life, knowing there was hard work to be done. Anna Laura had instilled in them that anything of importance was worth working and patiently waiting for.

Arriving back at their homestead, they prepared a very healthy supper of fresh vegetables and fruit.

After supper was over and the clean up was completed, they sat on Anna Laura's mother's quilt of many colors and had devotions. At this particular devotion, Anna Laura taught them the ways of a virtuous woman.

"Ladies, the ways of a good woman are more precious than rubies."

By this time they knew what a ruby was as Anna Laura had exposed them to stones pictured in a geology book. Anna Laura continued to reinforce the importance of being reserved ladies, yet strong and not to feel above or beneath other human beings as God created everyone equally.

"Ladies, I also want you to know that just because you, as human beings, are created equally, you still must be careful who you become friends with. Show yourself friendly, but be wise. People sometimes get in trouble by associating with those who do not know good morals and do not change easily, if ever. Some we may be able to influence in a good way and then there are those that we cannot change. Young ladies, I have a surprise for you. I will be taking you to Cherry Valley on Saturday. We will go to the Hemlock Inn for lunch. Tomorrow I will teach you the proper way to engage in an elegant luncheon. I know you will be so dignified. Already you've learned so much of grace and manners. As practice, we'll spread a linen on the flat rock in Mary Jane's garden and properly set the table with silverware and dishes, even if we must use sticks and huge leaves to substitute. You will be aware of where each utensil is properly placed. In doing so, you'll know the correct silverware to use, as well as elegant table manners. Learning will be fun.

"I realize you are not improper at our regular meals, but we are using the ground and rocks for tables with limited tableware. I'm sure you feel uneasy about eating in a nice restaurant; however, you will not after we have finished practicing. We will reinforce as much as needed."

Saturday morning came quickly. Anna Laura, Selena, Crissy and Mary Jane beautifully adorned themselves in their favorite colors accented by matching lipstick and made their hair attractive with the special shampoo and soft mountain water and, of course, the use of their new hair brushes.

They wore riding skirts instead of jeans to look more graceful when entering the Hemlock Inn dining area.

Their trip down the mountain went smoothly as each had their own borrowed horses. Anna Laura had definitely enjoyed teaching them to ride the previous week.

They gradually entered the stable area. Jess was still working; he had not yet gone back to the university. He did a double take when he saw Mary Jane. She looked so sophisticated dressed in a light blue blouse that complimented her blue eyes. Dark hair and blue eyes were a very rare combination. The shiny pink lipstick enhanced her beauty.

Anna Laura could see that Jess was taken in to another realm of existence as he stared at Mary Jane even as he tried to care for the horses.

The four ladies gracefully walked toward the Hemlock Inn.

Jess stared after them thinking, "Looks like God loaned a few of his angels to Cherry Valley."

As the girls entered the Hemlock Inn dining area, their eyes took in a sight they had never looked upon before. Their hearts were touched by the beauty they saw.

Round tables with lovely linens of soft green and light pink alternated from table to table. Fresh pink roses sat in the center of every table. The dishes were fine cream-colored China, rimmed in light green with small pink flowers inside the green. They were stunned at the crystal clear stemware that would hold their drinks.

The four beautiful ladies were seated next to the huge window. Their table was covered with pink linen and the silverware shone. Their lovely faces revealed the comfort and peace they felt inside their hearts. The garden of pink roses beyond the huge window where they sat was enchanting. Being so caught up in the pleasant atmosphere, food was the farthest thing from their minds.

Anna Laura reminisced about sitting with Hank on the other side of the room the past spring when the mountain laurels and dogwood were in full bloom among the Hemlocks. That was their very first lunch together.

Anna Laura's mind returned to the present as their water approached. All four ordered tea. Selena, Mary Jane and Crissy had never drunk tea except that made from bad tasting herbs for a winter cold. They had certainly never drunk from crystal goblets. All ordered salad while waiting for their main course of roasted chicken, green beans, creamy mashed potatoes and yeast rolls.

The three young women remembered all that Anna Laura had taught them. They were as graceful as the linens, roses, China, silver and crystal that adorned the round table accommodating the four beautiful ladies.

As they sipped their tea and ate their salad their conversation turned to their future dreams for Brushy Mountain and its forgotten people. Joy and peace flowed through Anna Laura's soul just knowing she would be assisted by these three intelligent young ladies. Beyond a shadow of a doubt they would be her help in accomplishing her mission.

Anna Laura grinned as she looked at a radiant Mary Jane across the table.

"Mary, I believe the good looking Jess at the stables has an eye for you. I noticed the same look in his eyes on the mountain when he assisted me in bringing books and supplies. Even then I knew he was a bit taken by you."

Mary Jane blushed a soft rose color.

"Mary Jane I suppose you know Jess is studying to be a teacher."

"Anna Laura, are you sure that is a fact? You know that's what I want to be more than anything."

Anna Laura nodded as their meal was placed on the exquisite table. No one would have ever thought this was the first time the girls had eaten in a nice restaurant. After finishing their meal, the girls headed to the powder room to freshen up. While they were gone, Anna Laura would take care of the tab.

The cashier replied, "Your bill has been taken care of."

Anna Laura turned to walk away.

"Ma'am," the cashier called out, "someone called the Hemlock Inn and reserved the most luxurious room in the Inn for your friends and you, to say the least it's also the largest."

Anna Laura stood in wonder, but suddenly thought of how the girls had never slept in a nice room or a real bed, only small shacks or maybe a cabin. Neither had they had the opportunity to bathe in a real tub with running water.

She accepted. She could not deprive the girls of this luxury.

Crissy, Selena and Mary Jane came from the powder room radiating grace with every step they took.

"Young ladies, we'll be staying here in the Inn tonight!" Anna Laura exclaimed.

"Anna Laura, can this be true?"

"Girls, some generous person paid for us to enjoy the extravagance of the Hemlock Inn's largest room, as well as dinner. We'll first go to the department store and buy nightgowns with the money that was to be spent for dinner."

When entering the clothing store, their eyes went in all directions.

"Will you please show us the sleep wear?" Anna Laura requested of the clerk.

Crissy chose a soft pink gown that would be cool. Selena chose a soft pastel yellow with cream lace edging the sleeves and the bottom of the gown. Mary Jane chose a lilac cotton that was soft to the touch. For a moment Anna Laura was undecided. She located a pale mint green similar to the others. Of course, new undergarments were purchased as well.

After leaving the store, Anna Laura related to the girls, "Let's go see my friend, Hank."

As they walked to his office, Anna Laura realized that Jess must have headed straight to Hank's office when they left the stables letting him know the ladies were in town. Hank must have phoned the Inn and informed the personnel to reserve the biggest and best room in the Inn and to take care of their dinner as well. She was touched by his generosity.

Hank was delighted when Anna Laura, Selena, Crissy and Mary Jane walked into his office.

He was shocked by his own behavior; he could not stop staring at Selena. He was moonstruck by her beauty, realizing that she was part Cherokee. He forced his attention back to Anna Laura immediately letting her know he was delighted to see her. After talking about the progress in Brushy Mountain for a short time, Hank walked the ladies back to the Inn.

Afterward, walking back to his car to head home, the image of Selena seemed to be trapped inside his head.

He thought, "I suppose I am surprised to think a beautiful, part Cherokee girl grew up on Brushy Mountain." He viewed her as a beautiful girl without any prejudices. He was bewildered to say the least. Hank experienced confusion in his heart, soul and mind. He could not comprehend his feelings as he had such deep emotion for Anna Laura as well.

At the hotel, the four ladies took turns bathing and dressing for a night of sweet sleep and lovely dreams as they rested on soft, clean beds.

All of them slept like princesses.

As the morning sun filtered through the crystal clear windows, they came alive with as much beauty as the morning glory, a vining flower of many colors that opened when the sun shone on them in Brushy Mountain.

Anna Laura called from the bathroom as she finished putting on her lipstick. "Girls, we'll have breakfast then head for the stables for our horses and head up to Brushy Mountain, leaving this lovely place until we are privileged to visit again."

As she walked from the bathroom into the luxurious room, she softly spoke, "We have lots of studying to do as well as hard work helping the people in Brushy Mountain, but we will succeed. Even there shall God's hand lead us and His right hand shall hold us until our mission is accomplished."

Jess brought their horses one by one when they made it to the stables after a lovely breakfast. Mary Jane's was the last to be lead out by Jess. As the others mounted, Jess assisted Mary Jane. Softly he spoke, "I hope to see you again one day."

Mary Jane smiled a smile that warmed Jess' heart. Never had he experienced such feelings for a young lady.

He asked himself as he watched Mary Jane and the others ride away, "Is there such a thing as love at first sight?" He watched till Mary Jane was out of sight.

"I cannot believe what I am feeling." Neither could he believe how refined three girls were that had lived among the forgotten people of Brushy Mountain. He suddenly realized Anna Laura worked hard and fast and the girls were blessed with brilliant minds and caught on very quickly.

The four lovely ladies enjoyed the ride up the mountain, even thought the skies became cloudy and warm rain began to fall. The soft rain wetting their faces as they looked upward was soothing.

Reaching their camp high on the mountain, they found everything was dry as the rain had taken a turn in a different direction. They bathed then sat near the fire, letting their hair dry as Anna Laura quizzed them from advanced text books.

As daylight began to turn to darkness, they prepared their beds on the ground under the open sky filled with many stars.

Tomorrow would be a new day and they did not know what it would bring; living in the mountains was unpredictable. It certainly had been as Crissy, Mary Jane and Selena grew up, but now they experienced it in a more positive fashion since their lives had changed in such a wondrous way.

They all had drunk from cups of bitterness in their lives, but they were survivors. Their self-motivation and will to dream of a better life had carried them through the hard times.

Chapter 24

Hank received a call from Lieutenant Adams.

"Hank, the revenue agents will be coming to the mountains Saturday."

"Lieutenant, do you think you could ride up with them?"

One hour later Lieutenant Adams called Hank. "Hank, I've given serious thought to the situation and have decided to accompany the men."

Hank walked to the stables to find Jess. Of course Jess was busy caring for the horses, mainly the ones that belonged to Paul Green that were often rented out.

"Jess, do you think you could ride up to Brushy Mountain on Thursday and inform Anna Laura that the revenuers will arrive Saturday?"

"Hank, I'll be happy to." He could, at that very moment, see sweet Mary Jane's face before him.

"Jess, please let Anna Laura know that Lieutenant Adams will accompany the other men."

On Monday morning Anna Laura had the girls study for several hours before going to the settlement to help wherever they were needed.

When they arrived at the settlement, Steve informed Mary Jane, Selena and Crissy that the horses they sat upon were now theirs, a gift from Lilly and him. The unselfish decision had been made by Steve and Lilly while the girls were in Cherry Valley.

"Thank you, Steve and Lilly," came in unison from the three delighted young ladies.

"Sir," Selena replied, "we will help in gathering corn from the fields to winter the horses."

"We sure will," Crissy and Mary Jane confirmed. Anna Laura was proud to see the girls taking on responsibility.

On Tuesday and Wednesday, the four young women helped in every way possible to finish the cabin. The men were putting the roof on and if all went well, they would finish that task by the end of the day.

Anna Laura and the three girls were working so hard, the cracks between the logs would be filled about the same time as the roof. It was exhilarating to know they would have a real shelter when winter came to the mountains. Crissy, Mary Jane and Selena knew how bitterly cold the winters were and how the snow seemed to pile up for an eternity in Brushy Mountain.

They were very excited to hear from Lilly that the settlement women would be honoring them with a house warming when they were ready to move into their new home.

Lilly invited the four for supper after their hard day of work. Anna Laura suddenly remembered she had brought Susie and Joel the new clothes that she had purchased for them in Nashville.

It was a heartwarming experience for everyone to see the faces of the two awestruck children as they held their store bought clothes from Nashville, Tennessee. Anna Laura's heart was filled with joy as she observed the children.

The ladies later returned to their camp having no idea at all that Jess and Hank would be coming to their mountain in a couple of days or so. Hank had decided to ride up with Jess.

Anna Laura's plan was for the girls to spend their usual time studying early next morning then head out to help with the ongoing projects. Some were working on the church, some the school and others the medical cabin, as well as Anna Laura's cabin. There was much to be done. Anna Laura, Selena, Crissy and Mary Jane worked as swiftly as they could. Mary Jane worked at the school house, Crissy the medical building, while Selena and Anna Laura continued getting their home ready. Some of the men were building beds, a table and chairs, shelves and cabinets for their cabin.

Rob and Steve were focusing on finishing the fireplace, while others were doing detail work to refine the cabin a bit.

The cabin was near a fresh water spring. One nice lady, Emily Gibbons, had already donated a galvanized tub for bathing in front of the fireplace when it was bitter cold outside.

Many families were preparing for the house warming. Mandie Smith would be donating a huge black iron kettle that would hang in the fireplace to keep hot water at all times.

Before long autumn would come and go and the frost would show itself. Harvest time was drawing near in the mountains.

Anna Laura and the girls would definitely be involved. Their cellar would be filled by the giving of the kind hearted mountain people.

Chapter 25

Thursday morning seemed to come quickly. The breeze was perfect; the air was an ideal temperature at the waterfalls. The flowing water was warm from the day before. The leaves on the surrounding trees lightly fluttered as the birds flitted from tree to tree. Their red, yellow and blue colors were delightful to look upon.

Anna Laura, Selena, Crissy and Mary Jane finished their showers one by one, enjoying the soothing sound of the water splashing on the rock beneath.

They had worked hard all week, now they were filled with an unsurpassable peace that God granted them by just being among His given blessings in the mountains.

After they were dressed, they sat eating mulberries, blue berries and sweet bread baked in an iron skillet over the fire between the rocks. Anna Laura never let a moment pass to quiz them on their advanced studies, even during meals. They could not let a moment be lost. She was absolutely amazed with their progress.

By midday they heard familiar voices coming near.

The ladies listened in anticipation, recognizing the voices of Hank and Jess. The two men got off their horses and found a place to sit. Needless to say, the girls were excited to see the two handsome men sitting in their camp.

Anna Laura exclaimed, "What brings you two to the mountains?"

"Well, Anna Laura," Hank began departing knowledge of what would be happening, "Lieutenant Adams and a force of revenuers will be up the day after tomorrow. As you already know, moonshining has gotten out of control in the mountains. We're here to help you plan a strategy. We need a couple of strong young men that know the mountains."

Immediately Anna Laura thought of Cold Tater and Rock Head. She believed that getting them involved would change their lives. For a moment she was sad as she remembered when in the valley below as a youngster how some children were stereotyped as no one had taken time to nurture them. At that moment she knew she would endeavor to learn the real names of Cold Tater and Rock Head and something of their background. She imagined a little hungry, ragged boy asking the people, "You got any cold taters left over from supper?" Then, he would carry them in his pocket and sparingly eat them to keep from starving.

"How could a child grow up to understand anything related to a normal life if they have only been told they are stupid and good for nothing?"

At that moment, Anna Laura vowed that she would work to change the lives of these two young men. She would help them understand that Jesus died on the cross for them, as well as others and they could be picked up from the dust and become good men. The hurt they had done to others would be forgiven and they could begin new lives, leaving their pasts forever behind them.

She entertained the idea that they were much aware of the moonshiners in Brushy Mountain. She also thought that it could be possible some women living alone with children might make moonshine and take it off the mountain, selling it to survive; if this was so, she wanted to help change their lives by moving them near the settlement where they could survive without breaking the law.

Hank, Jess and the ladies visited the settlement, which took up the biggest part of the day. It was getting late when they returned to Anna Laura's place.

"Jess, we had better get going," Hank quietly whispered.

Anna Laura realized it was later than she thought. In Brushy Mountain she had experienced how darkness could move in as if a huge curtain dropped suddenly to block the light of day. She was uneasy about the men traveling off the mountain after dark.

"Hank, Jess, you can spend the night under the hanging rock. The girls and I will sleep under the sky as we usually do. The leaves and blankets under the cliff are very dry and clean."

The girls built a fire; the flames danced and flicked casting light toward the hanging rock. Everyone had a snack of fresh fruit and vegetables and drank the clean spring water before lying down to sleep.

After the men said goodnight and found their beds, they found the dwelling beneath the hanging rock cozy and comfortable. They did some serious thinking while relaxing before falling asleep. Jess fell into dreams thinking about the beautiful Mary Jane. Hank found himself almost in shock before falling asleep, as he knew he was attracted to Selena. The bewilderment was almost torture because of the deep feelings he also had held for Anna Laura for so many months. He experienced a lot of guilt as he laid thinking. Hank was a man of high morals and not used to being so confused in his feelings.

After learning the circumstances of what happened to Selena, he believed she deserved special treatment. He knew he could give a woman an exceptional life. He also knew he would love the woman he married with all his heart. He believed that one day he would transfer to an office in Nashville. His emotions were extremely mixed. Hank saw the high character of Selena, as well as her strength and strong principles. He fell asleep still thinking.

At the break of dawn, Hank was awake. He eased out into the openness of the mountains, the only sounds being that of a dove and the rippling stream nearby. He went toward the stream captivated by such beauty. He followed the sound to the waterfalls. As he looked down, he saw clothes hanging nearby and realized this was where the ladies showered. The place was curtained with small bushes.

As he walked farther down away from the waterfall, the calmness of the water changed its sound to one of wrath. Upon reaching the origin of the sound, different streams merged, rumbling over a huge rock which was where the streams had met for many years. Hank perceived this as an absolute work of art and he knew who the artist was.

He could almost feel why the people had not yet left the mountains. "It's a different world on Brushy Mountain," Hank thought as he stood looking from mountain to mountain. He also realized among all the beauty there had been years of struggle, hurt and pain for the mountain people.

Only a small connection to the world below the mountains had made it more durable for those who managed to bring a few things into the mountain to make life easier. As he looked into the higher ridges, he wondered how much suffering the people had experienced. He then bowed his head and thanked God for allowing him the opportunity to be of help to these people.

He could now plainly see why Anna Laura was so adamant about preparing the children for a different life by opening a door for education.

Suddenly, Hank smelled the aroma of boiling coffee flowing through the fresh early morning breeze. He walked back to Anna Laura's place to find the four lovely ladies preparing breakfast, it smelled great.

He awakened Jess, "Jess, rise and shine. We'll be leaving in a short while. You will need to prepare the horses for the revenuers as they'll need them tomorrow."

As they sat with Anna Laura, Crissy, Mary Jane and Selena sharing fresh eggs, fried fritters and some of Lilly's fresh blackberry jelly, they talked of how the revenuers would arrive the following day and would possibly need someone to set up camp, all depending on their progress in the matter.

"Hank, we'll have Steve and Rob set up camp for the task force in case it is needed."

"I'll take Steve and Rob to the perfect place," Mary Jane replied as Jess watched her closely.

Hank and Jess saddled their horses and rode out of sight as the young women watched.

The four high spirited ladies had a big day ahead of them.

"Mary Jane, I have different plans for you. Selena, I want Crissy and you to go tell Rob and Steve all that is happening tomorrow and they will need to set up camp in the event it is needed. Crissy, the two of you know the area. You can take them there."

Crissy and Selena headed for Steve's.

"Mary, let's go searching for Cold Tater and Rock Head. I know you have wandered far and near in these mountains. Do you have any idea where they can be found? Perhaps, if we involved them in something of interest, their lives might possibly change."

"Anna Laura, I recall seeing a cave a couple of years ago when exploring the mountains. The area looked as though it was occupied since clothes hung on the branches of small bushes to dry. Rocks were arranged into a fireplace for cooking. I was sure someone lived there. I hid a ways from the cave to watch. I just know it was Rock Head and Cold Tater."

"Do you think you could find it again?"

"I believe so."

It was around noon. Anna Laura and Mary Jane saddled their horses and headed the direction where Mary Jane had seen the cave. They rode about an hour before reaching the place.

Cold Tater whispered, "Rock Head, I think I hear the sound of horse's hooves hitting on rocks."

Both listened intently as they sat beneath a huge oak tree.

When nearing the cave, Anna Laura called out, "This is Anna Laura and Mary Jane."

"What you a wantin'?" Rock Head called out in his strong voice.

"We need to talk with you. We have a job offer for you," Anna Laura called out.

"If this be true, come closer," Cold Tater yelled.

Anna Laura rode in front of Mary Jane. Their horses were swift and quiet as the terrain had changed for the better.

"Can we get off our horses and talk for a while?" Anna Laura asked.

"Sure, get off your horses," Rock Head responded.

Anna Laura felt secure so she left her rifle on her Arabian. Mary Jane dismounted, feeling a little anxious.

As they all stood near each other, Anna Laura asked, "Do you have names other than Rock Head and Cold Tater?"

"We sure do," both answered at the same time.

"I was sure you did."

Rock Head immediately began to feel guilty for harming Mary Jane. He experienced sudden remorse and shame. His chest tightened as he thought of what they had done to Anna Laura as well.

Anna Laura could see the regret and hurt in his eyes. She interrupted his remorseful thoughts.

"We know you did us wrong, but we forgive both of you and want to see your lives change. I know you've been alone and mistreated since you were small children. Your lives will be changing if you will allow me to help you. Rock Head, what is your real name?"

"My name is Bobby Hatfield."

"What about you, Cold Tater?"

"Mine is Billy Smith."

"From this day forward, I will let everyone know they are to call you Bobby and Billy."

The two young men grinned from ear to ear. They were first cousins. Their mothers had been sisters, both dying of the fever when the boys were small. The story went that their fathers had disappeared not long after their mothers passed.

"Now, Bobby, Billy, let's talk about the job. Tomorrow there's a Lieutenant Samuel Adams and a group of revenuers coming to Brushy Mountain to do away with the moonshine stills. Joel and Susie's mother, Martha, was killed because the shine drove her husband crazy, as well as Mary and others that were harmed and are still suffering because of it. Also, that fine Indian Joe was killed because the 'shine put a demon spirit of hatred in the drunken men to kill him simply because he was an Indian. Women and children are suffering far too much because of the moonshine. The task force that will be coming tomorrow will need a couple of guides. I believe you are the best men for the job. You will be paid well."

Billy immediately thought, "Reckon we could build us a cabin? One for Bobby and one for me? Might be close to the settlement. We sure would like to live like other folks and people could call us our real names."

Bobby was having the same thoughts. "Now, Anna Laurie, let us walk up yonder behind that big ole maple tree to talk."

"Take all the time you need," Anna Laura replied.

Mary Jane hadn't spoken a word. She still held a little fear inside due to her past ordeal. She found it easy to forgive because she knew the boys were ignorant and had been mistreated as well. She knew in time she would trust again and her emotions would be set free of the trauma.

As the young men stood behind the tree, Billy said, "First thing now, Bobby, remember to call me Billy and I'll sure call you Bobby."

Bobby replied, "It'll sure take some gittin' use to, but I think you can remember and I'll remember, too. Billy, do you think we can do that job?"

"Sure do, Bobby!"

"That Anna Laurie might learn us to talk good if'n they'll let us go to that school when they git it built."

"Might do that, Bobby. Now, Bobby, do we want that job they's a talking bout?"

"Billy, I'll sure do hit if'n you'll do hit."

"Let's go and tell her."

They walked slowly down the hill without showing any excitement. They very seldom had experienced positive excitement during their nineteen years. When reaching the cave where Anna Laura and Mary Jane patiently waited, both young men said, "We'd sure like to do this job."

Anna Laura shook hands with Bobby and Billy to show her approval. Mary Jane smiled, but remained silent.

Bobby sorrowfully turned toward her, "Mary Jane, you won't never get hurt again; you won't neither, Anna Laurie."

"Come to my place about the break of dawn," Anna Laura told the boys. "I will have food for you and horses prepared as well. The revenuers will arrive shortly after breakfast."

The two young men were speechless. No one had ever been this kind to them. They had actually survived from the bounty of the land. They learned at a very early age to seek out food on their own.

Anna Laura and Mary Jane met Crissy and Selena at the campsite and related their accomplishments to them.

"Everything is good with Rob and Steve."

"Thanks, Crissy."

The four ladies prepared themselves for what hopefully would be a good night's sleep. They slept under the starry sky. The night was perfect and hopefully the following day would be as well.

Anna Laura and the girls were up at the break of dawn. Billy and Bobby arrived just as Anna Laura, Selena, Crissy and Mary Jane were preparing breakfast. The flapjacks filled with fresh raspberries that Selena had picked the day before smelled unlike anything they had ever known. Their mouths watered. Billy and Bobby were served first, not only flapjacks, but milk that had been kept cold in the stream nearby.

Bobby and Billy ate a big breakfast; never had they tasted anything as good in their entire lives. Not a word was spoken between them as they shoveled the food into their mouths.

Anna Laura could not resist giving them a toothbrush and toothpaste and taking them to the nearby stream. They brushed exactly as Anna Laura did.

"Thank you an awful lot," Bobby shyly told Anna Laura.

"You are so very welcome, Bobby."

Anna Laura knew with all her heart these young men would be civilized and it would not take a great deal of effort as she could see they desired their lives to be different. All sorts of thoughts raced through her mind in a matter of a few short minutes as to how they could be helped to become functional in every way and maybe even leave the mountain one day.

Rob and Steve came with two extra horses. Just after their arrival, the revenuers and Lieutenant Adams could be heard coming up the mountain. With Jess as their guide, they arrived at Anna Laura's place. Lieutenant Adams was next in line behind Jess with five others following. All together there would be ten men involved in the hunt, including Rob, Steve, Billy and Bobby.

Anna Laura, Crissy, Selena and Mary Jane stood looking at their guests.

Lieutenant Adams introduced his men, "Meet the agents: Johnny, Buck, Jim, Conrad and Abe."

"I'm Anna Laura, gentlemen. Meet Rob, Steve, Billy and Bobby. Also, this is Crissy, Mary Jane and Selena, who at present are under my care."

Lieutenant Adams was captivated by Crissy's beauty; her natural blonde hair, her eyes as blue as the sky. He definitely did a double take, even while being introduced to Mary Jane and Selena he found it difficult to focus on the introduction.

"Crissy is my prodigy. All the girls are stunningly intelligent, but Crissy amazes me," Anna Laura related to the lieutenant. This intrigued Samuel even more. He was sure she had been in the mountains all her life, but had no idea how hard her life had been before Anna Laura took her into her care.

The plan was discussed. Everyone mounted the horses that had been prepared for the hunt.

Anna Laura hurriedly informed Lieutenant Adams that Bobby and Billy had lived high in the mountains and knew them like the backs of their hands. They had likely scouted around enough to know where most of the moonshine stills were located.

"Billy, why don't you lead Rob, Conrad, Abe and Jim? Bobby, you lead Lieutenant Adams, Buck, Johnny and Steve."

Billy took his crew up the mountain then turned west. Bobby took his followers in an eastward direction. Bobby knew exactly where Big Dan had a still.

"Now, boys, we'll be a gittin off our horses now. We can walk a piece and you'll see a big sink hole, that's where they run the shine off. Big Dan's wife Mury gives him one hard time. He works her like a horse."

The five men headed down the hill, sliding now and then as it was a bit steep. When they were in sight of the operation, they discovered the mountain shack that sat nearby. Bobby knew the ways of the moonshiners and was sure most of what they ran off into containers was carried to the shack and boards were raised from the floor for placing the shine in a huge hole which had been dug beneath.

Big Dan and Mary had a bunch of goats running around at the same time that ate the waste, or mash, from the finished product and got a little drunk.

Bobby related to Adams, "You see that big ole billy goat over yonder? It's near as good as a watch dog."

Since Big Dan and Mary were not at the still, they were likely to be in the house.

The men surrounded the house. "We are federal agents and we are coming in!"

They knew concrete evidence was necessary and the evidence was under the floor. Luckily, Big Dan didn't start shooting. He must have known the odds of winning that battle were against him.

Samuel yelled, "Open up in the name of the law!"

Big Dan flung the door open to see rifles pointing at him from different directions. All the men stampeded into the cabin.

Bobby yelled, "Buck, pull them there boards up, under that table."

Buck moved the table and pulled up the boards as the others watched.

No one had the slightest idea how spunky Mary was. Buck bent over to look for the moonshine, Mary booted him in the behind with her knee, and down he went head first. Luckily the white lightning was stored a little farther back.

Adams found an excuse to exit the shack as he could not contain his laughter as he saw Buck go head first into the hole and especially seeing the strange look on Mary's face. He stood outside bent over with laughter trying not to make a sound, it was almost painful.

Suddenly, he found himself meeting the ground face to face as the huge billy goat sensed he was interfering. The big goat had a long beard and beady eyes. He looked downright evil as he backed up to make a run toward Adams. As the goat butted the lieutenant in the behind, the man went airborne. The goat stood beside him as he lay there with his blond hair covered with dirt and debris. The goat eyed him warily, as if sending the message, "you better not move or there will be more to come!"

He lay very still, fearful the others might come out the door at any moment. Suddenly Adams smelled the breath of the goat and realized the animal had come from the still and was a little impaired. The goat began to stagger away from Adams and finally lay down on the ground some distance away.

He quickly got off the ground, brushed the dirt from his hair and combed it with his pocket comb. He then walked back inside as though nothing had happened. He would never reveal this secret except perhaps one day when he was old and had grandchildren.

As Buck got the worst end of the affair, he got the privilege of arresting Mary and Big Dan. They were put on horses and tied to the saddle horns as they needed their hands to hold to the guide rope.

Adams had a good sense of humor and he chuckled a little when passing the billy goat as they rode away.

Billy, Rob, Conrad, Johnny and Abe were around the mountain on the west side. Like Bobby, Billy pretty well knew where to lead the men. Traveling in a westerly direction was farther than the other route.

"Boys, I'm sure the men that killed Selena's dad has a still back yonder behind that big ole bunch of trees. They's a whole bunch of 'em lives in one big cabin. I'm thinking they take liquor all the ways off that other side of the mountain and sell it 'cause me and Billy slipped and watched um fetchin' good stuff to their cabin. Must've swapped the liquor for it. They's real mean men. We'll sure have to be careful or we might git kilt."

The others loaded their automatic guns. The last thing on Earth they wanted was to die while scouting out moonshiners.

Abe whispered, "Look! Smoke is rising behind those trees."

The men stopped at a distance and tied their horses to a tree. The moonshiners had their horses near the still. With the smoke rising, the men were likely making a run and the women and children were at home.

Billy, Abe, Conrad, Rob and Johnny made a plan to close in on the moonshiners as they worked.

They quietly moved in close enough to surround them. As the still was in a low area hidden by trees, the arrest would be easier.

Conrad yelled, "We have you surrounded! Faces on the ground!"

The moonshiners were staring into the barrels of five rifles. They could not go for their guns; they had laid them some distance away from the still. The risk would be too great and they knew it.

Billy recognized the one that actually fired the shot that killed Selena's dad. He so badly wanted to practice an eye for an eye and a tooth for a tooth, but knew it would be better for the man to go to jail. He had enough sense to know that two wrongs did not make a right. He had heard his Granny Maudie speak those words when he was a small boy.

The men hit the ground. Billy and Rob tied their hands behind them. Johnny, Conrad and Abe went for their horses. After securing them to their horses to prevent an escape, they headed for Anna Laura's place to meet Lieutenant Adams and the others.

When Billy and his crew arrived at Anna Laura's with the five most productive moonshiners on the mountain he was a little surprised that Bobby and his crew had apprehended Big Dan and Mary as he knew how sneaky they were. The thought crossed his mind, "I'll bet they didn't get them two without a bunch of rough stuff going on."

"We had better get going if we are to get these culprits behind bars before dark," the lieutenant stated quietly.

Anna Laura, Selena and Mary Jane extended their hands one by one to thank Adams for his assistance and thanked the others as well as Bobby and Billy.

Crissy hurriedly went to the clear stream for a bucket of fresh water.

"Would anyone like a drink of fresh water before you go?"

Quickly Adams replied, "I would appreciate a drink of cold water."

Crissy handed Adams a dipper of water. As he slowly drank he could not take his eyes off Crissy. Her sweet, innocent smile captivated his heart, mind and soul. He thought, 'Someday, somehow, I will see this beautiful young lady under different circumstances.'

Anna Laura and the girls waved goodbye to the revenuers, thanking them for what they had done.

Selena's heart ached with grief when she looked toward the man that had taken her dad's life; knowing he would now pay for his crime was her only consolation.

<h1 style="text-align:center">Chapter 26</h1>

The lawmen did their job by seeing the moonshiners were locked up. Adams would support them. The courts in Cherry Valley would see that justice was done.

Now, Anna Laura, Mary Jane, Selena and Crissy could really focus on the projects that were taking place.

Steve and Rob headed to the settlement. Everyone could feel safe now. Billy and Bobby had supper with Anna Laura and the girls.

As they ate, they made plans to spend two hours each day teaching Billy and Bobby the alphabet, how to read and spell, and their numbers. They would give the boys a foundation to spare them the embarrassment of learning the basics with the small children.

The girls and Anna Laura were surprised to see how fast Billy and Bobby were able to learn. Their lack of knowledge was basically a lack of education and opportunity. They definitely would not be placed as low achievers.

Anna Laura felt within a short span of time the young men could make something of themselves. Anna Laura also planned to ask Rob and Steve to teach them building skills. With an education and building proficiency they could do well, she was sure.

Billy and Bobby began to let their former belittling names, Cold Tater and Rock Head, fade from their mind. They only thought of themselves as Bobby and Billy. Their hearts felt so much lighter. They were finding it easy to put the past behind them. They were speedily changing from the inside out. Anna Laura was so filled with joy to see the change taking place. To her this was what life was all about, helping someone who needed guidance.

When returning to their so-called home at the cave each day, the boys were filled with remorse for their unkind acts towards Anna Laura and Mary Jane.

They knew there was a God as their Grandmother Maudie had taught them when they were very small before passing. They made a decision that very night to bow to their knees as they had seen their grandmother do and repent of their negative behavior they had practiced over the years.

Bobby said to Billy, "I feel real good inside. How about you?"

"Yeah, Bobby I feel light inside, like that cloud up yonder." Their speech was improving very quickly.

Surely God was using Anna Laura to teach the young men that everyone that might be counted as hopeless was not. Billy and Bobby would never be the same again. It was as though a new birthing of their spirits had taken place over a very short span of time.

Anna Laura had asked them to go to the settlement with her. Rob and Steve had already promised Anna Laura to be role models to the two young men.

Anna Laura gave them soap and shampoo. They had been using lye soap that an elderly lady who lived not far from the settlement had given them. She had always felt pity for the boys, but did not have the means to help them with much. The most she was able to do was offer lye soap to wash their tattered clothes. They were able to scrub them over the clean rocks in the mountain stream. With two outfits they could keep themselves fairly clean.

That very evening they bathed and shampooed with the good smelling shampoo. Their own mountain stream provided the shower. They tried modeling themselves after the neatness of the revenuers, especially Lieutenant Adams and a couple of others.

Morning came after a night of heavenly sleep. They felt accomplished from the help they had given toward making a better life for the less fortunate women and children higher in Brushy Mountain.

They mounted the horses that had been given to them and rode to Anna Laura's.

Anna Laura, Crissy, Mary Jane and Selena were shocked when they arrived. They were actually good looking young men, very tall and muscular.

Bobby's hair was dark brown. He had combed it to the side. Billy's hair was as black as a crow and combed back without a part. They looked as good on the outside as they felt on the inside.

Chapter 27

On the drive back to Nashville, Samuel could not get Crissy off his mind. Never had he felt the way he did now. He knew he had to see Crissy again.

Jess worked the stables with the image of Mary Jane's pretty face in his mind. He would find a reason to return to Brushy Mountain.

Hank sat in his office completely confused. He asked himself, "Why can't I get beautiful Selena off my mind and at the same time have such deep feelings for Anna Laura?"

At that very moment, Clint was on call at the hospital in Germany.

As he lay on his bed in a small room made available for emergency calls, he was grieved in his spirit, "Why can't I forget sweet Anna Laura? She has probably married some handsome man back in the USA by now."

He pictured her somewhere in the mountains with a handsome husband who was a doctor by her side through her endeavors as her mission was being fulfilled.

His heart ached with grief, but he still prayed that he could be wrong and their paths would cross again. He prayed to God that destiny would bring them together.

He hoped one day Anna Laura would realize they belonged together just as he did. He then vowed he would wait a while longer. He would pour his heart and soul into his work. He knew that being busy made living without Anna Laura a little easier.

As Samuel continued to drive, not even realizing how near Nashville he was, he could not stop thinking of Crissy. "Am I nuts?" he asked himself.

It wasn't just the prefect figure, the blond hair, the facial features of a goddess and the flawless skin tinted lightly by nature, there was more. He could sense beneath such outward beauty that past hurt surfaced from the inside out. A hint of loneliness lingered in her beautiful blue eyes. It was almost as though he had looked through those blue eyes into her soul and saw the hurt that was yet to be healed.

At the same time, he could see the high intelligence in every effort she exerted. He was sure a great dream existed somewhere in her human spirit.

Secretly, Crissy wanted to be a midwife. So many babies died in the mountains because of lack of knowledge or ignorance. Her dream had been to save the babies. Without Crissy realizing, Anna Laura had picked up on her secret dreams. Her plan was to have Crissy assist her when she was summoned to bring new life into the population of Brushy Mountain. As before, Anna Laura had no doubt that Crissy was a child prodigy and could definitely become an obstetrician if she one day left Brushy Mountain.

In the meantime, the mountain people needed all three of the girls that Anna Laura mothered. She knew God would bring all things that destiny held in His own time for these girls.

Anna Laura easily perceived Crissy's secret feelings for Samuel. She could see how Crissy's countenance had changed. As Crissy's heart sang a new song, it affected her on the outside as well.

Crissy did not truly understand why she viewed this Samuel as she did. Her first insight was, "How can this handsome, muscular man be so tender?" The men she had seen in the mountain where she had lived had been so heartless.

She was stunned to see a man with such kindness. He did not try to impress anyone. She could not forget the tenderness in his compassionate eyes when it came to Bobby and Billy. It was as though life had handed them a cup of bitterness and they had drunk from it for many years and Adams could see that. She saw a special gift manifesting in his spirit when visiting the settlement. She observed how he looked at the young boys and girls with eyes that revealed how much he would like to help these children believe in themselves.

In her imagination, beyond a shadow of doubt, in his line of work he had likely helped many to believe in themselves and what they could be.

Crissy was smart in mountain ways, but also in human relations as she had been so deeply hurt until Anna Laura rescued her. Anna Laura believed in Crissy. She believed Crissy could be all that she desired to be.

At the present the mountains held Crissy's heart, but she would one day be a woman of fulfilled destiny.

Chapter 28

It was now time for Anna Laura and her adopted daughters to become the closest beings to angels on earth as any human could ever be. There was less fear in the mountains with the most harmful people gone.

The four of them could even search the higher mountains for hurting women and children and perhaps families. Sunday morning after their devotions they would ride into the mountains, maybe Bobby and Billy would accompany them.

Presently it was Monday morning and they rode out to the settlement. Things were moving extremely fast. The ladies were extremely surprised.

Billy and Bobby were doing the work of four men as they were eager, young and strong. Rob and Steve insisted they build themselves a cabin in a vacant area behind the settlement on a piece of level ground that had a few oak trees sparsely scattered on the property. They could call their niche, the twin oaks.

With the experience they gained from helping with the projects, they would quickly be able to build a cabin to accommodate their needs. The older women would supply basic supplies for housekeeping. Billy and Bobby would help with the crops and in return would be given fundamental food supplies. Eventually they would earn or buy chickens, pigs and maybe a cow as some of the money from their first job of helping the revenuers would give them a start. Being members of the settlement population would mean the world to Billy and Bobby.

After seeing how well Bobby and Billy were doing, Anna Laura related to Steve and Rob, "Crissy, Mary Jane, Selena and I are here to help in any way we are needed."

"First, Anna Laura, you and the girls go on working with your own cabin. It won't be long till the fall of the year. Winter up here comes on so fast you can hardly believe there has been a fall and we will need to get the buildings done before harvest time." Lilly kept talking, "I'll tell you what, that Billy and Bobby are real workers. We'll have the school, the church house and the doctor's building done before you know it. Let's take a walk and see what you all think."

Anna Laura hadn't visited for a few days and was shocked to see the buildings were now finished. Their next project would be working inside. The men would begin building benches and tables for the school house.

Anna Laura knew she and the girls would need to make a trip to Cherry Valley before cold weather. She would have Hank get Jess to bring up a chalkboard, erasers and other necessary items that had not been brought up previously. The furniture for the doctor's office could be built without a lot of effort.

Anna Laura would draw a picture of church pews. She knew Rob and Steve were artistic in wood work and could do a good job. The two could build a simple pulpit for the Reverend to lay his Bible on as he spoke to the congregation. Everything would fall in place in due time.

When the moon was full, Billy and Bobby borrowed the tools they used during the day and worked on their cabin at night.

Copying from Anna Laura, Billy and Bobby prepared a campsite not far from their future home near a rippling stream that accommodated them well. To see the change that was taking place in Bobby and Billy's life was an absolute miracle. Again, this proved to Anna Laura what a little kindness could do.

Meanwhile, Anna Laura, Selena, Crissy and Mary Jane worked very hard helping with their future home.

"Tomorrow we'll help with the gardens," Anna Laura explained to the girls, "but don't forget after we're finished and have eaten and refreshed ourselves for bed, we must spend a couple of hours studying."

Anna Laura was thrilled to see the eagerness in the girls every time they opened a book. After the girls were settled for the night thinking Anna Laura was asleep, she overheard them having a wonderful conversation.

Crissy related to Mary Jane and Selena her dream of becoming a midwife.

"Seeing new life emerge is the most fascinating thing I have ever seen. I sneaked off with Josie Brown a few times when I was a young teenager; I actually helped her bring new life to the world. It was so fulfilling."

Mary Jane related, "I want to be a teacher more than anything. I can only imagine what it will feel like to the mountain children when the learning process opens a new world to them as it did for me after meeting Anna Laura. I so want to be a part of bringing this to the children in Brushy Mountain. Who knows, I may leave in the future and others will step up and take my place."

Anna Laura anxiously waited to hear Selena talk of her dreams.

"I feel my mind going in every direction," Selena stated. "Since my daddy was murdered for no reason at all, there are times I would like to be a part of bringing criminals to justice as I have read in Anna Laura's criminal law book."

Selena's unique personality, her ability to listen and be silent, her meek spirit, and her discretion would be a great asset if she should choose law. Anna Laura was sure if Selena ever left Brushy Mountain she could easily study at an accredited university.

Anna Laura lay staring from a distance at the three girls thinking of what their destiny would or could be. She knew it would take time, but was sure God would order their steps.

She prayed, "If Selena one day leaves the mountains let her be accepted in society as she deserves to be." Then, she remembered her previous thoughts, "If God is ordering her steps as I believe, then she will be a part of a whole new world when that day comes."

Chapter 29

Back in Germany, Clint was having second thoughts. He could not believe Anna Laura would marry anyone. He pondered on hiring a detective back in the United States to find her. He could not let her go; his love for her was far too great.

He began making contact in Boston, as Anna Laura had worked there for a short while.

He vowed, "If it takes ten years, I will find her!" He wanted to tell her she would be accepted by his family.

Finding someone at the end of the world on Brushy Mountain would be a huge task for any detective.

Never had anyone loved a woman more than Clint loved Anna Laura. He prayed a fervent prayer every night before falling asleep, hoping that one day Anna Laura would be beside him as his wife.

Meanwhile, back on Brushy Mountain, Anna Laura was doing everything possible to accomplish her mission. She and the girls went to the settlement and worked hard, gaining the respect of more and more mountain people. Anna Laura was filled with excitement to see Bobby and Billy happy and continuously learning new skills.

One beautiful Saturday morning, Anna Laura invited Billy and Bobby to ride high into the mountains with Selena, Crissy, Mary Jane, and herself. The boys showed up bright and early looking alert and eager. There were still mysteries to be found in those mountains; Anna Laura could feel it in her heart. Anna Laura and the girls prepared a special lunch.

Everyone mounted their horses after placing the food with Anna Laura. The most effective way of keeping food intact was to tie two bags to a rope, placing the bags on each end of the rope and attach it to the saddle.

Billy and Bobby's mouths were already watering from the smell of the fried chicken.

After riding upward for a half a mile or so, they turned east, riding another half-mile. When coming to a clearing, they stopped to spread their picnic on a muslin sheet over a huge flat rock. Baked sweet potatoes, fried chicken, flour fritters, and fried apple pies were spread over the rock. All six carried gourd dippers to a nearby stream to bring back clear water to drink with their lunch.

What a shock it was upon returning to find their food gone. The look on Bobby and Billy's faces were like those of children who seldom got candy and someone had taken it away.

"Anna Laura," Billy spoke loudly, "there are people living beyond the clearing. I know, because Bobby and me know a lot about these mountains."

"There is a family not far from here. We haven't seen them in two or three years. There was a woman, a man, and two young girls. They were hungry, is my opinion." Bobby added.

"Anna Laura, the two girls were real pretty the last time we saw them. But they were awful skinny. Didn't get enough to eat. We couldn't help them because their pa always came out with a double-barrel shotgun. I hope you can help them like you have us."

Crissy exuded an unusual amount of excitement, "Let's find them!" Selena and Mary Jane agreed.

"Okay, Billy and Bobby lead and we will follow," Anna Laura softly spoke. The boys hit the trail on foot and the ladies followed.

Billy was so hungry Bobby could hear his stomach growling as they walked swiftly.

The farther they walked, the more nervous Anna Laura became as she thought of the double-barrel shotgun. Suddenly Anna Laura asked everyone to stop, "Billy, is it okay if I lead? It may be possible that I can talk to the old man and he might not shoot, and you can guide me on the right path."

"That will be good, Anna Laura."

It wasn't long until they saw a small cabin.

The first thing visible was a double-barrel shotgun sticking through the slightly opened door. An elderly man appeared with the gun in hand, his finger on the trigger.

"What do you want?"

Anna Laura whispered, "Bobby, what's his name?"

"His name is Seth Jones."

"Seth, my name is Anna Laura. Will you please point your gun toward the ground?"

"Well, that'll depend on what you're wanting."

"Sir, I came to Brushy Mountain to try and help the people."

Selena saw two girls hiding behind a huge pile of firewood. They really looked pitiful; so skinny and pale. Both had long, dark hair. It appeared they were identical twins.

Anna Laura kept talking to Seth. He was mesmerized by her charm. He had never expected anyone like Anna Laura to show up at his cabin. Anna Laura was relieved as Seth opened the door and laid his gun on an old chair.

"All of you come in and sit for a spell. Sit on that wood bench."

Anna Laura began an introduction and told him who Billy and Bobby originally were. "I can't believe it – there's Cold tater and Rock head!"

"Yes, sir, it is."

"I got two girls. Reckon you can do a thing or two for them? They needs fixin' up like you've fixed them there purty girls. Come on down, children, and acquaint with Anna Laura. Come on, Sarah, you and Sadie."

The girls shyly came from behind the wood pile. They had a hard time keeping their eyes off Bobby and Billy. The two had seen them in the past. Bobby noticed as Sadie smiled, a small particle of chicken clinging where her two front teeth met.

Sarah tried not to be obvious, but she kept glancing toward Billy as everyone talked.

"Seth, where's your wife?" Anna Laura asked.

"Well, Gracie took sick a ways back and ain't too well. She's going down to nothing, just skin and bones. She's on that bed in yonder."

"Sir, can I go in to see her? I'm a doctor."

"Sure can. Can I call you Annie?"

Anna Laura was surprised to find Gracie on a clean bed as well as a clean room. Gracie was really sick but tried to smile. Anna Laura sent for her small medical bag. Crissy wasted no time in getting it; she liked assisting Anna Laura whenever possible.

Anna Laura had treated many cancer patients before, and Gracie had every symptom. She could barely talk, her breathing was shallow, and she was near death. Anna Laura knew it was only a matter of days until the stain of death would come.

The family only had rough grub, but Anna Laura began contemplating on what to feed her. She remembered a potato soup being made and fed to her mother before she died.

"Sadie, Sarah, do you have butter and milk?"

"Yeah, out at the spring."

"Please bring some." Anna Laura took an onion from a bunch that was tied together, hanging by a nail on the wall.

After mixing chopped onions and potatoes she added milk, butter and a little salt. She then took it outside where Billy and Bobby had placed rocks together as the fireplace was not burning inside. It would be too much heat for Gracie. After mixing everything in the small iron kettle, she carried it to the fire. After the soup was ready, she tried feeding Gracie a very small spoonful of the soup. Gracie was humble. She tried very hard to follow Anna Laura's instructions by swallowing the liquid. Her face lit up a little as she tried to show Anna Laura her gratefulness.

Gracie was unable to eat enough to gain strength. Anna Laura knew the sweet woman's life on earth was about to end, but sensed in her spirit Gracie was prepared to go to heaven.

Gracie tried very hard to ask Anna Laura to look in on her girls now and then after she departed this life. She knew it wouldn't be long. She managed to ask Anna Laura to read the Bible to her. Gracie had served God since her youth. She couldn't read, but she loved to hold the Bible near her, the one that belonged to her mother.

Anna Laura recited the 23rd Psalm to Gracie. Gracie looked like an angel as she listened. She could see the green pastures and the still waters. Her soul was as peaceful as the still cool clear waters that ran nearby.

Her voice was weak, but she whispered, "Anna, I see angels. I don't have no pain."

Anna Laura later learned that Seth had met Gracie down in the valley in Kentucky, near where Anna Laura grew up. He married her when she was only fifteen and brought her to the top of Brushy Mountain and down the other side a ways to the Tennessee side.

Seth was uneducated, but was good to Gracie, Sadie, and Sarah. He cleared new ground and produced enough food for survival. Hunting wild game also carried them through the years. He did the best he could.

The day was slowly wearing away. Anna Laura and Crissy went outside. Crissy's eyes were filled with tears. The situation had touched her heart greatly; an even greater desire to become a doctor engulfed her soul.

Anna Laura relayed, "Seth, I'm sorry, but your wife will only be here for a few more days. If you need me, I have a campsite not far from where the water runs down the mountain. If I should not be there during the day, come to the settlement."

Seth looked surprised. "I know right where you're talking about. There's a waterfall not far from it."

"We need to get going before dark," Billy said.

As they left, Anna Laura looked back to see Seth, Sadie and Sarah looking forlorn. She knew they stood, looking on without hope as she and the others rode away. She hated to leave sweet Gracie and the young girls who would soon be without a mother. The six young people were very sad as they made their way home. Billy and Bobby headed for their temporary home, as the girls turned toward their own.

As they sat around the small glowing fire under the sky filled with stars, Selena asked, "Can we bring Sadie and Sarah down sometime and teach them how to look pretty? We can share our shampoo, soap, toothpaste, and clothes. I know they're smaller than us, but I was taught by my mother how to alter sizes, especially for dresses. I brought my mother's sewing basket. That was one of her earthly treasures, and I will keep it forever."

Mary Jane and Crissy cut into the conversation, "We would like to share our belongings with them too!" Crissy said. "I want to teach them how to make that long, dark hair shiny and beautiful. And to care for their skin too! Though it looks to be in good condition already."

Mary Jane sat listening, "I would like to teach them the basics of education. I know, in my heart, they possess intelligence that has laid dormant their whole lives. Like us, they need someone to encourage them and bring their abilities to the surface."

"We will be going back in two or three days to check on Gracie." Anna Laura spoke sadly to the girls. Her heart was breaking for the family.

"Anna Laura, they are good people. I can sense it. There is something about Seth that reminds me of my own father," Selena spoke in a sad tone.

The women were all physically and emotionally exhausted. They ate the extra food that had not been packed with the picnic lunch. Everyone showered and would, hopefully, sleep peacefully under the open sky. Their sleep kept them in touch with everything they valued as it was the basis for their physical and mental strength.

As they lay on their beds of soft leaf pallets and blankets, they silently counted the stars to calm their restless minds and bodies.

As they grew weary, ready to give into slumber, they spotted a shooting star. "Make a wish," Selena called.

By this time, their minds were somewhat at ease about the family they had met that day. They had purposed in their hearts all that could be done and would follow it through.

Selena's wish was, "One day, I want to meet a charming, tall, dark, and handsome man, get married, leave the beautiful mountains and become involved in criminal law." Her mind was made up as to what she wanted to pursue as a career.

Mary Jane wished, "I want to leave the mountains when my work here is done and go to a real college to be a certified teacher."

Crissy's wish was, "I want to be a midwife here on the mountains, but one day, I wish to meet a good man, get married and live in the city of Nashville that I have heard so much about, the city that Samuel lives in, and become a doctor that delivers babies."

Anna Laura laid with tears flowing down her cheeks, privately wishing, "One day, I want to find Clint – or maybe he will find me when my God-given destiny is finished – and spend the rest of my life with him as his wife."

They had all fallen asleep finally, resting like newborn babies. It was as though God had given them much needed rest, for they all had a hard mission before them.

When waking at the break of dawn, they heard voices heading towards them. To their surprise, it was the twins who appeared at their camp.

"Anna Laura, we need you on the mountain. Mother needs you! Daddy's with her."

"Crissy, you come with me. Selena, you and Mary Jane feed the twins, let them bathe at the falls and provide them with clean clothes... and let them rest a couple of hours. They look really tired – maybe they can fall asleep. Afterwards, bring them up on the horses."

"We can do that."

When the two arrived on the mountain, Seth was standing at the door, tears flowing down his face. He seemed upset – as though he was grieving.

Anna Laura got her medical bag as they went inside, making their way to Gracie as quickly as possible. When she looked upon Gracie, it was obvious the angel of death was near.

"Gracie? Can you hear me?" The stricken woman slowly opened her beautiful azure eyes, giving a faint smile of acknowledgement.

"The angels are here," was the last thing Gracie whispered before her eyes closed, never to be seen again.

Anna Laura and Crissy's hearts ached as their own memories flashed to the forefront of their minds, grief taking hold of them as they remembered their own mothers. Crissy ran outside and leaned against the big Oak tree, remembering the day her mother went away. Anna Laura stood looking down on Gracie wishing she could have known her long ago. Her emotions were in turmoil as she thought of the death her own loving mother.

Gracie was gone to heaven now. Anna Laura covered her with the sheets then tried to comfort Seth.

"I tried to be good to her. I know I sure didn't do the best, but I tried."

Anna Laura collected her emotions and called Crissy in. They bathed Gracie, found a pretty flowered dress that must have been put in the cedar chest for a special occasion and dressed her. They washed and combed her light brown hair. As they finished, Anna Laura heard others outside nearing the cabin. Selena and Mary Jane had brought Sadie and Sarah home.

Crissy walked outside and stood among the daisies growing near the cabin and waited to tell the twins their lovely mother was gone. One saving grace was that she would never suffer again. The twins ran inside the cabin sat beside Gracie's bed, weeping for a time.

"Where's daddy?" Sara asked.

Seth had gone down by the stream and the twins went to be with him. They found him crying sadly by the water.

When he saw his girls, Seth wiped the tears from his eyes with his shirtsleeve. He had never seen his girls looking so lovely. "Sarah, you and Sadie look so pretty. I wish your momma could see you. She sure would be proud."

They embraced their father and the three of them wept together.

Later, they all came back to the cabin where Anna Laura and the girls extended their sympathies. Anna Laura kindly suggested they see to burial arrangements. "I'll have Billy and Bobby with the help of Rob and Steve build a coffin for your Gracie."

"I sure do thank you."

"Girls, you stay with Seth and the twins. I'll be back before dark."

Anna Laura rode to Billy and Bobby's cabin first. The boys were apprehensive seeing her ride in.

"What's wrong, Anna Laura?"

"Seth's Gracie has died. We need to go see Rob and Steve so the four of you can begin building a coffin for Gracie."

The two young men jumped on their horses and followed Anna Laura. She related the news of Gracie's death to Rob and Steve. They knew what had to be done.

"We have the wood we need and our wives will bring cloth to line it. We'll have it done in about two hours."

Anna Laura went to see Lilly, sharing the news with her as well. She fixed Anna Laura something to eat while they talked as she looked a bit pale. Anna Laura ate quickly and the two of them gathered together a few of the settlement women. They would begin working on the lining for the coffin. Unfortunately, this was a job they had been called upon to do many times before.

The coffin was carried by sled as far as possible along with food prepared for the family by the women of the settlement. When the sled could go no further, Billy, Bobby, Rob, and Steve carried it the rest of the way with Anna Laura trailing behind. They had to rest a few times, but soon reached Seth's.

Sadie and Sarah were sitting outside the door while Seth had already begun digging the grave beneath a huge hemlock tree. The Earth was rich and soft and easy to dig, yet this was the most devastating task he had ever performed.

Anna Laura suggested the men eat before finishing, she knew Seth needed the strength. After eating, the men took turns until the task was finished. Anna Laura had insisted that Sarah and Sadie eat although they had no appetite. Selena, Mary Jane, and Crissy took them down by the stream to eat with them.

Later, the girls pitched in to help Anna Laura gently lift Gracie from her bed to the coffin as Sarah and Sadie looked on with tears sliding down their faces. While tradition usually had the family sit up one night with the dead, Seth asked that they go ahead and bury Gracie.

Being the strongest, Billy and Bobby carried Gracie's coffin through the small cabin to the graveside. Steve and Rob tied strong rope around each end and together the men lowered Gracie to the bottom of the grave.

Selena began to sing, "If I could hear my mother pray again." Her voice echoed through the stillness of the mountains. Anna Laura then read the twenty-third Psalm.

While the men filled in the grave, the girls took Sadie and Sarah to the area where the wild daisies grew. They picked flowers to lay on their momma's grave. By the time they returned, the grave had been filled in and the top smoothed. Sadie and Sarah spread daisies from one end to the other as Seth stood leaning against a tree, his heart aching with grief.

Seth watched his girls, beautiful in their new clothes and with their hair shining in the sun. He knew in that moment they must go with Anna Laura. His heart ached to think of his three girls all leaving him on the same day, but they would forever be in his heart.

Seth walked over to Anna Laura and asked if they could walk down to the stream. "Anna Laura, Sadie and Sarah's momma is gone. I can't rightly say I'm able to take care of them. Will you take them? I'd be obliged. I can't stay here without my Gracie. My daddy is dead and gone; I'd sure like to go back to Virginia where he came from. I'm thinking you might help my Sadie and Sarah get a new life."

"Yes, Seth, I'll take Sarah and Sadie. They can start school when it begins in the fall. Selena, Mary Jane, and Crissy will teach them. You can be proud and know they are doing well even if you never make it back to Brushy Mountain."

They walked back to the cabin and Anna Laura explained the plans to the twins. They embraced their father as mixed emotions flowed over them. Even in this time of sorrow, Billy and Bobby's hearts raced at the thought of living near Sadie and Sarah.

They all said their goodbyes to Seth and filed down the mountain as Seth watched his lovely daughters go out of sight. He knew that Sarah and Sadie were going into a whole new world.

Chapter 30

Anna Laura awakened in the middle of the night. It was now August and the moon was new; it was as dark as dark could be with not a star in the hazy sky. Anna Laura could hear one of the girls quietly sobbing; she was not sure if she was awake or grieving in her sleep. She remained very quiet, allowing whichever girl it was the outlet of tears.

Anna Laura lay in the dark thinking how strange it was to find herself guardian to these five young ladies. She knew the other girls would soon teach Sarah and Sadie to read. School would start soon after the annual harvest and preservation of food. There would still be some things to do after school hours, like gathering corn and fodder for the animals.

Hopefully school would be in session by the first of October, a time when the trees lit the mountains in a variety of color. The mountains would truly be a sight to behold. Soon the wild geese would fly over the big mountains heading for warmer climates. The old-timers knew when the wild geese flew over, winter would soon be coming.

Suddenly, Anna Laura heard a voice from out of the dark. "Anna! Come to the settlement. Steve and Lilly's niece Elizabeth is ready to give birth!"

Lighting her bedside candle, Anna Laura called out for Crissy to wake up and come help. Dressing quickly, both mounted the Arabian, Crissy holding a candle inside a jar to give them enough light to see.

Steve and Lilly were already at Elizabeth's cabin. Lilly was like a mother to Elizabeth whose own mother, Hester, had died in childbirth. Lilly had the scissors sterilizing in boiling water along with cloth to tie the cord. Anna Laura quickly realized that this baby was breech; it would not be an easy birth. Explaining the problem to Crissy, Anna Laura told the girl what they needed to do. She needed Crissy to follow her every instruction.

As Lilly silently whispered a prayer of faith, Anna Laura worked to turn the baby into the head first position. Elizabeth was already exhausted, lying there with tears streaming down her face.

As daylight filtered in the window, the baby's head finally began to crown. Once the baby was on its way into the world, Anna Laura allowed

Crissy to finish the delivery. Shortly, a baby boy came into the world with a loud cry. Elizabeth relaxed as her baby was placed across her stomach.

Elizabeth's husband, Carl, yelled so loud the house echoed. Elizabeth quietly announced, "This is Carl Stephen Turner."

Never had Anna Laura seen Steve look so proud.

Lilly and Anna Laura walked outside. "Many babies and mommas have died from this kind of problem."

Anna Laura nodded, "I'm so thankful that Elizabeth and her son made it."

Riding back to camp later, Crissy said, "There is no doubt in my mind I want to bring new life into the world!"

Anna Laura knew this intelligent girl would get her chance. Arriving back at camp, they found the others were still fast asleep. Anna Laura suggested they get a little more rest as well.

Tomorrow would be Friday; Anna Laura decided they should have a day of leisure and perhaps teach Sarah and Sadie a little about eating in a nice restaurant. She wanted to take the girls to Cherry Valley soon. They could borrow Billy and Bobby's horses for the new girls; she knew Seth had taught them to ride. They could even begin to teach the girls the alphabet and the basics of learning to read.

Everyone woke around nine o'clock and the girls were surprised to discover what Anna Laura and Crissy had done in the night. Each of them took turns at the falls, Sadie and Sarah enjoyed the fragrance of the shampoo and soap mixed with fresh water. Anna Laura prepared new toothbrushes for the girls as well as baking soda to whiten their teeth and toothpaste to use afterward for fresher breath.

Returning from their showers, Sadie and Sarah looked much better. A little of the sadness was gone from their eyes. They smiled shyly as Anna Laura complimented them.

After breakfast, Crissy brought out the material they would need to help the girls learn to read. Selena and Mary Jane were just as eager to help their friends discover a new world. Listening to them, Anna Laura knew these twins were blessed with the ability to learn; it would only take time and direction. The girls were grasping the basics very quickly. Looking to the sky, Anna Laura silently thanked God for their blessings. She had no doubt that by October the girls would be doing fine.

After a long and fruitful day, they settled in for the night again.

Anna Laura announced, "Girls, I have a surprise for you. We're going off the mountain to Cherry Valley early tomorrow. We'll likely spend the night. Who knows? An angel of mercy may come on the scene as before."

Selena explained to Sadie and Sarah what had happened on their last trip.

Come morning, Selena, Crissy, and Mary Jane went through their clothing to find riding skirts and tops for themselves as well as Sarah and Sadie. They all helped Sarah and Sadie with their hair and makeup, which they had never used before. The twins were more beautiful than ever. The only way to tell them apart was the beauty mark, a small mole above Sarah's lip on the left side. With their beautiful blue eyes, fair skin and dark hair, the girls were a vision. This would be their first trip off Brushy Mountain. The excitement drove the shadows from their eyes.

Jess lit up like a Christmas tree when he saw Mary Jane riding toward the stable. After the women had stabled the horses, Jess asked Mary Jane, "Do you think Anna Laura would allow you to go to a square dance with me this evening?"

"Jess, I can't dance."

"I'll teach you. After the dance is over, I'll bring you back to the Inn. You are spending the night, aren't you?"

"I'm not sure."

Jess had some money saved and decided then and there that he would pay for rooms for the ladies if Anna Laura would stay.

Anna Laura asked the girls if they would like to window shop for a while. The twins had never heard of such a thing. Stopping in front of a huge shop window with beautiful clothes behind it, Anna Laura said, "I want to buy the twins something really pretty. Something that will be a perfect fit."

As they walked by the windows of the department stores, Sadie and Sarah were amazed by all the beautiful clothes. Deciding on a store, they went inside.

"Sadie and Sarah, I want you to choose complete outfits. Selena, Mary Jane, and Crissy will help you decide while I let Hank know we're in town."

Sadie's eyes were drawn to a blue plaid shirt and blue jeans, while Sarah liked the red better. They each chose new boots, sleeping gowns, and undergarments. The girls immediately changed their old shoes for their new boots. When Anna Laura and Hank came back to the department store, Hank had brought some of the grant money to buy clothes for the mountain people in need. The twins showed Anna Laura what they had chosen.

Hank took Anna Laura aside, "Have the girls buy more new clothes."

Anna Laura smiled and told the girls to pick out a few more outfits. The twins could hardly contain themselves. This was more than they had ever dreamed could happen. They chose three beautiful outfits each.

Anna Laura suggested, "Why don't all of you choose a new outfit for church. It won't be long until church services will begin on Sundays."

The five girls were very excited. They chose a beautiful dress each.

Hank really enjoyed watching as the girls made their choices, especially Selena. He was confused as he looked at Selena and their eyes met. This feeling of excitement still puzzled him. What he felt for Selena was different from what he experienced when he thought of Anna Laura.

After everything was paid for, Hank told Anna Laura about the rooms Jess had gotten them and suggested she take the girls there to leave their things. They would meet with Jess at the Hemlock Inn restaurant. Anna Laura could hardly wait to see Sadie and Sarah's faces when they walked into the restaurant.

Once they reached the rooms, the girls freshened up. It was a bit early for dinner, but they were hungry and had skipped lunch. Anna Laura suggested they go ahead to the restaurant as the men were probably waiting.

Hank and Jess were waiting among the green and pink linen covered tables. Sadie and Sarah were totally overwhelmed to see such a beautiful sight but remained calm as they had been taught. Jess, Mary Jane, Crissy, and Sadie were seated together and the others took a second table. They were all close enough to carry on conversation. Anna Laura properly introduced Sadie and Sarah to Hank and Jess. The twins were very comfortable. The men were somewhat curious as to how the twins had come to be with Anna Laura, but she would save that story for another day. When it came time to order dinner, Anna Laura discreetly directed the girls. "Why don't we all have the roast chicken, salad, rolls, potatoes and green beans?"

"Good choice," Hank replied, following her lead.

Jess finally asked, "Anna Laura, can I have your permission to take Mary Jane to the square dance after dinner?"

"Sure, Jess, just have her back by ten o'clock."

Mary Jane could hardly contain her smile of pleasure.

"Would you ladies like to go to the theater and see a movie?" Hank asked. Crissy, Sarah, Sadie, and Selena were speechless. Selena and Crissy had read about movies before but Sarah and Sadie had no idea what they were. Anna Laura accepted knowing this would be a treat for all of the girls.

Once Jess and Mary Jane left for the square dance, the others walked to the movie theater. As they were seated, Hank somehow found himself between Selena and Anna Laura. Hank was a little uncomfortable. Sitting next to Selena, he experienced feelings in his heart and soul he had never known before. As they were shoulder to shoulder, the light touch convinced him his heart was truly captivated by Selena. All his earlier discomfort was gone. He knew he did not love Anna Laura nor did she love him. He sat through the movie thinking of how life had likely been very difficult for Selena. He wanted to nurture her, give her a nice home as well as love and care.

Jess and Mary Jane left the dance a little early to take a walk out by the lake.

"Mary Jane, are you always planning to stay on Brushy Mountain?"

"Jess, I'm not sure but I can't say that I want to. I do plan to help with teaching this fall as the new school will open."

"I'm glad you want to be a teacher, Mary. Can I call you Mary?" Jess was so nervous he did not stop for an answer before continuing, "Mary, I will finish my training to be a certified teacher in December. Do you think I could come to the mountain for the winter and be of assistance?"

"I believe Anna Laura would be happy to have a qualified teacher in our school. I'm sure Billy and Bobby will have the cabin finished by then and wouldn't mind you staying with them."

"I won't be able to get a teaching job in Cherry Valley until next fall."

"Jess, that will be wonderful."

Gathering his courage, Jess gently kissed Mary Jane as their conversation ended.

The girls took turns bathing in the antique tub. Sadie and Sarah were absolutely astonished by this world beyond the mountains as they dressed in their light blue nightgowns. They felt like princesses as they stood before the mirror brushing their long dark hair. Since they had two rooms, Anna Laura had suggested Sadie and Sarah share a room by themselves. Anna Laura, Crissy, Selena, and Mary Jane said their good nights. Sadie and Sarah felt safe and special as they closed the door that separated the two rooms.

"Sadie, did you ever think we would sleep in a bed like this?"

"No, Sarah, it's so different from corn shucks or the ground."

As they prepared for bed, the girls talked a little about Billy and Bobby. Sarah was relieved to find that Sadie liked Bobby, because she was very taken with Billy.

"Sarah, I miss Momma and Daddy so bad. I know Momma is in heaven with Jesus, but do you think Daddy is doing well?"

"Sadie, Daddy has what Anna Laura calls good common sense. He can survive."

"Do you think he'll be happy in Virginia?"

"I think he might need a good wife that will see his needs. I think he'll find a job easy enough; he can do about any kind of hard work."

"That makes me feel better, Sarah."

Together they drifted into a peaceful sleep.

In the other room Anna Laura, Mary Jane, and Crissy fell asleep quickly, but sleep would not come for Selena. She was worried about her feelings for Hank; she thought Anna Laura cared for him.

Still troubled, Selena drifted into sweet sleep.

As the morning sun lit the rooms brightly, everyone got up and made themselves presentable. They packed their clothes and went to the Hemlock Inn restaurant for breakfast. Sadie and Sarah enjoyed their breakfast far more than the others. The atmosphere was unlike any they had ever experienced. The fresh fruit, blueberry muffins, and the coldest milk they had ever drunk in summer were very special.

Once everyone was finished, they headed for the stables. The girls attached their new things to the saddles.

Jess kissed Mary Jane before she mounted her horse. As they rode up the mountain, the girls teased Mary Jane, but she did not mind. She knew they only wanted to have a little fun and she was too happy to worry about a little teasing.

When they arrived back at their camp at midday, Billy was anxiously waiting. "Bobby is hurt, it happened while we were working on the roof of the schoolhouse. He had a pretty bad fall."

Anna Laura went for her medical supplies and Sadie asked if she could come along. Anna Laura agreed and they headed to Bobby and Billy's new place.

"Billy, do you think Bobby has any broken bones?"

"I'm not sure, but I believe his arm's broken."

"When did this happen?"

"About an hour ago."

Once they reached the cabin, Anna Laura went straight to him. After checking the young man carefully she told Billy he was correct, Bobby's arm was broken. "I'll need your help as well as Sadie's."

Bobby was in so much pain that Anna Laura administered a light sedative; the bone had to be set.

"Now, Bobby, the medicine will help a little, but you'll have to be brave."

As Anna Laura set the bone with Billy's help, Sadie held a cold cloth to Bobby's head. Bobby was so taken by Sadie that he was especially brave, even though he wanted to scream. Anna Laura and Billy splinted and wrapped his arm to keep bones in place.

Shyly, Sadie told Bobby, "I'll bring supper and make sure you're doing better."

Bobby would need a couple of days rest. As long as Sadie came by to pamper him, he really did not mind.

Billy teased Bobby a little after the ladies left.

"Billy, you're sweet on Sarah and you know it," Bobby teased back.

For a while, Bobby was silent. "Can you believe all the good that is happening to us?"

"Bobby, I believe something good will happen. It's like miracles are happening all over the mountain."

Around noon, Sadie and Sarah came by bringing fried chicken and fried apple pies. Billy and Bobby were impressed.

The four of them talked as they ate, both young men finding excuses to sit near the girl they wanted to get to know better. The twins stayed long enough for the picnic but left soon after because Anna Laura told them it would be the proper thing to do. As they left the boys thanked them.

On Monday morning, the girls were up early and on their way to the settlement shortly after daylight. There was much work to do. As they got closer, they could hear the echoes of hammering and sawing. The workers were as busy as bees while the women prepared food. Bobby and Billy were there, Bobby doing his best with one arm.

They were working on the church. Several men were placing wooden shingles on the roof.

Anna Laura and the girls continued to chink their cabin with clay to keep out small animals and the cold weather. Steve suggested that Bobby help the ladies as it would be an easier job for him. When they got low on clay, Bobby volunteered himself along with Sadie and Sarah to go for more. Taking their buckets, they walked through the woods to the clay banks.

Bobby related, "Girls, me and Billy used to make toys out of the clay. When they dried we played with them."

The girls were amazed at the amount of work Bobby was able to do with one hand. Of course, Bobby had a hard time keeping his eyes on the clay and off Sadie.

As they worked, Bobby suddenly said, "Sadie, do you think you could be my sweetheart?"

Sadie blushed red, but ignored the fact that Sarah heard and said yes.

Suddenly Sarah said, "We'd better get going; Anna Laura will be worried." Sadie and Bobby shared in carrying the large bucket on the way back.

Sadie's heart was still pounding a little because of Bobby's question. Seeing the sparkle in Bobby's blue eyes made her heart warm.

The ladies were waiting for the clay and smiled at each other seeing the looks on Sadie and Bobby's faces. The love bug had truly bitten.

Around noon, Lilly rang the dinner bell. Billy took his chance and went to ask Sarah to join him for dinner. She agreed and they sat by the stream. After a while, Billy asked her if she would be his sweetheart. With a big smile, Sarah said yes.

By the end of the day, the chinking of Anna Laura's cabin was finished. The fireplace, the door and everything else was completed. Only the furniture was lacking.

The church and the school still needed clay chinking so Steve suggested that Billy and Bobby continue helping the ladies with that job. The boys were definitely agreeable to the task.

As Anna Laura and the girls headed back to camp later that evening, all they could think of was the cool clear water of the falls. They cleaned up, prepared a snack and finally rested on blankets beneath the star filled sky.

Chapter 31

Anna Laura was startled from sleep by the sound of voices. At first she felt she was dreaming, but soon realized it really was voices that sounded like children. Taking her candle in its jar, she set out to investigate. To her surprise, she came upon six children. They looked to range from about three to eight years old.

"Children, where did you come from? What are your names?"

The tiny blond with curls replied, "My name is Erma."

A little boy spoke up, "We come from up yonder on the ridge."

"Where are your momma and daddy?"

"They left us three days ago, said they wouldn't be back. Said they's going to a better place."

"What kind of place?"

"We don't know. They just took off over the mountain that away."

The boy was pointing in the direction from which Anna Laura had traveled when she first came to the mountain.

"They told us to find that strange woman with that big horse. She'll take care of you, they said."

Anna Laura led the children towards camp; she was shocked by the children's situation but knew she had to keep calm. Once they reached the camp, she asked the children if they were hungry.

"Awful hungry. Haven't had no food since yesterday morning."

Anna Laura could not feed the children fast enough. They ate as if they were starving. As they finished their meal, she laid out quilts under the hanging rock. When the children finished eating, she put them to bed on the quilts and covered them carefully. Full, warm and safe, they went to sleep quickly.

Settling down again, Anna Laura wondered how she would handle this challenge. She promised herself that she would learn their names and ages in the morning.

In the early hours of the morning, Anna Laura thought about a couple that lived in the settlement. They had no children although they

[177]

were both nearly forty. Anna Laura thought about the Psalm that said, 'Children are an heritage of the Lord and the fruit of the womb is his reward. As arrows are in the hand of the mighty men; so are children of the youth. Happy is the man that has seen his quivers full of them; they shall not be ashamed.'

Anna Laura showered and groomed herself before the others woke up; she wanted to be prepared when the children rose. She smiled thinking of how Selena, Crissy, Mary Jane, Sarah and Sadie would react when they looked upon six abandoned children sleeping in their camp. She mixed up a batch of pancake batter and added blueberries that Lilly had canned in glass jars. She had brought cold milk from the spring.

As Anna Laura cooked breakfast, the rich aroma began flowing into the area where the children were sleeping. Erma began to move first, it only took a short while for her to remember where she was. She got up and looked upon Anna Laura and the sleeping young ladies. She woke her brothers and sisters and they all stared as Anna Laura put pancakes on plates and poured cold milk into tin cups. The older girls were now awake and saw Anna Laura placing all the food on the table that Billy and Bobby had built for them not long ago. They were puzzled to see their camp had grown overnight. Anna Laura asked them to head to the falls to shower and get dressed for the day. In the meantime, the children marched down to Anna Laura. They were very dirty, but she knew they were also very hungry.

She directed the children to wash their hands in a pan of water she had placed on a rock. They each did as she asked and then took their places at the table. Sitting on a stump at the end of the table, Anna Laura asked Erma if she would like to say grace.

"What is grace, Anna Laura?"

"We give God thanks, just say what you feel."

Erma began, "God, I know you're out there and brought us here to this good woman. Thank you for what you've done."

Anna Laura encouraged the children to eat and asked Erma to introduce her to the others.

[178]

"This is Ruthie next to me, she's three. That's Harold and he's five; over there is Annie, she's seven; next is Rodney, he's four, and that's Will and he's eight. I'm six years old."

Anna Laura's mind was occupied with everything that needed to be done for these children. The five young ladies returned, looking fresh, clean and rejuvenated. Anna Laura could hardly contain her laughter seeing the bewilderment on the faces of the girls as they looked at the six children sitting at their table.

Anna Laura made the introductions and the children seemed a little in awe of these beautiful young women.

"These are the prettiest children I have ever seen," said Mary Jane warmly.

While the girls got acquainted with the children, Anna Laura searched in the stored clothing for things that would fit each child. When she found what she needed, she rounded up the three boys. "Follow me; I have a surprise for you."

She took them to the falls and gave them shampoo, soap, a towel and instructions. She stepped back into the woods to wait. It was obvious from the noises she heard that while the boys were scrubbing themselves they were also taking time to play. Once they were dried and dressed, she showed them how to brush their teeth and combed their light blond hair. They were very handsome and she told them so.

As she walked the children back toward camp, she heard a voice in her spirit. "I will lead you to a destiny of hope and lasting nurturing for these six innocent children. I will heal their broken spirits and restore peace."

Anna once again thought about the childless couple she had considered the night before. She knew they were good people with tender hearts.

As they entered camp, the little girls looked at their brothers in amazement. Crissy and the other four girls headed toward the falls with Erma, Ruthie, and Annie. They helped the little ones wash and groom themselves. An hour later, six little children that had been so desperately dirty and hungry looked as if they had never experienced such physical and emotional pain. It would, of course, be a while before they would fully heal.

Each of the young women mounted their horses and a child was placed in front of them. They rode slowly toward the settlement, the children becoming quieter as they drew nearer. They had lived secluded with only their parents for company all of their lives. They had never seen so many people. Neither had they ever seen such level land or so many houses before. All they wanted was to run and play in the tall green grass, but they were also afraid.

"One day, you will be able to play with the other children in the meadow," Anna Laura assured them.

When they reached Phoebe and Samuel Britton's cabin, Anna Laura and the others stopped. Phoebe's eyes lit up.

Samuel walked over from where he was working and called out, "Anna Laura, where on earth did you get all those children?"

"Samuel, they showed up in my campsite last night. Their parents left them and sent them to me."

Phoebe's eyes filled with tears. Her heart yearned to say, "I want these children, all of them." Samuel saw the tears on her face and his heart was touched.

"Anna Laura, I have a big extra bedroom; it's real big. I could divide it and make two rooms. One for the boys and one for the girls."

Anna Laura's heart was pounding as her eyes filled with tears. Erma was crying softly in a way that would touch the heart of anyone. It was a cry of happiness.

"Get off them horses," Samuel said firmly but with a little break in his voice.

As everyone dismounted, there were smiles all around. Will said to Rodney, "Is this real?"

"I sure hope it is, Will."

"We were just about to sit down to dinner," Phoebe said. As they entered the house the children could hardly keep from licking their lips seeing the yellow and white ears of corn, green beans, potatoes, cornbread and big slices of red tomatoes. There were custard pies on the shelves nearby. Samuel and Phoebe had a long table with benches so there was plenty of room for the children. Everyone was invited to sit.

As they ate, Samuel asked, "Anna Laura, can the children start staying with us right now?"

Anna Laura was a little surprised when the children lifted their voices, "Can we? Can we?"

Anna Laura smiled and nodded her head. God never ceased to amaze her. He truly was a miracle worker.

Samuel asked the children if they would like to see the schoolhouse being built.

"School?" Rodney cried out. "You mean we might can go to school?"

"Yeah, Rodney, and we'll look at the new church too."

Erma cried out, "Oh, I want to go to church!"

All of the children joined in enthusiastically. They wanted to go to church too. They wanted to learn about the one that Anna Laura said had helped them so much.

"You can do just that," Phoebe replied.

Anna Laura sent the girls on to work at their cabin while she helped Phoebe clean up so they could talk about the children.

Samuel and the six children walked, the breeze gently blowing across the meadow. It was strange to see so much flat land even though they were on top of the mountain. The children held hands by twos and walked with Samuel as he told them about how the settlement emerged years ago and how the flat lands were present even then. There were mountains to the north and west that were much higher.

Will spoke up, "Samuel, we lived up toward the top of that mountain over yonder."

Harold chimed in, "We never want to go back there. When mommy and daddy drank that clear stuff in jars, they were mean to us. We didn't get much to eat for days."

Little Ruthie said softly, "Samuel, I'm glad that good woman that mommy and daddy talked about brought us to you and Phoebe."

"Children, I know God sent you to me and Phoebe," Samuel spoke as tears welled in his eyes. All six tried to wrap their arms around his legs, hugging him tightly. "Come on, children, over here is the springhouse, let's have a cool drink of water." Samuel folded cups for them from huge wahoo leaves.

After everyone had a drink and the children seemed calmer, Samuel said, "Well, children, we'd better get back. Phoebe's probably waiting to dish out that custard pie!"

The children laughed out loud knowing this was something new and good. They knew now they would have a good bed, food, love and affection.

Anna Laura had a camera in her saddle bag. She took a snapshot of Samuel, Phoebe, and the children. It might be a while before she could get it developed, but it would be a memory of a very special moment. She was so happy these children had found a home, and she thanked God for the wonderful couple who had taken them in.

Chapter 32

Progress was rapidly moving for the settlement, autumn was near. Soon the mountains would be ablaze with the glorious colors, the construction would be finished, and the crops would be harvested and preserved for the winter.

Anna Laura could feel fall in the air as she sat on her Arabian outside their cabin where the girls were working. There is a special feeling in the air even before fall comes, a serene feeling that is within, that cannot sufficiently be described by man or woman.

Anna Laura sat watching Samuel taking his Rodney, Will, Harold, Erma, Ruthie and Annie inside their cabin as Phoebe was standing back inside a ways smiling. Anna Laura knew their lives would be forever changed. She would bring more clothes for the children the following day.

Anna Laura dismounted and went inside her cabin. "Girls, you are making the place homey and cozy. I can't believe that some of the men took time to build our furniture. The table, benches and beds are absolutely amazing. The women are donating feather beds for us to sleep on and we have enough bed linens, blankets, quilts and pillows."

The light purple curtains that Selena had sewn were hanging in the windows. Late pink wild roses were placed in a fruit jar that was in a light purple pouch that Selena had also made. A rocking chair sat by the fire place that Steve had donated. Straight backed chairs were donated to accommodate the girls if they were not working at the table sitting on benches. Cushions stuffed with feathers lay on each chair covered with cloth of more colors.

It definitely wouldn't be too long before they could move into their cabin and also get on with school and church.

Anna Laura exclaimed, "Your talents amaze me." The girls smiled proudly.

Even though an unreal amount of good had taken place Anna Laura experienced emptiness somewhere in the corner of her heart, or perhaps the center of her soul. Deep within she believed God would send a divine intervention that would make her feel her life was complete.

She believed she would reap what she had sown and knew she had tried to sow good seeds. Perhaps a little might fall on stony grounds because it was not accepted. Most seeds, no doubt, would land on good ground.

"Girls, the clouds are beginning to pass over fast toward the east and it is looking a little dark. Perhaps we had better head home."

"We're ready Anna Laura," the girls called out.

They made it to their temporary home, got their showers and made their beds under the open sky as usual to sleep in the coolness of the night. They were sure the dark clouds would pass over. The moon was also new and of course there was not a star to be seen. The only light was their flickering fire.

Each fell asleep thinking of what they could accomplish the next day.

Around midnight they were awakened by a loud roar. It sounded like gushing waters.

Anna Laura shouted, "Girls, get up quickly, I believe there has been a cloud burst upstream, and the water is coming."

They grabbed their things and headed for cover where they would be protected. The water was moving rapidly. Anna Laura was last as she put the girls in front to be sure they all made it. Suddenly, a huge flood of water swept through, carrying Anna Laura away before she made it to the cave.

The girls screamed with fear when they realized Anna Laura had been swept away. Luckily, Anna Laura was thin and the water carried her down through an area that did not have many trees. She was able to lock her arms around a slim poplar tree.

The five girls were devastated. After what seemed an eternity, the breath of dawn began to show itself.

Selena had experience dealing with mountain emergencies.

"Girls, you stay here, I am taking the path to the left of the flowing water to look for Anna Laura."

Selena was light and graceful on her feet even on the side of a mountain. She made her way downward whispering a prayer as she went. As she continued on, she began to cry out, "Anna Laura, can you hear me? I'm coming for you."

There was no response. She continued downward for at least half a mile.

Suddenly she heard a faint voice.

She yelled loudly, "Anna Laura, Anna Laura, where are you?"

"To the left!"

Selena walked as she scanned the area with her sharp vision.

The water had receded somewhat, and Selena saw Anna Laura near the base of a tree surrounded by water. She was too weak to let go of the tree and wade out. Selena waded in and got to her quickly.

Anna Laura's eyes portrayed more gratitude than Selena had seen in her entire life. She checked Anna Laura for broken bones but everything seemed to be intact. After helping her to safety, Selena noticed Anna Laura was limping, she practically carried Anna Laura, stopping to rest several times. Hopefully it was only a sprain.

The girls were still under the huge rock praying fervently and at the same time terrified.

When they got close enough Selena cried out, "Girls, please help us."

The girls did just that and brought Anna Laura to the cave and covered her with warm blankets as she was shaking uncontrollably. They built a fire at the mouth of the cave with wood that was stored inside.

Mary Jane made peppermint tea from plants they had gathered in the summer and gave some to Anna Laura and Selena. When the chill had eased, Anna Laura began to respond normally.

"Girls, I thought my life was over when the rushing waters carried me away. As I locked my arms around that small tree, I knew God was directing my path as it was so dark. I remembered my assignment and knew it had not been finished. This gave me hope in the darkness. As I held onto the tree, the swift waters almost took my breath away but I knew I had to keep my head above the water and hang on.

"This gives me more faith than ever that our God given destinies will be fulfilled. We are going to continue to bless the lives of others here on Brushy Mountain for a given time. Earlier I felt an emptiness in my heart but it is now gone."

Their camp was wiped out but all their goods to help others were safe beneath the huge cave.

"Perhaps the ladies will get those feather beds ready real soon and we'll be moving into our cabins sooner than we thought," Anna Laura hoped.

"Anna Laura, can we go to Lilly and Steve's now that it's daylight? I would feel safer." Mary Jane asked.

"Girls, get our horses. I believe my foot is okay, the pain isn't too bad." The girls were already dressed but didn't prepare breakfast as everything had been washed away. Anna Laura would not be working today as she needed to spend the day resting after the trauma of the night. The girls could continue getting the cabin ready.

Riding into Steve and Lillie's yard, Lilly was uneasy about them showing up so early. She noticed Anna Laura was tired and pale. She noticed the limp as well.

Lilly swung open the door, "Are you alright, Anna Laura?"

"We'll explain inside."

Lilly had enough breakfast and coffee for everyone. As they sat at the cherry wood table, Lilly was shocked as the near disaster was related to her. She could visualize Anna Laura being tossed down the mountain by the raging waters. She also knew a miracle had taken place; otherwise Anna Laura would have drowned.

"Girls, let's join hands and give God thanks for sparing Anna Laura's life and for Selena's bravery in rescuing her." Each joined hands as they sat at the table. Tears slid down their pretty faces.

"After breakfast," Lilly insisted, "Anna Laura, you go into our spare room and rest today. The girls can work without you."

While the girls were working, word had gotten around fast about their camp being washed out. At least six women came to help. Many shared their housekeeping supplies with the ladies. By mid-afternoon the beds were intact. Many mountain women thought ahead and prepared extra for themselves or for their children when they married. They could hardly wait to tell Anna Laura they could move into their new cabin that very evening.

After they reached Lilly's house, she soon announced, "Supper is on the table."

Anna Laura joined the others at a long table loaded with fresh cooked food. Before eating, Sarah spoke out, "I have something to tell Anna Laura," she paused for a moment controlling her emotions. "We will be moving into our new home tonight. The ladies of the settlement did a real house warming; we have beds and everything we need."

Walking into the cabin and looking it over later that evening, Anna Laura was in tears as she looked at the fluffy beds covered with muslin sheets and quilts of many colors that had been pieced together by hand. Anna Laura was speechless but everyone knew what her heart was saying by the look on her face.

The pantry had been filled with food preserved by the neighbors. Fresh squash, tomatoes, corn, green beans, cucumber, onions and potatoes were laid on the flat board nailed to a post on the back porch.

The back of the cabin faced the mountains; the inclining hills were decked with such beauty of nature. This would be the perfect place to sit and have morning coffee and watch the wild game roam the forest - turkey, deer, and much more. The prettiest sight was the abundance of blue birds which folklore said represented peace. The tall oak tree in the back yard served to shade the cabin.

The horses in the corral at the edge of woods were sheltered in part by the trees. The grass was green and tender covering a large area.

Anna Laura lifted her eyes toward the skies, "I thank you, God, for your work of art."

Anna Laura and the girls rode out to the falls for their showers and would continue to until winter. They would then bathe in front of the fire place. They wanted to be clean when their tired bodies lay on the soft clean beds.

When morning came, they would enjoy preparing breakfast inside although it might seem a little strange. They had decided that since the weather was still warm they would place rocks close together and cook as they did at their former campsite. This too would allow the cabin to remain cool as the breeze flowed through the open windows freshly scenting the curtains. The fireplace would be perfect for cooking over during the winter; this would be a new experience for Anna Laura.

After going to bed, all six ladies felt so blessed not to be sleeping on the ground. They had loved and appreciated their private camp but they felt for the moment they had died and gone to heaven. The cool night air breezed through their rooms soothing their tired bodies. Hearing the dew dripping from the huge oak tree in the stillness of the night was relaxing, almost like a slow soft rainfall.

Anna Laura had learned much about nature just as the girls had and all definitely were appreciative of God's works.

Chapter 33

Anna Laura, Sadie, Sarah, Crissy, Selena, and Mary Jane now yearned to begin making preparations for school. The chinking of the schoolhouse had been completed. Now it was time to work inside and organize.

Time was of the essence and it was passing so swiftly. The tables, desks, and chairs had been completed. The teacher's desk was perfect. Shelves were ready for storing books and supplies. The slate board had been mounted to the wall.

Rob and Steve would bring the books and other supplies from storage soon. The girls were filled with excitement when they arrived. They began arranging everything in order; they had a long day's work before them.

By now, Bobby's arm was mostly healed. He and Billy were putting their time in at the doctor's office and missing Sadie and Sarah.

Many, many settlers and children were harvesting and preparing food for winter. They knew from experience when October ended, winter was just around the corner.

As the girls worked, Selena told the others how she had always loved watching the wild geese fly over the mountains in October. "I imagined following them to see what existed beyond those mountains. I was so sad when I saw them pass over."

Crissy had her own opinion. "Girls, we have been blessed just to visit Cherry Valley. That's far more than I ever dreamed would happen in my life. I figured I would never leave these mountains. I didn't really expect to make it to the settlement, but I admire your thoughts of days gone by."

Selena nodded. "I always feared not being accepted by anyone. Coming from higher ground to the settlement is more than I dreamed could happen in my life. Sometimes I lay awake at night and wonder what Nashville, Tennessee that Anna Laura speaks of is like. I even dream of going there for a visit one day, especially the plantation that Anna Laura visited with Hank."

As the girls worked at the school, Anna Laura cleaned then fried chicken and apple pies for their lunch. She then stopped by the medical building and invited Bobby and Billy to go to the school to eat with the girls. Sadie and Sarah's eyes lit up when they saw Bobby and Billy with Anna Laura. The young men spread the linen and placed the food on one of the tables.

Anna Laura admired and complimented the girls on how well they were organizing the supplies. As the others took their places, Anna Laura informed them that she had already eaten. She stood looking out windows as far as she could see. Her thoughts were miles away from Brushy Mountain. She imagined Clint, busy in the hospital saving lives, but wondered if he had met someone and was possibly falling in love.

At that very moment, Clint stood by a window staring out over the huge city that was lit up as far as he could see. He wondered where and what his lovely Anna Laura was doing. As his heart ached and many months had passed, he could not suppress the fear that he would never see her again.

"Girls, I feel that I'm ready to work again."

Rob and Steve arrived with another load of supplies and Billy and Bobby carried them in so the men could go home for lunch. They were all very excited. They knew they could look forward to more learning when winter came on. Crissy, Selena, and Mary Jane knew they would be teaching with Anna Laura as their supervisor when she was not busy tending the sick or performing other duties.

Mary Jane could see herself imparting knowledge to the children and how fulfilling it would be. She thought of how Jess would soon be certified by his college and hoped she too would one day have a degree.

Sadie and Sarah thought of how they, along with Bobby and Billy, would one day leave Brushy Mountain to find jobs.

Crissy thought of Samuel Adams in Nashville and dreamed of marrying him one day. She wanted to be educated in the care of pregnant mothers and their babies.

Selena still dreamed of Hank as she worked. What would their destiny be?

As Anna Laura worked alongside the girls, she suddenly called out excitedly, "Ladies, perhaps in October before we begin our teaching, Hank will take us to Nashville."

The girls were ecstatic. This was more than they ever dreamed could happen.

It was difficult to snap back to reality and finish the work of organizing supplies. The mountain children would soon begin a wonderful new school year. As they learned to read, they would vicariously go places they had never been or perhaps never would go. Through books they could explore the world.

The small schoolhouse stood at a short distance from the cabins. A huge oak tree shaded the playground and Anna Laura would teach them games. She knew the value of taking time to play.

A short distance from the school was a spring of water that bubbled from the earth near a Hemlock tree. The children would bring gourd dippers for drinking and their names would be written on them. For some of them, this might be the first time they would see their names written out.

The children of the settlement were already excited. The very air stirred with it.

The harvesting of crops would be done soon. Potatoes were being poured into holes that had been dug in the ground beneath outbuildings, turnips would also go underground. The cabbages would be buried beneath the earth in the rows where they were grown. Tomatoes and other vegetables were canned in glass jars and stored away. Corn was canned or dried to be ground into cornmeal for making cornbread. Apples, strawberries and blackberries would be made into jelly or jam for a sweet treat. Green beans were dried all summer long to make shucky beans. Come winter, the dried beans would be soaked in water and cooked with cured bacon to make a delicious meal. Along with meat and eggs from their farm animals and wildlife, the settlement people would fare well until spring.

Chapter 34

It was now October and Anna Laura had been on the mountain for eight months; a fully lived and very productive eight months.

The mountains were lit up with the first luminous golds, crimsons, and other colors of nature. The children gathered walnuts, hickory nuts, and hazelnuts with enthusiasm. Their hands would be stained from shelling walnuts, but they did not mind as they thought about cracking the nuts on rock hearths when the snow began to fall.

This winter would be different for the settlement children, they would be in school. Anna Laura and the girls joined in the harvesting crops after the school supplies were organized and the lessons were planned. They worked hard to help where they could; after all, they would share in the food.

Anna Laura was not yet fully recuperated from being carried away in the water. She became tired easily and would often stop to rest near the stream. She lay back on the grass looking toward the sky; the peach and blue colored clouds floated over looking as though they were brushing the mountain.

She saw a flock of wild geese flying south. She was mesmerized by the beauty and pattern of their flight. As the colorful leaves sailed down to alight on the surface of the rippling water of the stream, she knew her destiny still remained in Brushy Mountain and with its people. It was time to get back to work.

Walking toward the cornfield, she thanked God for their lovely cabin. Birds flitting from tree to tree nearby were small dots of color that calmed her mind. Life here was a struggle, but it was like a little piece of heaven as well.

They worked a few more hours, but her injuries slowed her down somewhat. Finally they were finished, and ready to head to the waterfall for a shower. The water was a little cool but was very rejuvenating.

As they returned to the settlement, Lilly called them to come for supper. The perfectly cooked meal of garden vegetables was wonderful to taste after the long day.

Later, when settling into their cozy cabin, all six of them sat gazing through the windows as the sun slowly faded over the mountains.

"Girls," said Anna Laura, "we should take our trip to Nashville as soon as the crops are in. It would be nice to see the beautiful fall colors across the state. We'll go off the mountain Saturday and speak to Hank and maybe even Jess about going next weekend. This beautiful weather is slipping away and soon it will be too cold to go."

"Do you think Bobby and Billy could go?" asked Sarah.

"I don't see why not," Anna Laura replied. "I'll pay their expenses. We'll also work with them a little more on etiquette. They've come a long way in a short time, but we want them to be comfortable among other people. I'll also buy them a couple of outfits when we go to Cherry Valley this week."

After a week of hard work, Saturday finally came. The girls and Anna Laura were up at the crack of dawn, as the roosters began to crow. They all dressed nicely and put on a little makeup then all six of them headed for the road that would lead them off the mountain. It was always a wonderful experience but even more so this time as the fall colors surrounded them. The girls felt almost like princesses as they rode through such beauty.

The young ladies were a little giddy as they got closer to town, but they always carried themselves well. Anna Laura enjoyed their giggles and the conversation which included talk of the special young men in their lives. Anna Laura was very glad these young people had found each other. Before they knew it, they had entered Cherry Valley. They met Jess at the stables and left their horses in his care then headed for Hank's office.

Hank was pleasantly surprised when the girls showed up at his office. "What brings you ladies to town? It looks like God let a few of his angels off Brushy Mountain."

Hank could hardly keep his eyes off Selena. His heart seemed to skip a few beats until he regained some control.

Anna Laura was very glad to see this connection between her two friends. "Hank, could you go to lunch with us? I think it's time I treated you."

The Hemlock Inn restaurant was as lovely as ever and the girls were very comfortable. They sat at a round table covered with mint green linen. After ordering chicken salad and sweet tea, Anna Laura got to the point just as Hank was about to ask them what had brought them to town.

Anna Laura explained that they were interested in the trip to Nashville before winter. She mentioned she would pay for the hotels and other expenses.

Hank was more than agreeable. "I believe that can be arranged." They would make the trip on the next Friday.

Hank knew the trip would do all of them good, including Billy and Bobby. He also knew that Crissy would be able to see Samuel in Nashville. It went without saying that he would enjoy spending more time with Selena.

The girls went clothes shopping for Bobby and Billy; Hank joined them to offer a man's opinion.

All too soon, they were on the way back up the mountain. The girls were very excited. Anna Laura thought about how a whole new world had opened up for these young people. It had been a glorious day they would dream about the entire week.

They walked into their cabin, thankful for so many things. Once they were in bed, Selena called out, "Anna Laura, who will ride in which car on our trip to Nashville?"

"I have been thinking about that. Crissy, Bobby, Sadie, and you can ride with Hank. Mary Jane, Billy, Sarah, and I will ride with Jess."

That was exactly what Selena wanted to hear, she was delighted she would be riding with Hank.

As the girls quieted down and went to sleep Anna Laura lay awake thinking how she could make Hank feel comfortable enough to tell her he was in love with Selena. She decided she would tell Hank she would never love anyone but Clint. That was her answer. As she drifted into sleep, Anna Laura knew God would take care of things in His time.

The day dawned bright and beautiful; the air was serene as the October clouds drifted over the mountains where the trees glowed in the morning light.

Everything was falling into place; Anna Laura lifted her hands toward the sky as she had so many times before and gave thanks that her mission was being fulfilled. She hoped that by late spring everything would be organized and she could leave. She was sure she could teach Steve, Lilly, and their niece Alifair what they would need to know to tend to the medical needs of the people. She had spoken to Alifair several times and knew the girl had a gift for healing. Anna Laura would teach her as much as she could through the winter.

They would need a pastor for the church and Sunday school teachers. A young settlement couple, Elizabeth and Carl, would be wonderful teachers she knew. She was sure there was a man somewhere that would be capable and willing to oversee the church.

She could not leave before her mission was complete and she knew God would let her know when it was finished.

Chapter 35

Anna Laura and the girls worked diligently all week long, and rested well at night. They wanted to feel they had earned their trip to Nashville.

Bobby and Billy accomplished the work of four men, lending a hand wherever Rob and Steve needed them.

When Thursday night finally arrived, the girls were in a whirlwind as they chose and packed the outfits they would need for the trip. Anna Laura knew this trip would be an adventure for all the young people.

On Friday morning, the girls headed for the waterfall to shower and dress. In the meantime, Billy and Bobby got ready for the trip as well. The clothes the girls had bought the young men suited them well. The boys saddled their horses, secured their bags, and they all met on the trail.

As they traveled along the trail, they were all very excited. The girls were very impressed to see Billy and Bobby looking so handsome in their new clothes. The two young men had come so far and worked hard to overcome their past.

When they reached Cherry Valley, they left their horses at the stables and met Hank and Jess for lunch. Soon it was time to leave.

Jess' car was a little older than Hank's, but in good condition. Sadie, Bobby, and Anna Laura took their places in the backseat and Mary Jane slid in beside Jess. In the other car, Sarah, Billy, and Crissy took the backseat so Selena could sit beside Hank. Shortly, they were finally on their way.

As the fresh air from the windows blew through their hair, the young people barely paid attention. There was so much to see! As they traveled, Jess and Anna Laura told them a little about what Nashville was like. The city sprawled out for miles, Jess told them. There were many tall buildings, department stores, and nice restaurants. There was a huge river and long bridges unlike anything in the mountains. The farms and flat land Anna Laura described were unimaginable to them. The young people could almost visualize the city from their description.

In the other car, Hank had described many of the same things to his companions, but he also told them they would be spending Saturday at the plantation. When they crossed the long bridge leading them into the city, they were filled with excitement. They arrived at the Andrew Jackson Hotel and met outside. The four gentlemen carried their luggage as they walked inside. Many of them had never seen carpets before much less antique furniture and long velvet drapes such as those that decorated the lobby. It was everything they had imagined and more

Billy, Bobby, and Jess would share a room; as would Anna Laura, Crissy and Selena. Sadie, Sarah, and Mary Jane would share another room. Hank went out to the plantation for the night, but would return in the morning.

Shortly after they settled into the rooms, there was a call for Crissy to come to the lobby. Anna Laura walked down with her. As Crissy walked into the lobby, not knowing what to expect, someone called her name.

"Crissy, Crissy."

She turned to see Lieutenant Samuel Adams walking toward her. "Lieutenant Adams, what are you doing here?"

"Please call me Samuel or Sam. Hank told me you would be arriving this evening." Adams could not stop himself from lightly embracing Crissy. He asked her if she would walk down the street for a soda and sandwich.

"That would be great, I am a little hungry."

As they walked slowly, Samuel spoke softly, "I haven't been able to get you off my mind since you gave me that drink of water before I left the mountain. I've thought of you constantly."

"Samuel, I feel the same way too."

"Crissy, I truly feel in my heart and soul that I am in love with you. I never dreamed this would happen to me; my career has always been so important."

Crissy agreed that she too had fallen in love at first sight. As they walked, they talked about their future. Crissy told Samuel about her desire to become a midwife or obstetrician. Samuel realized that Crissy was very intelligent and remembered how Anna Laura had referred to her as a prodigy. There were many colleges, including a medical school, in Nashville. He was sure in his heart he would one day marry this beautiful intelligent young lady, but he would give it time. He asked her if he could come to Brushy Mountain in the spring to see her. She happily agreed.

They continued talking as they reached the restaurant and had their meal, sharing their hopes and dreams. Afterword, Samuel walked Crissy back to the hotel, and kissed her good night. Crissy knew this was the greatest evening of her life.

When Crissy returned to the room, Anna Laura and Selena could see the joy on her face. She shared her feelings for Samuel with her friends.

The ladies were very tired from their trip and decided to turn in early.

Morning seemed to come quickly; they had rarely rested so well. After bathing in the fancy tubs, they dressed and met the men in the lobby. Hank and Samuel were waiting for them there. They decided to get breakfast at the hotel. Once they were seated and food had been served, Hank extended an invitation for them to have dinner at the plantation. He said his aunt and uncle insisted. He tempted them with the promise of great food.

"Aunt Daisy and Uncle Joe are really looking forward to this. They're very anxious to meet you."

After brunch, the girls went back to the rooms to brush their teeth and freshen up. Returning to the lobby, they headed out to the plantation. With the addition of Samuel's car, they were able to split up into groups of four in two cars and three with Samuel.

When they reached the winding road that would lead them to the huge house, the young people from Brushy Mountain were speechless. They had never seen a house so large and grand. As the three cars came up the long drive, Joe and Daisy stood on the porch. Hank was the first to get out with Anna Laura not far behind. Joe and Daisy embraced Anna Laura, they were still very fond of her and a bit confused that she was riding in a different car. Hank opened the passenger door of his car for Selena and they were stunned by her beauty. Hank introduced her to his aunt and uncle. They could tell from the look in Hank's eyes that this girl was special to him. Hank managed to introduce the rest of the group, adding a little information about each one.

The older couple invited them all inside. The young people from Brushy Mountain had never seen such a home. Just one of the small shacks most of them had grown up in would fit in this cavernous living room.

Joe suddenly announced, "You'll be staying here tonight. No need to pay for a hotel bill when you're more than welcome to stay with us."

Anna Laura could see the delight on the faces of her companions.

Daisy asked Hank to show the four men to the guest house while she had one of the maids show the ladies to their rooms. The young ladies were amazed that every room had its own bath. The views from each room were beautiful, flower gardens, trees and fountains surrounded the gorgeous, old house. They freshened up and met to go back downstairs again.

Everyone gathered back in the living room and talked while dinner was being prepared.

Daisy once again noticed the emotion passing between Hank and Selena. She suggested he take her for a buggy ride across the property. The other four couples also decided to walk around before dinner; each couple going their own way.

Crissy and Samuel chose to walk out to the corral to see the many fine horses. As they stood together, Samuel asked, "Crissy, do you think you could ever be happy living here?"

Crissy paused, remembering the mountain, her parents, and her life back home. "Samuel, time will help me to get used to the idea of leaving the mountains. I believe I could."

"One day, if we are married you can come live with me in Nashville and fulfill your dreams. Crissy, I love you, and someday hopefully you will be my wife and we will grow old together."

"Samuel, I love you too, but I want to help others on the mountain the way that Anna Laura has helped me. I must at least be there for fall, winter, and spring."

"I can accept that, Crissy, I love you enough to wait."

As Hank and Selena rode the buggy across the plantation, Selena's long black hair blew softly in the October breeze. Hank could hardly guide the horses he was so captivated by her beauty. He halted the horse and buggy near a magnolia tree then took Selena's hand.

"Selena, I love you as much as any man could love a woman. I want you to be my wife. Do you think you could be happy here? Aunt Daisy and Uncle Joe are getting up in years and I am their only kin. Someday this plantation will be mine."

"I think someday I want to become a lawyer. I know women are not a big part of the profession, but I know I can be."

"There are several good schools in this part of the state."

"Hank, I love you and will marry you, but not until spring. I am going to be needed in the mountains for a while."

"I will wait, Selena." Hank softly kissed Selena's pretty lips. She gracefully sat close to him in the buggy as they continued their tour.

Billy and Sarah walked through the many trees and flowers, smelling the fragrance of the fall air. Billy asked, "Sarah do you think we could be married in the spring?"

"Yes, Billy, but I feel in my heart we are meant to stay on the mountain and pass on what Anna Laura has taught us. I know your life was much harder than mine, and I feel the six of us, Sadie, Bobby, Jess, and Mary Jane will make many good things happen on the mountain."

Billy shyly put his arm around Sarah as they walked through the garden.

Sadie and Bobby were walking not far from Sarah and Billy having an almost identical conversation.

[201]

Billy looked at his Sarah and said, "Sarah, I am so lucky to be able to look forward to marrying someone like you. I never dreamed life could turn out this way."

Jess and Mary Jane were walking through a stand of white oaks, admiring the lovely scenery.

Suddenly, Jess asked, "Mary Jane, will you marry me in the spring? I'll probably be there on the mountain in December as we planned before. I feel our careers are going in the same direction."

"Yes, Jess, I will marry you come springtime."

As they stood among flowers, Jess gently kissed Mary Jane and told her how much he loved her.

Mary Jane thought of how much her life changed. She had grown up much differently than Jess, but knew it made no difference in how he felt about her.

"Jess, I truly love you and can see myself with you for as long as I live."

Jess smiled broadly. "Mary Jane, I believe the government will pay me to teach the children of the mountain. We'll stay as long as we're needed."

Joe and Daisy watched the couples from a distance. They too had once experienced such new love. They hugged one another thinking that very exciting times were ahead for these young people.

Anna Laura stood on the hillside above the plantation surrounded by nature's beauty. She could not help thinking of Clint.

Toward the blue sky, she said, "Dear God, if your will is for us to be together, let my mission be fulfilled on Brushy mountain by late spring. Please allow destiny to lead Clint to me or me to him. I know you have guided me this far and I know you can guide a woman's journey according to your plans for her life and I'm putting my trust in you. You're my navigator through this awesome journey."

She glanced at her watch and realized it was nearly dinnertime.
Upon reaching the plantation house, she saw everyone was there. There was
a new look on the faces of her companions which led Anna Laura to
believe serious discussions had taken place. Just knowing she had a part in
bringing such happiness to these young people settled her spirit.

The butler appeared to announce that dinner was ready and they
made their way to the dining room. The table was splendid. The men
graciously seated the ladies and then themselves. Joe and Daisy began a
pleasant conversation about the mountains and asked many questions.
They inquired about Jess and Samuel's careers as well as Bobby and Billy's
expertise in building. The young ladies were asked about their future
careers. No one was left out.

While Joe and Daisy were somewhat puzzled about Hank and Anna
Laura's relationship, they were not going to ask.

Anna Laura sensed their confusion and knew this would be a good
time to bring up Clint. Not only would it clear the issue for Daisy and Joe,
it would reassure both Hank and Selena. She briefly said what was needed.

Daisy and Joe could see more clearly now that Hank was in love
with Selena; he would definitely be given their blessing. They trusted their
nephew's choice. Daisy was sure they would have beautiful children.

After dinner, everyone moved to the huge front porch and enjoyed
the evening until darkness settled in.

By this time everyone was tired and said their good nights.

At the break of dawn, Anna Laura awoke feeling rested and
peaceful. She dressed then went quietly downstairs and out the door for a
morning walk. Sitting under a huge oak tree, she looked to the east to see
the most beautiful sunrise. She thought about the splendid weekend
everyone had experienced and was suddenly startled by something behind
her. She jumped to her feet to find Hank standing there.

"Anna Laura, I need to talk with you. I'm sure you're aware of my
love for Selena." She nodded. "I feel that I have betrayed you."

"No, Hank, you haven't betrayed anyone. You've been blessed to find love that few people find in a lifetime."

Anna Laura, do you think Daisy and Joe will accept Selena?"

"Hank, their faces light up when they see you together. They only want you to be happy."

"What about you, Anna Laura? Were you ever the least bit in love with me?"

"Hank, at one time I probably was a little. I learned very quickly that I only loved you as a friend. You're someone that God put in my path to help in fulfilling my destiny. Hank, truthfully I have never gotten over Clint and probably never will."

Hank took Anna Laura's hand. "If it had not been for you, I would never have met Selena. She's more than I ever dreamed would enter my life."

As dear friends they walked back to the house and prepared themselves for breakfast.

As they ate, Joe began to talk. "You are the finest young people I have ever met, and believe me, I have met many during my life. You're my kind of people. I like your simplicity, that you're happy being who you are and don't try to be something you are not. Each of you is so well matched as couples. It's as though you were put on Earth for each other. You remind me of Daisy and myself many years ago. Hank, we approve of your Selena. We can all see that you love and adore her. She's the only girl we want here on the plantation with you when we depart to the great beyond. Anna Laura, you're very special to us. We believe in miracles and one day you will cross paths with your Doctor Clint again."

After breakfast everyone got their things together to leave. Daisy and Joe stood on the porch watching them until they were out of sight. They had surely enjoyed their time together.

Everyone was very quiet as they traveled home, thinking of the wonderful weekend they had just experienced. Crissy and Samuel would not see each other again until spring. Selena knew she would see Hank from time to time depending on the weather this winter. Come December, Mary and Jess would be together again. Billy and Sadie and Bobby and Sarah would be going back to the mountain together.

Upon reaching Cherry Valley, they were excited to see familiar ground again. They had enjoyed their weekend away but it was good to be home. They had lunch together then headed for the stables. Everyone said their goodbyes and headed for Brushy Mountain.

It was a much quieter ride going back up the mountain than it had been coming down a few days before. As they rode into the settlement, it was as if they'd been gone away for a long time. Everyone smiled and welcomed them home.

They spent time with Lilly, Steve, and some of the neighbors telling them about their wonderful trip. Everyone enjoyed learning of the big city so far away.

Chapter 36

It was the end of October. The corn was gathered and in the cribs. Soon they would be putting up fodder for the animals. Winter was just around the corner. School would begin the week before Thanksgiving. Deciding it was time for some sort of celebration, Anna Laura suggested a pig roast. Steve and Rob knew just what to do.

It would soon be time for Anna Laura to bring out the winter clothes that she had stored. The clothing would be hauled in by horse and sled. The news of winter clothing and a pig roast was spreading fast. As usual around this part of November, Indian summer showed itself on the mountain. It was a perfect time to celebrate and receive warm clothing for the vicious winter months ahead.

The big day arrived after all the finishing touches were added to the new buildings. Excitement was mounting as this day was drawing near.

A fire was built of hickory wood and a pig prepared and hung by metal poles that would allow the men to turn the meat regularly. The ladies had prepared every mountain dish imaginable. Shuck beans, cornbread, and chicken with dumplings were just a few of the dishes that would be available. About an hour before the pork was done, the women and children carried in the food.

Anna Laura and her group were stationed in a clear area not far from the celebration. Before the festivities, everyone would come and choose clothing of the correct sizes.

At last, the dinner bell rang. Everyone headed for the food, filling their plates in an orderly fashion. There was so much food the tables had been extended with extra boards. Anna Laura was asked to say grace.

Anna Laura and her group sat in a small clearing nearby to eat. The school children gathered around and everyone talked about school and their future plans. The young mothers and fathers and some of the older folks talked about winter coming on and of harsh winters they had survived in the past. They believed they were as prepared as they could be for the winter season.

As the festive day ended, everyone headed home with their precious gifts of clothing and food. There were plenty of leftovers, so everyone was able to take roasted pork home for supper.

As Anna Laura and the girls sat in their cabin later that night, they made lesson plans for school appropriate to the different age groups. They felt they might be able to set up special times for the preschoolers to come learn socialization, their letters and numbers.

As they finished, Anna Laura said, "We must find a preacher for the church."

Selena spoke up, "I remember a man called Jeremiah that used to visit my father. He carried a King James Bible and read and talked with my father about it. He lived up in the North Woods. I just know Billy and Bobby could find him. They called him the old Reverend Jeremiah. He definitely knew how to read the Bible and did a lot of preaching on the written word.

"He used to stand on the mountain and preach. The moonshiners had no other choice but to hear him since his voice echoed from one ridge to another. Daddy and I sat outside and listened a lot. When he came to our place a few times, we enjoyed it when he talked quietly from the New Testament. He certainly enjoyed our fried chicken as a token of our appreciation."

"We'll have Billy and Bobby go find him and bring him to the church to meet Steve, Rob and the rest," Anna Laura replied.

.

Chapter 37

The coldness began to move in from the north; the higher the elevation the colder it became. Anna Laura had given out much of the winter clothing that she had in storage. She now realized they were nowhere near adequate for the harsh winter weather that was sure to hit the Brushy Mountain.

She called Billy, Bobby and the ladies together. "We must go to Cherry Valley and have Hank take us to the provider to get more clothes for those in need. Even we will need more clothes as we'll be outside a great deal."

Mary Jane spoke gently, "There are several young women expecting babies during the winter months. Crissy and Anna Laura will often be out in the cold weather and must be suitably dressed. "

"Mary Jane, that is so thoughtful of you to think of us."

Even though it was cold, the eight of them headed off the mountain to bring back more durable winter clothes for those who would face a great deal of exposure. The ground was covered with dry leaves that crunched and rustled as the horse's hooves disturbed them. The mountains looked so different now that the trees were bare, the many hemlocks, white pines and other evergreens were the only spots of color among the gray trunks and branches now.

Upon reaching Cherry Valley they were able to find Hank. To their surprise, the grant still covered as many winter clothes as they could carry back. He stuffed several burlap sacks full. After they had finished purchasing supplies, they took them to the stables; Hank asked if they could go to lunch at the Hemlock Inn. He had a surprise for Mary Jane.

"Mary Jane, I worked out something wonderful for Jess. The federally funded education program has agreed for him to come to Brushy Mountain after graduation in December. He will be a head teacher at the settlement school."

Mary Jane sat speechless, but bubbled inside like an artesian spring. Selena, Mary Jane, Sadie, and Sarah would be his assistants. Billy and Bobby would keep fires, clean, and do any heavy work as well as attend classes as time allowed. They would be able to continue their building trade whenever work was available. They would have a chance to learn math which would be important to their building trade. Anna Laura would personally work with them in math and reading

Looking out the huge window after finishing lunch, Billy exclaimed, "Look at the snow clouds!"

Anna Laura hurriedly went to the provider and loaded up on the free blankets, matches, and other items needed for emergencies. She had a feeling deep inside that the weather was about to make a drastic change.

Selena found a way to spend a few minutes with Hank before heading to the stables. "I will see you as soon as winter breaks."

Just as they were mounted and ready to leave, a few snowflakes began swirling through the air.

"We'd better get on our way!" Bobby exclaimed.

Billy agreed. "The higher we climb the harder the snow will fall; I've seen big ones in the middle of November right after Indian summer."

Hank was sad to watch Selena go out of sight. He experienced such emptiness to know it would be months before he saw her again.

About halfway up the mountain, the snow was so thick the group could hardly see. It would be dangerous to continue. The ground was covered within an hour and the horses began to act out. By this time the drifts were at least a foot tall as the snow had been coming for a while at higher elevation. Anna Laura had never seen anything like it. She remembered the cave where she and Jess had sheltered from the rain months ago, and related to Bobby and Billy where it was. There was another more spacious one very near where the horses could be stabled. Billy and Bobby had brought small bags of shelled corn for the horses; their plan was to let them rest and eat on the way back as they would be carrying a heavy load. The corn would be enough to sustain them as well as provide a little body heat. The clothes, blankets and other necessities were placed in the cave with Anna Laura and the others.

[209]

Bobby and Billy built a fire at the mouth of the cave where they would hold up for the night. Perhaps the snow would stop falling by morning and enable them to see where they were going. Once bedded down for the night, Bobby and Billy were on the side near the fire. At some point someone had left an ample supply of dry wood and they would take turns keeping the fire going through the night. They were all thankful for the blankets Anna Laura had gotten to bring back to the mountain.

As daylight crept in, Anna Laura exclaimed, "The snow has stopped! I have never seen it snow so hard I could not see through it. This is an experience I will always remember. Billy, I am so thankful that you and Bobby are with us." The young men smiled and knew they were needed

"Lilly and Steve will be worried sick."

Bobby and Billy brought the horses by twos and loaded the goods then helped the ladies mount. Then the men bound their goods to the saddles and slowly led the way through the deep snow. Anna Laura fell in line last, this way she would know the girls were safe.

As they traveled, the horses were obedient; they wanted to make it back to the settlement too. They spent hours plodding through the snow as the horses were so heavily loaded. As they reached the top of the mountain, everyone sighed with relief and gave thanks to God, their navigator. As they reached the level land to the settlement there was no cloud cover which enabled cold weather.

Steve and Lilly were anxiously pacing back and forth from the big rock fireplace to the window.

"Steve, I'm going to fry ham, bake biscuits, make redeye gravy and fry some fresh eggs. I know they'll be hungry."

"Lilly, I believe you're right."

Knowing it would take them a while to reach the settlement, Lilly knew she could have breakfast on the table when they reached the house. As they drew closer, the aroma of the food reached the noses of the eight travelers.

"Lilly, I see them!" Steve yelled, as he looked out the window. "They are fine."

The group was elated to say the least as Steve motioned them to come in. Knowing their own cabins would be cold and they were very hungry, this was more than they could have hoped for. Warmth and food were just inside the door. Tethering their horses, they walked in to see the table spread with ham, eggs, biscuits, gravy and jellies. Removing their coats, the tired young people sat at the long table near the fireplace feeling the warmth of the fire soothing their chilled bodies. They enthusiastically devoured Lilly's wonderful food.

Billy and Bobby could hardly believe this was happening to them. They had spent many winters shivering in the cold with their stomachs empty. This seemed almost unbelievable. Childhood deprivation had taught them to appreciate any act of kindness. Not one of them forgot to bow their heads and offer a silent prayer before they began to eat. They thanked Lilly and Steve for their kindness.

After the meal, they sat around the fire.

Steve asked, "Where did you stay last night to get out of the cold?"

Immediately, Bobby spoke up. "There was a cave about halfway down the mountain and the horses stayed in a larger one nearby."

"Boys, you may not believe this, but me and Rob had the same experience years ago when coming from Cherry Valley around this time of year."

"No, Steve, I believe you're mistaken. It was later in the year; it was December and a lot colder."

"I guess you're right, Lilly." Anna Laura smiled as Steve agreed with Lilly. "Our wives were worried sick when we got home."

Lilly spoke up, "I believe you were about as worried last night as we were when you and Rob were stranded."

"I can't deny that, Lilly. These young people are like my real family, you know. You all seem like my own children."

They were all deeply touched to hear those words; especially Bobby and Billy who had never known a real dad. Their expressions spoke volumes without a word coming from their mouths. Steve read their thoughts and gave a nod letting them know he truly cared for them.

Lilly sat in silence thinking how Anna Laura had changed so many lives.

"I think it's time we get going with school, church and health issues," Anna Laura stated as she looked toward Steve.

"You're right, Anna Laura, I'll get all the help you need to get the goods to the families this very day so the children can be in school."

Lilly chimed in, "We'll get the word out this evening that school will begin tomorrow."

The girls were overly anxious; they had waited so long to see the look on a learning child's face. There would be a great deal that Bobby and Billy could do to help as well. The fire would have to be built early and wood carried in, then they could get on with the learning process. They had already come a long way; Anna Laura would teach them more. These eight people were about to start on a journey that would change lives of all the youth in the mountain.

As she looked at the young girls around her, Anna Laura believed God had picked the young people that had entered her life. Even though they all suffered some sort of trauma, great changes were coming in their lives and the lives of the children of the mountain.

Lilly spoke up, "We'd better get to work there's a lot to be done."

They each thanked Lilly and Steve again for their hospitality and headed for home.

"Me and Steve will help!" Lilly called after them.

"Yeah, ten people can get a lot done!" said Steve.

A new day was about to dawn over Brushy mountain.

Anna Laura's thoughts extended far beyond the settlement. She would bring those in the higher mountains down before she left the mountain, she was sure of that. She had a way of putting words and thoughts into action. She believed all things were possible with God's help.

Chapter 38

The settlers began to offer their help; it seemed there was a job for everyone. There were so many ways they could be involved as a community. In the early 30s, fruit jars were available on the mountain. They now had more and more ways to store food so there was less worry about starvation in the settlement. Anna Laura worried about those who lived beyond the settlement, how would they survive?

The church, the school, and the medical office were all up and running. Everyone was so happy with this new addition to life on Brushy Mountain; the children especially were bursting with anticipation. News had traveled by word of mouth that there would be a meeting at the church house since it was the largest building.

Anna Laura took the stage. "Ladies, gentlemen, and children, I want to thank all of you for your physical labor as well as your moral support. Tomorrow all the children will be in school. Sunday morning at 10 o'clock, Reverend Jeremiah will conduct our church services." There were a few whispers around the room as some did not know Jeremiah. "We will also choose Sunday school teachers today before we leave."

Joel raised his hand as he had been taught by his parents. "What is Sunday school?"

"Joel, at Sunday school you will learn about Jesus and his miracles as well as about the men who followed him called his disciples. You will learn many beautiful Bible stories that little boys and girls need to know. You will learn how God provides when there seems to be no way."

"I believe Jesus has already helped Susie and me," whispered Joel. Around him tears could be seen in many eyes.

Susie spoke up, "Who will teach us at school and what will we learn?"

"Remember, Susie, the day of the pig roast," asked Anna Laura. "Selena, Sadie, Sarah, Crissy, Mary Jane, and me told you how we would be teaching."

"Oh, yes, now I remember. What will we learn? "

"You'll learn how to read enough to know about other countries, towns and cities that lay beyond these mountains." The older people in the audience had looks on their faces that said they had silently yearned for the same thing. Anna Laura made it clear to all the parents that paper, pencils, readers, spellers and arithmetic books would be available for everyone thanks to the government grants.

Anna Laura turned toward Steve. "Do you have anything to add?"

Steve stood to his feet. "Everybody here should be thankful that this woman filled with love for the people has come to this mountain to try and make life easier for our young people and even the older ones, that change will come to this mountain, and one day the children will grow up and desire to leave. This wonderful woman is preparing them for that day. She's preparing all of us the same way."

After Steve finished, Anna Laura announced that the children could tour the school if they should want to. She also added that school would begin at nine o'clock the next morning.

"Remember, school is not only for children. Adults are welcome too, that's why we built an extra room." Of course that one was a little bit smaller. "Remember also, on Sunday morning we'll meet at the church and give praise for all the good that God has done for us."

Everyone clapped their hands.

Bobby was at the back of the building and suddenly spoke out. "Anna Laura, when I was a boy wandering the mountains with no place to go, I used to sit near the last cabin on the east side and listen to the most beautiful voice I ever heard. As mean as I was, I took time out to sit in all kinds of weather. Bobby did too. Victoria and Luke lived in the cabin. Victoria sounded like I imagine angels will sound. My favorite song was 'Amazing Grace'. Being orphan boys, mine and Bobby's lives were hardened by the knocks life gave us but that voice and the words to those songs humbled Bobby and me. I know we did some bad stuff when Anna Laura came to the mountain and we're ashamed, but she has forgiven us and just taught us so much. What I'm trying to say is those songs are filled with meaning that had already set a place on hearts to know that everything

[214]

couldn't be bad. It took us a while but we have changed and learned so much good from Anna Laura's teachings. We are miracles. You think Victoria could sing in church on Sunday?" he asked.

"Would you, Victoria?" Anna Laura asked.

Victoria nodded with tears in her eyes. "Yes, I will sing in church come Sunday."

The others stood up and told of their own life changing experience and how God loved the mountain people enough that He sent someone to help bring hope and change.

Finally Steve stood on his feet. "Does anyone else have anything to say? If not we will go home and pray that school goes well tomorrow and the moms and dads trust all these wonderful people to care for and teach their children."

Anna Laura and the girls were looking forward to resting in the coziness of their home. Billy and Bobby had gone ahead to be sure the fire was ready to take the November chill from the air. Sadie and Sarah insisted they stay for supper.

That night Bobby and Billy felt so blessed. As they lay down to sleep in their cabin, they remembered the previous winter of struggling to stay warm and thought of being called rock head and cold tater only a few months ago. In time, they would be completely healed from the shame they had faced in their earlier years. Most encouraging to them was that Anna Laura helped them realize that they had innate abilities that were normal and their problems were not impossible to overcome. She helped them believe that their only real problem was a lack of normality as they grew up.

Daylight filtered over the mountain and feet hit cold floors as fires began to diminish the chill. This would be the first day of school that included every child of all ages in the settlement. Eight-thirty came, and many children and teens gathered from all directions. The air was extremely cold but the kids were all dressed warmly enough. As they walked together talking, their breaths swirled into a fog that surrounded them. The children were so excited they purposely blew out their breaths into the cold air. The closer they got to school, the faster they walked or skipped.

Upon reaching the schoolhouse steps, Joel spoke up pleasantly. "Let's get in line and walk in as quiet as we can. That's what my dad and mom said to do." It was very obvious Joel and Susie were going to be good influences on the others; their new parents had taught them well.

Little Erma was also going to be a positive influence; she could talk a mad dog into being calm or an angry person into humbleness. There was something very special about this child.

Anna Laura, the girls, Billy and Bobby greeted the children as they entered and directed them to their assigned seats on the benches and tables. Their names were written on rough tablet paper and taped in front of where they would work. After learning to write the alphabet, they would learn to spell their names. It definitely would not take long for them to recognize their names.

Anna Laura began by asking the children their names. After that, they recited the Lord's Prayer and next she taught them to sing 'Jesus loves me.' Later she would teach them short Bible verses and other short songs that would enhance their imagination; they would also learn traditional children's songs like 'All around the Mulberry Bush.' To help with any shyness, she would also have them recite short Bible verses.

Unbelievably, forty children had shown up the first day; Sadie was amazed after counting them. Selena passed out the alphabet books. There were ten children at each table. Sadie and Sarah took a table together; Crissy, Selena, and Mary Jane would instruct ten children each. Anna Laura, Bobby and Billy would help wherever needed.

Today the children would learn their first three letters. The children learned to print the letters, and they would add more each day until they mastered the entire alphabet. As many children as there were, there were still empty chairs. Hopefully more children would come in the days ahead.

After about a week, adults showed up. They too wanted to learn to read and write.

Not long before Christmas, the children mastered their alphabet. Now was the time for some fun. The children would be introduced to a Christmas play. Anna Laura remembered well the Nativity scenes performed every Christmas at the little church in the Valley of Sampson. There would be a place for all the children as she could use as many as she wanted for angels and of course Erma would be the angel of the Lord; her white-blond curly hair would be perfect for the part and she would be able to say the lines. Shepherds, wise men, Joseph and Mary would be special parts as well. They would practice the play in the church. Even the preschoolers could take part.

Costumes could be made from muslin cloth for the angels with flexible wire to shape wings. Glenna, Fannie, Ruthie, Liddie, and other women in the settlement that were good at sewing would help them prepare for the play. The men would deck the church with holly bows with lots of red berries in clusters. Soft hemlock boughs could also be used around the doors, windows and stage. The most work would go into accommodating forty children. It could be done even though Christmas was not too far away. Anna Laura had some candles of red, white, and green for a special occasion in storage. They would be arranged in special places throughout the church. Bobby and Billy would bring a hemlock in for a Christmas tree. Sadie, Mary Jane, Crissy, Sarah, and Selena would direct the children in making decorations of paper chains, bows, and strands of holly berries. They could color the chains with crayons.

Steve, Rob, Bobby, Billy, and other men from the settlement who were good with woodwork were going to carve a toy for every child and extras in case they were needed. Anna Laura also had colorful tissue paper stored away that would be used for wrapping the gifts. Giving the children as many of these jobs as possible would encourage them to work hard in school before the Christmas break. As word spread of the play, old and young alike were filled with the spirit of Christmas. There had never been anything like this on the mountain.

As Christmas break began, play practice would start. Everyone worked hard getting ready for the big event.

"We must all work together," Anna Laura explained. "We'll make a beautiful Christmas happen on Brushy Mountain. One that will forever be remembered and become a tradition from year to year."

The children were excited and promised to be on their best behavior as they got ready for the play.

To everyone's surprise, Anna Laura sent Billy and Bobby off the mountain with the narrow wagon to purchase dolls and little trucks and even colorful wrapping paper for the forty students and the preschoolers. Even the babies would get colored rattles. Bobby, Billy, Sarah, and Sadie would be in charge of wrapping the presents. They would also wrap extra in case the children from higher on the mountain showed up.

Anna Laura had noticed a couple of young boys lurking around the schoolhouse trying to listen, but they always ran away when she tried approaching them. One day soon she would have Bobby and Billy ride into the higher ridges with her to find out where the children lived. When she asked Billy and Bobby about it they looked worried.

"Anna Laura, we will but it may be dangerous. These people are like we were in the beginning; they don't take to strangers."

"We must have faith that God will allow us to help others," said Anna Laura. "Surely He will shield us. We may have a battle but we will come out winners."

The entire settlement took part in preparations for Christmas. The costume makers met at different homes with patterns that Anna Laura and Lilly had cut for them to follow. Lilly would be the overseer; she could go from house to house giving instructions where needed. Everyone loved Lilly; she was a pillar of the community.

Things were going well but Anna Laura could not get her mind off the people high on the ridges battling cold and hunger.

"If we can get the hurting people to listen as we talk, perhaps they will become motivated to bring the children off higher ground. It's possible they may want to go to school. Eventually they could build cabins at the edge of the clearings of the settlement. They could clear more land for crops. I really feel the settlers would help them in getting started. We must try; I cannot leave this mountain knowing there are people suffering."

"You're right, Anna Laura. Where would Billy and me be if you hadn't cared? We must care about others too," Bobby said. They all agreed to go up the mountain on Saturday.

Gathering her assistants together, Anna Laura enthusiastically told them, "Young ladies and gentlemen, we have a new assignment. With the help of God and our guardian angels, we will find time and strength. We're going to have the best winter ever. It may not be easy, there may be unexpected incidents from time to time, but you are strong mountain men and women. You are no longer boys and girls; in the mountains, when you turn eighteen you are men and women."

Each of them smiled proudly as they knew Anna Laura spoke only with truth.

Saturday came quickly. Anna Laura, Billy, and Bobby dressed warmly, fed their horses, then saddled up for the climb. Uncertain how it would come out, they were nonetheless ready for a new adventure. The higher they went up the mountain, the colder it was, but they were all used to the cold.

Arriving at the first shack, Anna Laura knocked on the door. As the door cracked open, she was staring into the barrel of a shotgun. Holding the gun was a thin man with a beard. Behind him stood a young woman that would probably be pretty if cleaned and groomed. A little boy stood off to the side. Behind them were two little girls who were close in age, and almost looked like identical twins with their beautiful fragile faces and curly blond hair. They appeared to be around six or seven years old and the boy around four or five. They all looked sad and undernourished. Anna Laura's heart immediately wept for them.

"Please put the gun down, we want to help you. I am Anna Laura; I came to the settlement several months ago. With the help of others, we've been able to get a school started. Since Christmas is soon coming, we are having a special event for the children. Would you bring your children down for Christmas Eve?" The children's faces lit up. They must have been imagining what it would be like.

The man lay the gun down; he was a humble man but trapped not knowing which way to turn. He had never known anything except a harsh way of life. He looked at his wife and asked, "What you think, Esther?"

Like the children, Esther also looked excited in her tired way. "I'd sure like that, Isaiah, and the children would too."

Anna Laura believed in her heart this was a real beginning. "Isaiah, would you and Esther help us to talk to others up here?"

"Ma'am, we sure will."

Isaiah went to five families with Anna Laura, Bobby, and Billy. It turned out these were the only families remaining on the mountain. It was getting dark; this was as far as they could go before it would be too late to come off the mountain. What a glorious day it had been, all the families agreed to come down to lower ground.

Billy, Bobby, and Anna Laura went down the mountain filled with joy. "Boys, I was a little scared when I saw the barrel of that gun. I wondered if I would leave Brushy Mountain alive!" The boys laughed just a little. Hearing this from brave Anna Laura was a little funny.

"Now, Anna Laura, you said God would go before us and He did," Billy replied.

"I know, Billy, but he also teaches us that laughter is good for the soul. I was happy to see you laugh a little, I also know we're human and our faith does waver at times and mine did a bit. I could hear my heart pounding."

Billy still grinned like an opossum as he thought of the look on Anna Laura's face when she stared at the barrel of the shotgun. They reached the Valley at dusk and, of course, Lilly and Steve were pacing the floor. After a good supper, they went to bed.

Anna Laura counted the number of people they had met on the ridges. There were ten adults and eleven children. How were they going to get twenty-one people off the mountain before the blizzards set in? Where would they live? She thought of the outbuildings on each farm that were far warmer and in better condition than the ramshackle houses on the mountain. The biggest problem would be heating the buildings. She had faith that Steve and the other men would figure that problem out. A miracle could happen, perhaps close kin would move in together and loan a few cabins until spring. When spring came, they could camp like Anna Laura did, even at the same place until cabins were built. She knew the settlers were caring and helpful.

She would call a meeting the next day and hopefully it could be worked out before Christmas. Anna Laura prayed the rest of the night. A still voice spoke in her mind, "I will give you the desires of your heart, miracles still happen." Anna Laura knew this act of kindness from the settlers would be a miracle and believed it would come to pass. She finally fell asleep toward the end of the night.

Chapter 39

A new day had emerged. Anna Laura related her ideas to the men of the settlement. The settlers began emptying their buildings and putting their goods in the barns. All week long the men carried rock and clay even though fires had to be built near the clay banks to soften the earth. By Saturday, all five buildings had working fireplaces. It was a hard job and took a lot of manpower.

On Saturday morning, one week away from Christmas, settlers headed to higher ground to bring the last of the suffering people down. Anna Laura, Billy, and Bobby went along. As they rounded families up, Anna Laura could see how excited they were to know they were going to a different world even though it was not that far away.

She was fascinated when one couple said, "Come on in." Anna Laura recognized their two children as being the boys she had seen hiding behind the schoolhouse listening. This really made her day.

At times the journey seemed long; Anna Laura could see the anticipation of the children. They didn't know what to expect. Tears filled her eyes more than once as she saw all the children shivering from the cold, their clothing too thin to warm them. She knew she had clothes stored at the settlement that would fit them and keep them warm.

The men remaining at the settlement had built fires; the buildings were cleaned by the women and ready for the new families. How wonderful this would feel for the five families, the last of the forgotten people from the mountain ridges. Cold wind was rising as snow began to fall; they had arrived just in time to escape the bitter cold. All the women had cooked and brought out food to each of the buildings. They had also brought small tables from their canning sheds to set the food on and benches were brought as well. Knowing the newcomers would likely only have bedcovers and a few clothes, women brought in two feather beds for each family. Dishes, sheets, cookware, and silverware were also donated. Anna Laura had extra blankets in storage that would probably be needed. Dried and preserved food was brought to each cabin as well.

Isaiah and Esther and their three children decided that Esther would sleep with the girls and Isaiah with the boy for the time being. The little girls, Ruby and Judy, were happier than they had ever been. The word 'school' had brought tears to their eyes until they finally fell asleep. Jasper, their son, was happily cuddled up with his dad. They had a wonderful night's sleep, their stomachs full and their bodies warm.

The other four families were just as happy. The adults were pleased that they would be able to feed their families for the winter. The good people of the settlement would give their family a chance the mountain never would. They all gave thanks to God for sending the stranger and her unusual horse to bring them to this safer place.

Sunday morning came quickly, everyone would be at church. The newcomers to the settlement were some of the first to set foot inside.

Jeremiah taught a beautiful lesson about the mercy of God. Victoria sang like only she could. The notes of 'Amazing Grace' floated over the mountain. Elizabeth and Carl taught the younger children while the teenagers stayed with the older ladies and gentlemen.

As soon as church ended, Anna Laura asked if anyone else was in need of more warm clothing and led them to the extra room. The new children were elated as they and their parents were given boots, socks, underwear and other clothing. This was like Christmas before it even came! They all left quickly with their parents to try on their new clothes. For them this was a glorious day.

After dressing warmly, the new settler men headed outside to chop wood while the mothers cooked. They had no desire to be deadbeats. They wanted to be hard workers and not disappoint anyone, especially Anna Laura. Later that day, Anna Laura came by and led the children, now dressed in their new, warm clothing, to the schoolhouse. She wanted them to be comfortable their first day of school. "Boys and girls," she told them, "you can also come practice at the church for the Christmas play. I know you'll enjoy being in the play on Christmas Eve."

[223]

On Monday morning, Anna Laura walked across the barren ground. She came upon a graveyard marked with the rocks taken from the large streams nearby. She noticed many small graves which made her think of how pale and skinny many of the settlement children were. She wondered what could have caused the death of so many young people. When she went back to the medical building, she scanned her medical books over and over. She thought about the flies that lived on food in the summer; this might not be the reason for parasites but could cause other illnesses. She had already planned a trip to the Valley to bring back Christmas treats so she could also pick up medicine for the mountain people and herself.

Along with Bobby and Billy, Anna Laura headed off the mountain the next day.

On the way down the mountain, Anna Laura explained to Billy and Bobby, "so many children are pale and thin; at least seven out of ten. Have you ever noticed how many small graves there are in the cemetery?"

"No," Billy answered, "I guess we've always been used to seeing the children as they are and thought nothing of it. When we heard about deaths we always thought it was from some type of fever."

"Most of it was I'm sure," Anna Laura responded.

In Cherry Valley, Anna Laura went to Hank's office. She explained the situation with the children. After getting the medicine, the group loaded the small wagon with oranges and small candies. Before they left, Hank could not resist asking about Selena.

"Hank, Selena is doing wonderfully and looks forward to seeing you."

"Tell Selena I love her and I will see her in the spring."

Anna Laura promised she would pass the message along. She was happy for her friends and glad to have a friend like Hank.

Their return trip went well; they reached the old campsite in time to store the oranges and candies in the cave. Fruit would not spoil there since the air was fresh and cool but not freezing.

Anna Laura called a meeting at the church for ten o'clock Wednesday morning. She explained about the parasites and that she had brought back medicine to help keep them and their children healthy. Anna Laura also promised screen to cover the windows and doors, and the women smiled at the thought of no more flies in their homes.

Chapter 40

Christmas was near. Practice for the play was going well. Since it was only two days away, the men began decking the church with holly and hemlock. Costumes were finished. The best thing was that the children, after only three days taking medicine were already feeling better and their appetites were increasing.

Christmas Eve arrived. Everything was ready. With the whole community working together, there was no way this would not happen.

Joel and Susie were dressed as Mary and Joseph, Hattie and John's baby was a month old and was laid in the manger as baby Jesus. The angels were in their assigned places and formed a semicircle on the stage. The wise men and shepherds came down the aisle to where Mary, Joseph, and baby Jesus waited. Erma, the Angel of the Lord, came and spoke, "Lo, I am the Angel of the Lord and bring good tidings of great joy!"

Making the scene complete, a choir of boys sang 'Away in a Manger.' Selena and Victoria had been working with them for weeks. The candles and decorations were breathtaking. The glow of candlelight was so cozy the people could have sat among them for days.

Anna Laura had made Steve a Santa suit from red and white material she had purchased back in November. Wrapped gifts lay beneath the Christmas tree. There were piles of them and, of course, the children had been tempted from the moment their eyes lit upon them.

Steve burst through the back door with a huge sack of oranges and candy so big he could hardly carry it. He made it to the tree by the fireplace, sat down, and began passing out presents. The children hugged him and thanked him; they had never experienced anything like this.

"Now, boys and girls, I have something really special for you." The children were so busy opening their gifts that it took a moment for their minds to register that there was more. Bobby, Billy, and the young ladies had put oranges and candy in paper bags for each child and adult.

What a glorious Christmas Eve this was! As everyone walked home, the stars were shining and the moon lit their way. The night was clear and cold, but everyone was dressed warmly enough. Steve, Lilly, Crissy, Sadie, Sarah, Mary Jane, Selena, Billy, and Bobby stayed to help put the church back in order. They would leave the decorations for a few days. Even though Christmas was on Sunday, everyone gathered as Jeremiah spoke from the book of Luke about the birth of Jesus.

Every family prepared a wonderful Christmas dinner. The children played with their toys and enjoyed a special treat after church.

Anna Laura and her group spent the rest of the day with Steve and Lilly. The women helped Lilly cook knowing she was tired after all the preparations for the Christmas play.

"I thank you, Jesus, for the joy You have brought to the people in Brushy Mountain," Anna Laura prayed before they began to eat. "I know You have smiled when looking on their faces in church during the play. Jesus, I know You are looking down on every person on this mountain and know their destiny is in Your hands. I trust You will guide their lives in future years. If they leave this mountain one day, I pray Your blessings on them wherever they go. Amen."

After eating and enjoying a time of fellowship, talking about how perfect Christmas Eve had been and how thankful they were that five new families were not alone, cold, and hungry on the ridge tops but were now in the presence of people who had already come to love them.

Suddenly there was quiet at the table. Billy spoke up, "Bobby and I have something to say."

"Feel free to speak what's on your mind," Steve replied.

After a few minutes of silence, Bobby shyly spoke, "Sadie, Sarah, Bobby, and me will be getting married when springtime comes."

Congratulations echoed from one end of the long cherry table to the other. Sadie and Sarah's faces glowed almost as brightly as the candles in the church the night before and everyone was smiling.

"Let's pitch in and help Lilly clean up; I know both she and Steve are tired," Anna Laura suggested.

[227]

After cleaning up, Anna Laura and the young ladies headed to their cabin and Billy and Bobby to theirs.

Lying beneath her mother's quilt, Anna Laura stared through her small window as snowflakes began to fall. It was a beautiful sight to behold as the flakes swirled in open spaces lit up by the moon. She wondered what was happening with Clint as she felt a hint of sadness.

At that very moment, he was contemplating the announcement of his engagement to a lady from a Royal family later that day. When evening came in Germany, Clint announced his engagement at a Royal gathering. Standing in silence after the announcement, he couldn't help thinking sadly that this should have been Anna Laura beside him. But his life had to continue and he had no choice but to conform to the wishes of his family. His marriage would take place on June 20th of the coming year.

Back on Brushy Mountain, Anna Laura wiped the tears from her face, turned back to the beautiful scene outside, and fell asleep.

The day after Christmas, the snow was ten inches deep as daylight came. Everyone was snuggled comfortably in their homes still reliving the wonderful Christmas they had experienced. It was something they would remember for years to come. Fires glowed in their homes, as the blanket of white covered the mountain bringing serenity to everyone.

The only movement was the men trudging around in the snow to feed livestock and bring in wood. They gathered eggs from the chicken coops to prevent them from freezing and bursting.

Anna Laura and the girls had not yet exchanged gifts. Each had crocheted beautiful hats, scarves, and gloves for each other. Sadie and Sarah had also made scarves for Bobby and Billy. The boys came by to bring in wood and the girls presented their gifts. The young men were overwhelmed; these were the first gifts they had received since their grandmother, Maudie, passed away.

Selena asked, "Anna Laura, what were your Christmases like when you were young?"

"Since momma was gone, daddy did everything he could. He mostly gave me money. I hid it away for my future, that way my stepmother didn't know. We had special food; daddy always killed a wild turkey. Stepmother did a lot of baking; I have to say she was a very good cook. Christmas was okay, but I was always sad remembering Christmas with momma. I suppose being loved is the most important gift. Momma made special things for me; a ragdoll was my favorite gift. Daddy always got special candy from the sawmill office where he worked. Everything changed when momma died, a part of the excitement that lived in my heart also died. My dreams for my future were enough to sustain me through the holidays as well as other days.

"Momma taught me at an early age when my personality was being formed that without a dream we would all perish. She wanted me to dream of heaven but of my future as well. Many times I dreamed of past Christmases which made the present ones more real for me. I could feel the presence of my mother's spirit if I thought those thoughts."

Selena told how her dad always brought in a tree and stood it in the corner, always managing to put some type of gift beneath it for her, sometimes beaded jewelry or other things.

The others had a few memories except for Mary Jane. Her memories were always of being left out. This did not leave her bitter; she never failed to count her blessings. "God has made up for all the bad by putting Jess in my life."

"Mary Jane, I feel the same way. God has made up for the hard times in my life by putting Samuel in my life," Crissy responded.

Sadie spoke up, "Sarah and I never dreamed Billy and Bobby would be transformed into two tall handsome hard-working men with tender hearts. And in six months they will be our husbands. God has truly blessed us."

Selena said softly, "Hank is more than I ever dreamed could enter my life. I am so happy that the two of you were only friends, Anna Laura."

Crissy turned to Anna Laura. "You still love Dr. Clint? Do you think you will ever see him again?"

"I still love him, Crissy, but he most likely has found someone else by now. It's been eleven months since I left Germany." Anna Laura's eyes welled up with tears. This touched the hearts of the young women; they almost felt guilty for being so happy. They sat in silence thinking where they would be if it wasn't for this woman who so often put others before herself. One by one they told her their life changing experiences would not have come about without her. That slowed the tears falling from Anna Laura's eyes as she smiled.

Sadie and Sarah made fresh biscuits and brought out the fresh strawberry preserves that Lilly had put up the past summer. They ate then sang Christmas carols. Suddenly Selena began to sing a song she had written about Christmas in the snow on Brushy Mountain; she had a beautiful clear voice. Crissy read about the birth of Jesus from the Bible. This was a special morning, their time of true celebration for themselves.

"No more tears," Anna Laura said at last. "Let's get dressed and take a walk in the snow, when we return we'll feed the birds. The red ones are so beautiful, the males are as red as red can be. It never ceases to amaze me how they take care of the females. This is probably the best Christmas season I have ever experienced!"

The eight of them waded through the snow enjoying the feelings of happiness radiating from every home. As they walked, children and young adults began to emerge carrying boards with thick pieces of wood nailed to the lower end to brace their feet in order to slide down the hills; they named them "scootie boards." The eight of them joined in, taking turns sledding with the children.

The day was spent filled with laughter. Everyone went to their homes feeling peaceful. The mountains were so still one could almost imagine hearing heavenly angels singing. Anna Laura lay down on her bed as darkness fell, looking at the Eastern Star through her small window. She quietly prayed, giving thanks again for all that God had allowed her to experience on Brushy Mountain.

Chapter 41

With Christmas now over, everyone was getting back to work and school. One day around noon, Anna Laura left school and dropped by to check on Steve and Lilly. Sitting by the fire, Steve looked at Anna Laura.

"I've got a feeling in my bones; this is going to be one of the worst winters we have ever seen. I know it will not stop what you're doing. There are babies due this winter, but you will have no problem getting to mothers when time comes for delivery."

Anna Laura nodded. "Lilly, when you can I want you to go with Crissy and me to deliver babies. Crissy is learning fast to be a midwife and I know she will one day be more than a midwife. I think you can be a great mentor for her."

Lilly nodded her agreement and Steve spoke up again. "We'll make it fine through the winter as long as we use our God-given abilities."

As winter progressed, there was snowfall after snowfall. The able men of the settlement volunteered to shovel paths and school continued. Church was in session every Sunday and Jeremiah preached really hard and was clearly an excellent teacher. Many gave their hearts to God, both young and old. Selena put together a children's choir and they sang like angels under her direction.

There were a couple of deaths in early winter. Old man Bill was one hundred years old and old man Truman was ninety-eight. They both had viral pneumonia and Anna Laura could not save them. The funerals were difficult but mountain people were survivors and managed. Everyone spoke about how wonderful Bill and Truman had been. Hearts were touched. Old man Jasper added a little comedy telling how Truman had cut a grape vine almost in two and asked everyone to see who could make it to the vine first and swing out over the big waterhole. Of course Bill went first, the vine broke and he nearly drowned in the waterhole.

On another occasion Truman had taken a powerful laxative tea just before he and a bunch of boys went scouting in the mountains. As they were walking, he stopped. "Now all you Fellers get under this tree and I will climb the Mulberry tree and shake off those big juicy berries." Once in the tree, he yelled "here they come" and everyone bent over to pick them up. But what fell from the tree was not berries. To say the least, the boys were in a hurry to find the nearest waterhole. Truman did not come down until everyone was gone and did not show himself for weeks.

As he got older, Truman got away from his devious ways and became a more serious man. His good deeds were spoken of far and wide. Myrtle Jones told about how her baby lay on a quilt as she worked in her garden one day. Truman happened to be passing by and saw a rattlesnake near the baby. Truman got a rock, got close to the snake, and smashed its head.

Many stories were also told about how old man Bill was always helping people in need.

Not long after the burials, a flu epidemic broke out. School had to be closed for a couple of weeks. Anna Laura and her team nursed everyone back to good health, thankfully there were no deaths. Everyone worked together to take care of the elderly and sick. These mountain people were true survivors.

Once school was back in session, Anna Laura and her group were amazed at how quickly the children were learning. Anna Laura likened them to dry sponges soaking in water.

Mary Jane was getting a little uneasy because Jess had not made it to the mountain yet, but she knew he was smart enough to wait until it was safe to travel. On the first of February he was there. He paid Billy and Bobby to board with them a while, knowing they could use the money as well as the company. Mary Jane was elated when Jess became the head teacher.

Chapter 42

Spring was in the air, the melt was taking place very fast. The melting snow raised the level of the many streams and water was running high on the banks. Birds were beginning to sing their mountain melodies again. Children were shedding their winter clothing as they skipped to school. By the end of March, the trees were beginning to bud; dogwoods, redbuds, and sarvis would soon be in full bloom. The fields were being turned with plows to prepare for early crops. The mountain people sat on their porches cutting seed potatoes, sharing pea seeds, and other garden starters for early planting.

As they worked, Steve talked about the past winter saying it was the worst he had seen since 1910. They were lucky the livestock survived and that only two deaths had occurred. Things were so much better now that Anna Laura and her group were on the mountain.

The children at school really liked Jess and wanted him to stay on the mountain. Even little Erma spoke out one day telling Jess was the best teacher they had ever had. This was very fulfilling for Jess and he was very glad he had been led to major in education. He was amazed at the innate ability of the mountain children; they just needed a chance. Life was not perfect in the mountains, but illiteracy was disappearing.

Early one morning, Anna Laura sat sipping coffee while the others slept. She thought back to a year ago when she had first come to the mountain, remembering where she had set up camp. She wanted to return there again. Walking outside, she saddled her Arabian and rode out into the mountains.

Riding slowly, Anna Laura entered her small utopia and dismounted. She walked through the spring wildflowers and dogwood saplings thinking only God could create such beauty. She was filled with joy; it was almost as if the happy feeling in her heart would burst right out.

Listing to the rippling water of the stream running down the mountain, she looked toward the blue sky and asked, "God, is my mission here almost complete?"

A gentle voice in her heart spoke, "Anna Laura, it won't be long until you will be leaving these mountains. You are one of my special people that I sent here to change lives. You see, everyone is important to me but I must have people to use on Earth. I sent you here to help change lives; I love these people just as I love the most educated, the most wealthy or the most prominent. Thanks to your endeavors, generations to come will know you could only have been sent by me to accomplish so much in fifteen months by the time you leave the mountain."

Anna Laura realized at that moment she would only be there two or three more months. Looking toward the east, she felt empty inside thinking that one day soon she would depart from those she loved so much. Tears slid down her face as she remembered how she met Selena, Crissy, Sadie, Sarah, Mary Jane, Billy, and Bobby. She knew leaving them would feel as though she was leaving part of her spirit behind. Walking toward the falls where she had bathed so many times before, Anna Laura stood on a flat rock, her long dark hair flowing away from her face. As the gentle wind spoke to the mountains and the rays of the sun filtered through the trees, she stood as tall and beautiful as she had when arriving a year ago.

Her thoughts seemed to cover a million miles as she stood thinking of everything she had encountered over the past year. She wondered if someday these mountains would be empty as the older generation passed away and the younger ones went off to find a new life away from the mountains. She was sad thinking so much beauty would be left behind, but also remembered the hard work it had taken to live among this beauty.

Chapter 43

Heading back towards the settlement, Anna Laura could hear the sound of cowbells as cows returned home to be milked. Bees buzzed in the trees industriously making the sweet honey she enjoyed so much. In the distance, she could hear horses neighing, hens cackling as they laid eggs, and familiar voices calling gee and haw to their horses or mules as they plowed the fields. Most beautiful of all was the laughter of the children as they walked to school. She held the sounds close to her heart, wanting them to remain in her mind forever.

At school the children were learning about faraway places, giving them a taste of what lay beyond the mountains. Their progress so far had been unbelievable; the basics of reading, writing, and arithmetic had worked wonders giving the children a foundation for continued learning. Little by little, Anna Laura had brought books and arranged a small library in the extra room so the children would have access to reading at different times. By the end of May, school would end and the children would go to work helping their parents prepare and preserve food for the coming year.

Riding up to the schoolhouse, Anna Laura dismounted and eased into the classroom. She had brought back a bouquet of wildflowers and sat them on the teacher's desk, making the children smile.

Later, Anna Laura and the girls sat at the supper table. They were all yearning for a trip off the mountain to Cherry Valley. Anna Laura could read between the lines.

"Selena, I know it's about time for Hank to come on the mountain. I have a better idea, why don't we surprise him?"

Selena smiled, her entire face and her ebony eyes sparkled. If the weather permitted, they would head to Cherry Valley the following Saturday.

Mary Jane wondered if Jess, Bobby and Billy would come along. Crissy wished Samuel could be there, but knew it was impossible. Sadie and Sarah were perfectly happy knowing Bobby and Billy would be present.

The following week was very busy. Between teaching and medical examinations and gathering records from testing the children with the parasite medicine, days were very full. After hours of testing, Anna Laura was able to verify everyone was now clear of the parasites. These records would be kept in her office, and random testing conducted regularly from now on.

Jess also began compiling records on the children's academic progress. These records would also be stored in Anna Laura's office. They were all amazed at how well the children were doing.

Chapter 44

Friday, after the school day ended, Anna Laura, Selena, Sarah, Sadie, Mary Jane, Crissy, Jess, Bobby, and Billy prepared to leave for Cherry Valley early the next morning. Anna Laura let Steve and Lilly know they would be spending the night. She wanted to surprise the girls so she had not told them yet, packing extra clothing and sleep wear for them. She told the young men they would be staying over and warned them not to tell the girls.

Saturday morning found them riding off the mountain toward Cherry Valley. True to its name, the abundant cherry trees were in full bloom. The hemlocks did not bloom, but always had a light green tuft on the tips of their branches. It seemed strange for them to ride to the town stable and allow someone else to care for the horses.

Mary Jane asked permission to walk out by the lake with Jess. Sarah and Sadie also asked if they could walk over to the old Gristmill with Bobby and Billy. Town life was fascinating to them.

Noticing Crissy was a little sad, Anna Laura said, "Crissy, come with me and Selena to Hank's office. He works half a day on Saturday so I have a feeling he'll be there today."

Selena's eyes sparkled. She had dressed in a pretty purple blouse just in case she might see Hank. Reaching Hank's office, Selena looked disappointed when no one answered the knock at the door. Anna Laura knocked a little harder, and Hank appeared at the door. He was clearly shocked to see Selena standing before him.

After everyone said hello, Anna Laura asked, "Hank, could you excuse Crissy and me? We need to pick up a few more rolls of screen for the doors and windows in the cabins of the settlement."

"Wait a second, Anna Laura. I will give you a voucher saying the screen is vital for health issues."

"This is wonderful! I'll use the money I had for screen so we can spend the night at the Hemlock Inn."

Crissy smiled, she loved staying at the Inn.

As soon as Anna Laura and Crissy left, Hank turned to face Selena. "Selena, I love you more than you'll ever know."

"What about Anna Laura?" Selena still worried that Anna Laura might care for Hank.

"Selena, you are my God-given destiny for the rest of my life. Anna Laura loves Dr. Clint."

"I have never loved anyone as I do you. You are everything to me. Hank, but I love Anna Laura so much; I would never want to hurt her."

"Selena, you must stop worrying. Anna Laura doesn't love me. We are only friends and I mean that. Promise me you'll stop worrying."

"I promise."

"Selena, my dear strong mountain woman who has overcome so much, you are as beautiful in your heart and soul as you are on the outside."

Selena stood tall her long silky hair shining, her olive skin glowing as tears slid down her face. She was touched by Hank's reassurance. Hank told her again how much he loved her and gently kissed her. Taking her by the hand, Hank led her toward the cherry grove.

Anna Laura found an excuse to leave Crissy at the store. She went to the grove and asked Hank to call Lieutenant Adams and tell him they would be spending the night in Cherry Valley. If he left soon, he could arrive before dinner at the Hemlock restaurant.

"I will do that now!" Hank said as he hurried to his office to make the call. As luck would have it, Adams was not on duty and said he would leave immediately.

Crissy was in for the surprise of her life.

The group met again at the stables as the screen was delivered and packed into the wagon. Hank suggested they walk down to Cherry Tree Lane. Anna Laura and Crissy walked together.

Walking along the lane, the cloud of pink blossoms surrounded them. As the couples each went their own way, Anna Laura watched as each of the men knelt, clearly asking the ladies to marry them. June would be the perfect time since school would be out and the weather would be clear. Anna Laura knew Crissy was still sad and watched as she sat on a bench near the stream. Dressed in a pink silk blouse, she blended with pink blossoms around her. Anna Laura knew she was thinking of Samuel again, perhaps worried his feelings for her may have changed. Anna Laura thought about Clint, her tender heart aching with grief.

In the stillness of the moment, a voice spoke to her spirit as it had before. "There is a time for all things." Anna Laura was startled for a moment by what she had heard.

Walking back to the bench by the stream, she found everyone waiting. She announced, "Everyone, I have a surprise for you. We'll be staying at the Inn tonight."

The girls were ecstatic.

"Let's all go to our rooms and get ready. Hank, we will meet at six p.m." Hank smiled a little and nodded, they both knew Samuel would arrive around that time.

The ladies bathed and relaxed, then dressed for dinner feeling rejuvenated from the ride off the mountain. The girls dressed in their favorite colors. Anna Laura looked at each of them marveling at their beauty. Life on the mountain had served them well. Tonight they would look angelic in their soft colors with their hair hanging loose. When they were ready, they went out to the restaurant looking for the others. The round tables were covered with mint green and pink linens with cherry blossoms in beautiful centerpieces.

They saw the men sitting at the tables. Samuel was there at the restaurant waiting with Hank, Billy, Bobby, and Jess. As the ladies entered, every eye was upon them.

Crissy could hardly hold back her tears as she smiled. She took hold of Anna Laura's hand; she actually thought her eyes were playing tricks on her.

"Hold your head high, Crissy, and take a deep breath. What you see is real." Crissy smiled again but tears filled her eyes.

Samuel stood to his feet and seated Crissy; the other men did the same.

"I can't believe you're here, Samuel. How did you know I would be here?"

Hank smiled and Crissy knew Hank and Anna Laura had arranged for Samuel to be there. At Anna Laura's suggestion, Hank had pre-ordered dinner so they would not have to wait.

As they ate, Crissy whispered to Samuel, "I can't believe you're here."

"Neither can I, Crissy. I wondered at times if the past was a dream and I would ever see the girl I love so deeply again."

As the others talked and enjoyed their food, it seemed that Crissy and Samuel could not concentrate on their dinner.

"Will you excuse us?" Samuel asked.

Everyone nodded as the couple walked away.

Leading Crissy to a bench beneath the huge hemlock outside the restaurant, Samuel took a small box from his pocket. As he opened it, a diamond sparkled in the dim light.

"Crissy, will you marry me in June?"

As he placed the ring on her finger, she said, "Yes, yes, yes."

The lieutenant kissed his bride-to-be. He knew that Hank and Selena along with the other couples at dinner would all be getting married in June as well.

When Crissy and Adams returned to the table, none of them had ever seen Crissy smiling the way she was at that moment. As she reached for the crystal glass holding her water, the diamond sparkled and congratulations began. They all began to realize they had set their weddings for the month of June.

Anna Laura's imagination ran wild. "Why don't we have all five weddings at the same time on Brushy Mountain? The air will be cool; there will be all kinds of flowers blooming. We can choose a special place outdoors. There's a huge meadow behind the settlement where wildflowers are abundant and benches can be carried from the school and church. There's a massive flat rock that resembles a stage and I can have Steve and Rob build an arch wide enough for five couples. Lilly and the other ladies could cover the arch with all kinds of flowers."

Everyone agreed it was a wonderful idea. After some discussion, they discovered Samuel would be free in mid-June so the date was set for June 16th on a Saturday.

The men would ride up on Friday afternoon. Hank and Samuel could stay with Lilly and Steve since they had plenty of room.

Anna Laura suggested, "Girls, let's go to the fabric store and get what you'll need for your wedding attire. The purchases will be my gift to all of you."

They were happy to find the store was still open. They all chose patterns for Victorian-style dresses as well as cream-colored Victorian silk and lace. Ballerina style shoes were available in the same color. They would need flat heels for the outdoor wedding. They also purchased material for the veils; Selena would do those as she was very creative.

On Sunday morning, everyone said their goodbyes to Samuel and Hank.

"We'll see you in ten weeks," Anna called back as they rode away.

Chapter 45

As Anna Laura, Billy, Bobby, Jess, Sadie, Sarah, Mary Jane, Crissy, and Selena made their way up the mountain, they were a little slow. Billy's horse pulled the narrow wagon filled with screening and the wedding goods that were wrapped safely inside. Everyone was very excited.

"We have a lot to do in the next ten weeks," Anna Laura said during a break to rest the horses. "School will be in session for six more weeks. After school ends, we'll have a month then to dedicate completely to preparation for the weddings. I feel I must tell you now, I plan to leave after the weddings in June."

Everyone was quiet and not able to contain the tears that slid down their faces. The girls especially were upset. Billy and Bobby were all choked up, their eyes showing such sadness. They each told Anna Laura what she meant to them and how their lives would be forever changed because of her.

Anna Laura smiled sadly. "Let's enjoy the time we have and do all that we can to continue bringing hope to the people."

"Anna Laura, you seem as young as us sometimes, but you feel like a mother to all of us." Billy's voice broke a little.

Anna Laura smiled. "I must see Clint one more time and explain why I really had to leave. I'm sure he's probably married by now. Over a year has passed. There was a time when I thought I would never return, but I must. My destiny is in God's hands and I must accept whatever lies ahead."

They arrived home just before dark and unloaded the screen in Steve's barn. The girls carried their wedding materials to their cabin. Coming back to the settlement brought them back to reality; they had much to do in the coming weeks. Tomorrow school would be in session and Anna Laura would check each child to make sure all was well. Young Tisha White's baby would be due any day so Crissy and Anna Laura would pay her a visit.

The teachers rose early the next morning, feeling excited about school. They would concentrate on school and not their upcoming weddings. Despite trying to act very professional, as they were getting ready for school they giggled realizing that they had each been honorably and officially proposed to over the weekend. This seemed so ironic. But they suspected a little planning had taken place after the men got together in Cherry Valley.

As they ate breakfast, Anna Laura said with a smile, "Girls, I would like to counsel you as we have our meal. Please do not take marriage lightly. Purpose in your heart that it will be until death do you part." The girls listened intently and pondered in their hearts at the love they had for these five wonderful men.

Crissy spoke up, "Anna Laura, no matter where my destiny leads me I will follow the vows I make all the days of my life. I know I will leave the mountains to be with my husband. I will become a doctor, just you wait and see."

Sadie shared her future dreams. "Bobby and I will live on the mountain as long as we're needed to help with teaching."

"Billy and I will always go wherever Sadie and Bobby go," Sarah said. "I'm sure one day we will leave the mountain. I feel in my heart everyone will leave as the old people die off. Families will spread out through Tennessee and Kentucky to find work. They will learn trades and get an education that will carry them through."

"Jess and I will see to it that the children that are presently attending school will be a generation forever changed. One day they may even go to college. Jess will be able to help them there," Mary Jane softly shared.

Selena had been listening quietly and now said, "I know I will be leaving in June. Hank will be working for the government in Cherry Valley until he is needed in Nashville. His aunt and uncle are getting older and he is their only family." Selena dreamed about being a mother and housewife after earning a degree in law. She also wanted a challenge and knew she had the ability to be whatever she wanted to be. She was very happy as she thought of where she came from and where she was headed.

Anna Laura knew the girls and their husbands would continue to change lives. "You know, Mary Jane, you are so lucky to have met a man like Jess who is willing to spend a large part of his life on the mountain. Hank told me that Jess has a sister named Janie who is a nurse and her husband is a teacher. Perhaps they will come to the mountain and live here for a time to take care of the sick and teach with Jess."

"Oh, Anna Laura, all five of us lost our mothers. God sent you as a divine intervention into our lives. You have been a mother, a Christian mentor, a teacher and so much more. Do you have any idea what you have done for us? You've changed our lives."

"Selena, I only follow the calling in my life."

"Anna Laura, time has passed swiftly but it seems like a lifetime when I think of all that's happened in my life." Mary Jane's eyes filled with tears.

Sadie and Sarah thanked Anna Laura not only for the changes in their lives but the lives of their future husbands as well. "I know they will regret some of the things they did all the days of their lives, but they will not let it take away their joy," Sarah said.

"Now is what counts," Anna Laura said very seriously. "The Lord has freed their hearts from their old ways, they are now new creatures."

Sadie spoke with tears streaming down her face, "Where would Sarah and I be if God had not ordered your steps to these mountains?"

Smiling, Anna Laura replied, wiping tears from her eyes, "We'd better get going. Girls, you go ahead, I'll follow later."

The mountains were full of life after the long hard winter. Birds were singing, chickens cackling, cows mooed and the breeze stirred through the leaves. Anna Laura remembered a day like this not long after she had come to the mountain. As the girls walked to school amid the beautiful spring morning and all the sounds of nature, a different sound echoed their way. It was an angelic voice flowing across the settlement. One of the settlement women named Naomi was milking a cow in her field. As Naomi sang, the girls stood still and allowed the music to flow over them as she sang about what Jesus meant to her.

Anna Laura came up behind the girls as they stood entranced by Naomi's voice. "Can you think of any sound that would be more appropriate for a wedding?"

"If anyone could get her to sing for our wedding, it would be you, Anna Laura," Mary Jane replied. "Naomi was very nice to me when I was a little girl. She was always kind and helped soothe my spirit. She said life would not always be like it was because she had walked a mile in my shoes and, by God's grace, had a good life now."

"After school, you and I will pay her a visit," Anna Laura exclaimed.

Later in the school day, Joel and Susie came to Anna Laura as she observed their class. Sitting in a chair during a break, they each stood at either side of Anna Laura and put their arms around her.

"We love you," Susie said.

"We sure do!" Joel agreed as he hugged her. "What would have happened to us if we hadn't found you?"

"Children, there is a higher power far beyond what I can do. Do you understand?"

What you mean?" Joel asked as Susie listened intently.

"God led you to me. Remember how you showed up at my camp?"

Susie nodded and Joel shyly said, "We love you, Anna Laura."

"You are two very intelligent children and were blessed to get parents like Steve and Lilly."

Anna Laura was experiencing the fruits of the spirit each day as it was being manifested to her. She was absolutely amazed to see the progress that had been made so far during the school session and knew there would be more. She was sad as she thought that one day the mountain would be desolate when everyone was gone. She knew that day would come.

Scanning the classroom, she wondered how each life would turn out. She was very proud of how the teaching was going and how all her protégés contributed so well.

As the day came to an end, Anna Laura needed some alone time. She entered the cabin and told the girls that she was in the mood to go for a ride. "I'll be back before dark."

"Be careful," Selena whispered quietly.

Riding to her former camp, Anna Laura dismounted and sat among wildflowers. She laid her blanket in the clearing and lay down to watch the clouds. The sounds of nature helped her to relax more than she had in some time.

She wondered what her plans were once the girls were married. Of course, Clint was forever in her mind. The peace she had enjoyed turned to grief as she wondered if she waited too long. Watching the azure sky, her tears of sorrow dissipated as she was filled with peace. At that moment, she purposed in her heart that she would return to Germany when she left Brushy Mountain.

She had almost exhausted her funds but remembered she had some bonds she could exchange for cash in Boston. She closed her eyes, deep in thought. When she opened them again, she realized the last light of day was about to be overtaken by darkness. She grabbed her blanket, mounted her Arabian and headed out.

Chapter 46

Since they would be getting married soon, Billy and Bobby thought they needed to build another cabin. They were sure the settlement men would help out. The ladies would enjoy cooking for the men as well as the fellowship.

Jess and Mary Jane could live in Anna Laura's cabin since Selena, Crissy and Anna Laura would be leaving after the wedding in June. Not long after Billy and Bobby talked to Rob and Steve, the cabin was under construction. Some men got logs, some brought in rock, while others did the building. Nature seemed to provide almost everything they needed. Some of the women were making feather beds and pillows as well as other necessities for the new cabin. The best resource the mountain people had was their willingness to help each other.

Billy and Anna Laura made one more trip to Cherry Valley as there were a few things they had not anticipated. There were, after all, five couples. If all went well, this wedding would look as if it dropped right out of heaven. The many talented women of the settlement were working diligently to complete the wedding gowns. There would also be a feast after the wedding prepared by the wonderful cooks of the community.

Time passed swiftly, and school was finally out for the summer. The brides to be could now concentrate on wedding preparations. As they worked, Lilly and Phoebe gave the girls advice on how to hold a marriage together. The girls listened intently and also took in the advice of women who had experienced many successful years of marriage.

Hank and Samuel talked frequently about the wedding and were nervous as they could be. They would ride up on Friday and stay at Lilly and Steve's home. The men would wear cream-colored suits with brown pinstripes and ties.

Even though gardening and other chores were still going on, there was a great amount of time spent on wedding preparations. Steve and Rob constructed a trellis from wild grapevines gathered from the mountains. The ladies would cover the trellis with greenery and wildflowers. They were building it exceptionally wide since ten people would stand side-by-side beneath it.

Hank would bring Reverend Jeremiah a suit, shoes, and tie when he came up the day before the wedding. The Reverend had spoken with the girls earlier in the week about the meaning of the marriage vows. He would counsel the men when they were all together the day before the wedding.

The brides were anxious on Friday morning, it would only be a few hours before Hank and Samuel arrived. Billy, Bobby, and Jess were, in Steve's words, as nervous as chickens standing on a hot rock. The men could not seem to stay busy enough. Jess taught Bobby and Billy how to tie their neckties. Billy and Bobby styled their hair in different ways and let Jess be the judge. They wanted to look their best for their brides.

Anna Laura took her Victorian dress from its case. The dress was very special to her, but not as special as the young ladies she had nurtured.

The ladies of the community spent all of Friday evening decorating the arch. It was absolutely gorgeous with greenery and many colors of wildflowers arching over the flat rock surrounded by the green meadow in tiny wildflowers. The benches were all in place for seating during the wedding. The weather was clear and all signs pointed to a perfect day on Saturday.

When Hank and Samuel finally arrived, Selena and Crissy were ecstatic. They would not be spending much time together, just supper at Lilly and Steve's.

Friday night was difficult for the girls; they had no idea when they would see each other again. The girls sat in silence for a while, their eyes filled with tears. The hardest of all was thinking they would never see Anna Laura again. She had been a mother, a confidant, mentor and so much more. Eventually everyone slept and looked radiant on Saturday morning. The day was filled with sunshine and a breeze flowed gently through the settlement.

"What a beautiful day it's going to be!" Anna Laura called out to the girls. "We won't be sad about anything today. This is to be one of the most special days of your lives."

Anna Laura and Lilly helped the girls get dressed in their long, flowing Victorian wedding dresses. Since there were five brides, this took some time. Lilly had a wonderful idea just after dawn and had gone to a meadow full of wildflowers. She chose pink flowers for Crissy, purple for Selena, blue for Sadie, and Sarah, and yellow and blue for Mary Jane. The little flowers would be placed with the baby's breath in their veils. She also picked bouquets of many colors from her yard. She had tied the bouquets with lace and ribbon to match the dresses.

When the girls were ready, the veils were placed on their heads. With their hair loose and shining, and their lips highlighted with a soft colored lipstick, they were the picture of beauty. The final touch was their ballerina slippers; the flat soles would allow them to walk gracefully in the meadow.

At the same time, the men had dressed in their cream and brown suits. They were so handsome. When it was time, Steve walked them to the arch and positioned them in their places.

Naomi waited on the rock above the trellis. Beautiful in her new dress and hairstyle, she was ready to let her beautiful voice be heard as the brides marched to their grooms. The entire mountain seemed to be filled with the beauty of spring. Everyone smiled with happiness.

The girls filed out the door of the cabin, in the same order as the men they would be marrying were lined up under the arch. They made it to the clearing and could now be seen by their soon-to-be husbands and the crowd. The grooms were absolutely hypnotized looking at such grace and elegance as the five ladies walked the aisle of velvety green. The slight mountain breeze gently moved their long silky hair away from their faces.

As they began their walk, Naomi began to sing a beautiful mountain love song. Reverend Jeremiah was ready to step in as the brides reached their places, facing their grooms. Acting as their maid of honor, Anna Laura stood to the left. Jeremiah performed the ceremony, one couple at a time. When he told the gentleman to kiss their brides, there was not a dry eye on the mountain. More than just with joy of five wonderful matches, there was also a little sadness since it meant some of the ladies would be leaving. One by one, the couples were congratulated as they headed for the reception set up behind the church.

After the reception, the girls followed Anna Laura to their cabin to change. Selena, Crissy, and Anna Laura would be collecting their bags which were already packed. The men who were leaving headed to Steve's to do the same. Jess and Mary Jane would be going with the others off the mountain for a short honeymoon, but would return. Sarah, Billy, Bobby, and Sadie would be staying on the mountain; they were ecstatic to have their separate homes now. Jess and Mary Jane would bring Anna Laura's Arabian back to Steve. Before they left, Anna Laura wanted a little time alone with her faithful horse.

She rode to her special utopia to listen to the sound of the flowing stream and waterfalls, and gaze upon the many wildflowers that swayed in the gentle wind. She looked at the blue sky and thanked God for all he allowed her to do. She whispered, "Thank you, God, for allowing me to fulfill my mountain destiny. Please, God, order my steps from this day forward as You ordered them to this mountain. Please lead these mountain people in the direction you would have them to go. When the time is right, guide Jess, Mary Jane, Sadie, Sarah, Bobby, Billy, Steve, and Lilly where You wish them to go.

"God, I know the rest of my life is in your hands. Please guide me in the path you have laid out for me. Let me always hear your voice in the stillness of the night telling me what to do. I know I have a destiny on this Earth, but in the end heaven will be my final destiny and I'm looking forward to holding Your nail scarred hands. Amen."

She caught up with Hank, Selena, Jess, Mary Jane, Samuel and Crissy on the path down the mountain. They made it to Cherry Valley before dark. Selena and Hank headed out for the plantation in Nashville. The guesthouse had been completely redecorated just for them.

Samuel and Crissy were on their way to Nashville as well. Samuel had reserved a lovely cottage at a private lake near Nashville.

Jess and Mary Jane were not going too far. Jess had reserved a cottage in the country not far from the college he had attended.

Before everyone went their own way, Anna Laura bid them farewell trying her hardest to smile and not spoil the happiness the couples were feeling. Once they parted ways, she boarded the bus that would take her to Knoxville, Tennessee where she would catch a plane to Boston. As the bus rolled out of Cherry Valley, she looked back towards Hank's office, the very first place she visited in the town.

As the bus traveled through Tennessee, her mind seemed to cover a million miles. Memories of how she had driven into her long ago homeplace only fifteen months ago and had ridden her Arabian up the mountain toward the unknown. Visions of her mother flashed before her; scenes of their closeness when she was child. She realized just how many of her mother's traits she possessed: her looks, her spirit, and her adventurous nature.

It seemed only a short time before the bus driver announced, "Next stop Knoxville. Cabs will be waiting to drive you to the airport."

Walking to the cab, a sadness came over her and she asked herself, "Will I ever return to the mountains again?"

When the time came, she boarded the plane with mixed emotions but deep inside she knew she had made the right choice. She wondered whether she should get a job in Boston or head directly for Germany. When she arrived, she called a friend she had worked with in the past. The fifteen months she had been away in the mountains seemed like a lifetime.

As she sat waiting for her friend, Faith, she was thinking back to her work in the mountains. She was so deep in thought that Faith startled her as she called her name in excitement.

Faith was a tall, beautiful blonde, a researcher at the hospital where Anna Laura had worked.

As the girls rode to Faith's apartment, Faith asked, "Anna Laura, how long will you be in Boston?"

Suddenly, Anna Laura sensed an urgency to leave soon. "Faith, I'm going back to Germany."

The still voice in her mind whispered that she must be in Germany by June 20th.

[251]

Confidently, Anna Laura said, "I'll be leaving in two days." Given the time difference between the US and Germany, she wanted to give herself ample time to be there by the 20th.

Anna Laura spent a lovely, but short, time with her friend. Faith wanted to hear all about her mountain adventures. By the time Anna Laura finished her story, Faith replied, "Anna Laura, I can see how the good by far outweighed the bad."

Anna Laura made reservations to fly out June 19th. She would arrive around noon German time on the 20th.

She silently prayed as faith drove her to the airport, "Please, God, order my steps. I feel I am doing the right thing but I must have Your confirmation." She and Faith said their goodbyes and she boarded the plane. After settling in her seat, she began to meditate again. Suddenly that still voice impressed upon her, "When you arrive in Germany, go to the huge church north of the hospital where you worked."

Her flight arrived on time and by three o'clock she was in a nice hotel. She slept for an hour or so then bathed and shampooed her hair. She spent at least an hour enjoying the modern conveniences she had missed for so long. She brushed her hair staring at herself in the mirror. She had bought a dress in Boston; it was of a soft material with a pattern of tiny pink and green flowers on a cream background and fit snugly at the waist before flaring out to almost touch her ankles. She added pink lipstick and cream colored heels.

It was now five o'clock. She remembered she was supposed to go to the church, but wanted to surprise Clint. She took a cab to Clint's home and asked the driver to wait.

She was greeted at the door by the butler. He stood in awe. "Anna Laura, I'm surprised to see you! You are as beautiful as ever."

"Do you think I could see Clint?"

"Everyone is at church, Anna Laura."

Anna Laura immediately thought of how she had been told to go there; she thought this must be some sort of special service. She ran back to the cab as the butler called, "Clint is getting married!"

Unfortunately, Anna Laura could not hear what he said as the cab pulled away. The driver took Anna Laura to the church. Before going in she thought, "I'll wait in the vestibule."

When she walked in, she noticed there were flowers everywhere and the seats were filled. Someone lightly tapped her on the arm and asked if she was related to the bride or groom.

"I remember you. Weren't you engaged to Clint at one time? He's marrying Wilhelmina Anna Phista today."

Just as Anna Laura was trying to find an unobtrusive way out, the groom and best man walked in from an area outside. Clint caught a glimpse of her but thought perhaps this was only in his mind.

At the same time, Anna Laura saw him. She stopped in her tracks. She could not move. She wanted to run but her feet seemed stuck in place.

Clint blinked his eyes and stared again. He knew he had to touch her to be sure she was real. He touched her face and felt her tears sliding down.

"Anna Laura, is this really you?"

"I am sorry, Clint. I didn't know you were getting married."

The two of them stood in silence, staring into each other's eyes. Clint could not contain the tears that swelled in his blue eyes. He was in turmoil. Yes, he still loved Anna Laura but wondered, "What will I tell Wilhelmina?

He gently took Anna Laura in his arms for a moment.

"Please wait here."

Clint hurried to the other side of the church where his bride was waiting to head toward the aisle. He found Wilhelmina; she was deeply surprised to see him and knew something had changed.

"Wilhelmina, I hardly know how to tell you this. I cannot go through with the wedding."

She was a little stunned but knew their wedding was planned by their parents and neither of them was really ready or truly loved each other. In a way, Wilhelmina was relieved as she had loved someone else as well.

"Clint, I don't know what is happening but I appreciate your honesty."

Clint turned and ran for Anna Laura but she was gone. Running out the door, Clint could hear Wilhelmina rather cheerfully announcing to the crowd that the wedding was canceled.

Anna Laura was getting into a cab just as he made it outside. He ran for his car and followed the cab. As Anna Laura exited the cab at the hotel, Clint was parking his car. She was inside and gone by the time he reached the lobby but he managed to get her room number. When he neared the door, he could hear the sound of Anna Laura weeping. He tapped on the door and Anna Laura was startled. She wiped away her tears, composed herself, and opened the door.

"Clint? You should be married by now."

"Anna Laura, all is well. I never stopped loving you; I thought you were gone forever."

He took her gently by the hand. "Let's get out of here." First, he stopped and kissed Anna Laura's beautiful lips.

Clint took her to his home so they could talk.

"Anna Laura, I know you do not want a big wedding, I remember you never did. I'll call and have all the paperwork we need by tomorrow, you can have the guest quarters for tonight and tomorrow. Proper arrangements will be made and we can be married tomorrow evening at six. You'll have time to choose a dress and we can be married at the small chapel south of the hospital. I'll tell mother and father. They were so sorry when you left, their minds have changed in so many ways about you."

Clint kept his word. His mother and father were stunned at the news. They talked with him and related how happy they were for him.

"Clint, you haven't been the same since she left. We want you to be happy."

"There won't be many guests. Only close friends and those that were close to Anna Laura if I can get in touch with them."

In the meantime, Anna Laura had found a cream-colored Victorian dress similar to the ones her dear Sadie, Sarah, Crissy, Mary Jane, and Selena had worn on the mountain at their wedding.

Standing at the altar, Clint thought she was stunning. Walking up the aisle, she was the picture of beauty with her long dark hair adorned with Victorian lace. As he stared into her eyes as they took their vows, he silently thanked God for bringing his Anna Laura back to him.

Chapter 47

In the following weeks, Anna Laura told Clint all about her mountain destiny. She had followed her heart so the forgotten mountain peoples' lives would be forever changed.

In the meantime, Hank's aunt and uncle had decided to go abroad and asked Hank to transfer to a job in Nashville so he and Selena could live on the plantation. Hank took the transfer, but stayed in touch with Jess so they could meet the needs of the mountain people. Selena entered the university at Nashville and studied to become an attorney.

Lieutenant Adams was promoted to Captain. He and Crissy found a nice home in Nashville where she, too, entered college to become a doctor.

Jess, Mary Jane, Bobby, Sadie, Billy and Sarah were living happily in their lovely cabins, teaching school, helping the sick, building and helping wherever they were needed.

Six years later, Anna Laura and Clint were extremely happy. They practiced medicine, but last year Anna Laura took leave to give birth to a set of twins, a boy and a girl. Clint had agreed when she named the boy, Clint Steven, and the girl Lilly Anna.

Selena had become a lawyer. Hank's aunt and uncle passed away and the plantation was left to Hank and Selena. Selena gave birth to her first child.

Crissy was only a couple of years away from becoming an obstetrician, the next year she would be an intern. Captain Adams was now head of the Police Department in Nashville.

Chapter 48

Ten years had passed since Anna Laura left the mountain. The mountain people were beginning to leave Brushy Mountain.

Jess and Mary Jane moved near the college where Jess now held a teaching position. Mary Jane was in college becoming certified to teach.

Bobby, Billy, Sadie, and Sarah moved to Cherry Valley. Bobby and Billy began a construction company building log homes and were doing very well financially. Sarah and Sadie were both in nursing school. Samuel was still a police captain and Crissy was now a doctor.

The old-timers had died off and those left moved away and dispersed throughout Tennessee.

Lilly, Steve, Rob, and Jane chose to live in Cherry Valley. The men worked at the saw mill and both couples found a piece of land and built their own homes. Their children were now ready for higher education and would do well.

In the mid-40s, the couples planned a reunion. Of course, Anna Laura was in charge. When he received a letter, Hank let everyone know the reunion would be at the plantation. Crissy, Samuel, Sadie, Bobby, Billy, Sarah, Jess, and Mary Jane were all invited.

By this time, each couple had two children and the mothers had completed their education. Everyone was doing well.

Twenty-four people met at the plantation. The children were amazed at the spacious land as well as the plantation house.

The reunion lasted five days. This was five of the happiest days of their lives. They certainly had lots of catching up to do as well as some reminiscing.

Before leaving, Anna Laura had only a few words to say, "I'm glad all of you can see why I waited for Clint. He was part of my God-given destiny. We all have fulfilled our destinies so far on Earth. Just in case we never meet again here, let's plan our heavenly destinies where we will never part."

For a short time, eyes filled with tears. Again they said their goodbyes as the children hugged each other.

Hank, Selena, and their son, Clinton, and daughter, Annie, stood beside the huge white columns and watched as the five cars drove down the long winding drive that led them out of sight and back to their own homes.

The end

About the Author

Pauline Hensley Harber is also the author of Among the Mountain Laurels as well as Echoes from the Mountains and A Dog Named Pup. She is a retired Sociology and Psychology teacher and lives in Smith, KY with her husband.